AF413610

DON'T LOOK AWAY

A NOVEL

DANIEL KENITZ

SCRIBNER

New York   Amsterdam/Antwerp   London
Toronto   Sydney/Melbourne   New Delhi

Scribner

An Imprint of Simon & Schuster, LLC
1230 Avenue of the Americas
New York, NY 10020

This book is a work of fiction. Any references to historical events, real people, or real places are used fictitiously. Other names, characters, places, and events are products of the author's imagination, and any resemblance to actual events or places or persons, living or dead, is entirely coincidental.

First Scribner trade paperback edition July 2026

SCRIBNER and design are registered trademarks of Simon & Schuster, LLC

For information about special discounts for bulk purchases, please contact Simon & Schuster Special Sales at 1-866-506-1949 or business@simonandschuster.com.

The Simon & Schuster Speakers Bureau can bring authors to your live event. For more information or to book an event, contact the Simon & Schuster Speakers Bureau at 1-866-248-3049 or visit our website at www.simonspeakers.com.

Interior design by Jaime Putorti

Manufactured in the United States of America

1 3 5 7 9 10 8 6 4 2

Library of Congress Cataloging-in-Publication Data has been applied for.

ISBN 978-1-6682-0865-6 (pbk)
ISBN 978-1-6682-0866-3 (ebook)

Scan here to get book recommendations, exclusive offers, and more delivered to your inbox.

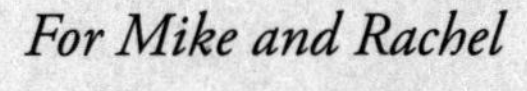

For Mike and Rachel

DON'T LOOK AWAY

PROLOGUE

Opening a paperback does nothing to settle Barbara Tiller's nerves. A beach read: that was the bright idea. Take Sarah out on Friday afternoon, watch her build a sandcastle, maybe get some sun and a solid two chapters in before bringing Sarah to her father's place by evening. But when had the weather ever cooperated with Barbara's plans? It's a gray, brumous, unseasonably cool day by Florida standards. If not for the two of them, the beach would be empty.

"Mom." Holding up her trowel, Sarah makes her voice a warning siren: "Ma-ohhhhhhh-om."

Barbara gives her daughter a little wave. *Very good, honey.*

"You barely looked." Dig, dig.

The paperback is a romance. Barbara checks the flowy illustration on the cover: a man in a nineteenth-century justaucorps is dipping a bare-shouldered woman in what looks to be either a dance or a burgeoning make-out session. Usually that's the sort of thing she'd enjoy, but she can't get past the first page without reading evil intentions into each character. Everyone who isn't the hero is a threat.

Barbara snaps the book shut and looks over the empty beach. Is there some hurricane warning she missed? She's tempted to go check the radio in her car. Her phone battery is dead and the clouds have gone sour.

"Castle or sea turtle?" Sarah asks, a bucket in each hand.

"Sea turtle for sure."

Sarah snicks her tongue. "Sea turtles are hard."

In truth, the reason Barbara hauled Sarah to a beach on a wet day is that her custody ends at 6:00 p.m. Then it's her ex-husband's turn—Friday, just in time for the weekend—and of course he'd take Sarah deep-sea fishing, or driving go-karts, or jet-skiing in the channels. His new girlfriend would be with him. Barbara is sure the two of them would keep Sarah giggling for three days straight. Sarah's eight now, and Barbara doesn't want her childhood memories of the Gulf Coast to be miserable school days with Mom in between kick-ass Saturdays with Dad and his endless parade of hip, twentysomething girlfriends. Kids don't remember routines, the countless PB&Js you carved them, the thousand books you read them to sleep. Childhood memories are always the outliers, the wild detours that stick pleasantly in the craw. Sometimes—usually Mondays, when Sarah comes home shouting about what an *awesome time* she had that weekend—Barbara wonders whether Sarah will remember her at all.

Hence this rainy beach, Barbara thinks. She can't conjure fun and magic the way her ex-husband does. The sun's probably waiting for him to show up.

"Maybe we should think about packing up soon," Barbara calls.

"Awwww."

"It's gonna rain, honeybee."

"I'd say we have about seventeen minutes," Sarah says, squinting at the horizon. Ever the little meteorologist.

"Seventeen, huh?"

"Sixteen." Sarah taps an imaginary watch on her wrist. "And fifty-five seconds."

Barbara stands and gathers their things. Then the answer comes to her. North Naples, not the threat of rain, would explain why no one's here. North Naples, scene of the most recent of the Gulf Coast Killer's murders as he stabbed his way up Florida, was less than a half hour down I-41. Barbara had spent a few late nights watching self-defense videos. She learned morbid things about the world. One doctor on YouTube quoted the depressing kidnapping statistics, saying that if anyone threatens you at gun-point and tells you to *get in the car*, you should tell them to go ahead and shoot you. Otherwise, you might regret missing your chance at a quick death.

"Pack up," Barbara says. "Time to go."

Another grumble from the ocean, the sound of water collapsing on water. Or was it thunder this time? Barbara has her beach bag packed and is about to start on Sarah's when she spots a black SUV pulling up near the dunes. A man eases out and waves at her. Barbara waves back, almost smiles. Having the company is oddly reassuring.

"Ma'am," he calls between cupped hands, his voice soft and fluty. "Band of rain coming. Just thought you should know."

"Thanks. We're headed home now."

The man flashes some sort of sign, maybe okay, maybe a goodbye wave. He's wearing a black button-up that's a size or two too large; the breeze plumps it up like a sail. His hair is soft and bleach white. As he gets back into the SUV and pulls away, Barbara rolls her eyes. As if she didn't see the rain coming herself, as if he couldn't see her packing up already. Another Good Samaritan of Madre: the island is full of widowers who use kind gestures as excuses to chat women up. Most of them mean well.

By the time Barbara and Sarah get up to their Subaru in the parking lot, the first few needles of rain start to sting. Barbara spreads a beach towel across the back seat for the sand Sarah is about to track in. Barbara will be vacuuming all weekend, sighing to the steady seethe of suction like it's such a pain, all the while counting the minutes until Sarah returns and she can fret about sand again.

Sarah calls out to her. She's pointing down to where the parking lot meets the road.

Barbara pulls out her head and looks. The same black SUV is idling near the sign announcing PRESIDIO HEIGHTS (PRIVATE BEACH). The driver's-side door has flipped open.

Underneath it, the white-haired man has collapsed on the concrete.

"Is he okay, Mom?"

"Stay here. Take the keys. Turn on the AC and lock the doors."

"I wanna hel—"

"Sarah! Just do it."

Thunder rolls like a passing train as Barbara jogs across the parking lot. She kneels beside the man. She can't tell if he's breathing. The SUV's radio is on (*come on down to Madre Island*

BMW if you want to give your lap a little luxury!) and the engine is still idling in park. Whatever it was, it happened suddenly.

Barbara presses two fingers to his neck. *Tha-dump. Tha-dump.* That catches her off guard: the steady, soft kiss of his pulse. She's no doctor, but wouldn't that rule out a heart attack? Then something else put him down. A stroke? Far away, she would have guessed he was old. But up close, the white hair doesn't quite match his age. She half expected to find a knife in his back and a trail of blood.

She's been spending too many late nights on YouTube.

Her phone is still dead. She'll have to plug it into her car charger to dial 911. She takes stock for a moment. The SUV is a Lincoln . . . Aviator, she notes. Someone might ask about that. *Aviator, Aviator, Aviator. A Lincoln Aviator,* she thinks, picturing Honest Abe flying a biplane, a ridiculous image—Lincoln aviating, donning aviator glasses, hot aviation wind blowing in his gunny Lincoln hair—to preserve the memory. The ambulance will need an address, and the vague answer of Presidio Heights will have to suffice. That could work. Wouldn't it? She turns to run back to her car.

But one leg doesn't turn with her. Her ankle is in his hand.

And as the realization darkens inside her, he stands, half a head taller, sinewy, lanky, healthy. He scratches his wrist through his long sleeves. Then he clutches her by the forearm and doesn't let go. He leans in as if he means to bite her, close enough for her to taste the piney burn in his breath. The obsessive way he works his wrists suggests a sudden, violent rash.

"Call your daughter over here," he says. "Then get in."

Barbara stares. Mouth open. Lips flexing. *If anyone tells you to get in the car, the best response is to say, "Go ahead and shoot me."* Does this man have a gun? What is she supposed to say? Nothing comes out of her but a hot trickle running down her leg.

"Mom!"

Sarah's voice is a shot of mom adrenaline. Barbara slips her wrist from his grip and runs to her idling Subaru. And, running up to the windshield, she catches her reflection as a figure explodes onto her from behind, his long arms cupping hers, his body weight crumpling them both to the concrete. Her veins go syrupy inside his reach.

Sarah screams.

Underneath the passenger's-side door, Barbara rolls over, freeing a leg she can drive into his groin. It's clumsy, but his groan tells her it landed. Barbara slides loose from underneath him and stumbles to her feet. She runs around the hood, over to the driver's side. "Sarah! Hit the emergency assist!"

Crying, shaking, Sarah's eyes dart around like every button is written in French. Barbara climbs in the driver's side, shouting. *"Seat belt, seat belt!"*—but Sarah's gone panic blind, feeling around for the button she can't find.

The man is on his feet again, dragging one leg as he circles around the front. Then he smiles and stops in front of the hood. Daring her.

Barbara fumbles with the stick. Park. Over to Drive. She's done it a million times. But her fingers are gummy.

"He's *coming*, Mom!" Sarah screams. Just a glance and Barbara sees him—walking to her side, now.

The stick *thunks* into place. Barbara kicks the gas. The engine roars. The RPM needle spikes—

—and they go nowhere.

Barbara looks down.

Neutral.

Then her door flies open.

"Run," Barbara screams to Sarah. "*Run*, baby!"

Sarah hesitates, then does what she's told, opening the door and running off into the rain.

It only takes him one arm to drag Barbara out and send her spilling to the ground. She tightens her fists, ready to kick his ribs, his pelvis, his legs, his groin, whatever soft spot he gives her, but when he stands over her, the blade in his hand catches a glint of the Subaru's headlight, and the fight goes out of her.

PART ONE

LESLIE

"Robert," I call. "Did you see? An eight-year-old got away."

Robert is in the den reviewing the bills, wearing rimless readers that age him beyond his sixty-two years. "Mm. Got away from what?"

"The Gulf Coast Killer." Self-soothing, I comb my fingers through my hair, rub a knot in my neck. "That poor girl. First witness."

"What happened to *Wheel of Fortune?*"

I turn the volume up. Though my gentle, squeamish husband, Robert Woodhouse, can barely unhook a bluegill without wincing, I grew up with a mother who worked in angiography. There's a social callus you develop when you see more veins and capillaries in a ten-hour-shift than most people do in a lifetime. I think she passed it on to me.

On the news, which I watch from our sofa with a bottle of rosé and a pile of cubed fontina cheese larger than my doctor would prefer, a breathy news anchor is relaying the key bits of information:

The woman had been at the beach with her daughter . . .

forty years old and divorced . . .

police are suspicious it's the latest of a series of attacks attributed to a "Gulf Coast Killer" . . .

though nothing is confirmed, this eight-year-old child would be the first witness . . .

Police use such lawyer-speak for the sake of the public. Suspicious? Of course it's the Gulf Coast Killer—and now we have to wait and see if an eight-year-old girl can describe him in any detail.

We would've heard if there was anything distinctive, if he were six foot six with a surgical scar, a blackwork scalp tattoo, and a severe case of Tourette's. No such luck. Until now, this killer has had the quiet precision of a Swiss watch. I've been reading about the case from Marco Island (single white male, age twenty-seven) through North Naples (married Hispanic female, age fifty-four), and though the killer is patternless with his victims, I've read enough from the headlines to know that this girl, eight years old though she may be, is the first loose end, the first to see his face without enduring ninety-six hours of dehydration before death. Ever since the news broke last night—I convinced Robert to walk with me down to Madre Beach Pier as far as the police barricade—we've heard nothing about the Gulf Coast Killer himself.

Robert rises behind me and walks to the kitchen. I hear the clanging of popcorn kernels swirling into a pot. This is the sign: the bills are done and soon it will be time to watch something we *both* like.

Once he fills his bowl, Robert drops a kiss on my head and sits next to me. The flare of the TV outlines his features: his narrow shoulders, his slick white hair, the subtle heterochromia of his eyes. The blue one is near-green, the green one is near blue, like different hours in the same sea. The combined effect is that sometimes when you look at him, two separate men return the gaze. He has a young man's smile, but it's mottled in wrinkles, his lips pinched and veiny like a folded old map. Follow the roads of it and you'll find a man who usually swallows his words. On nights like this, an ideal husband.

On the news, a reporter interviews frightened locals. Robert sets the bowl down without a bite. "Les. Really?"

"Just until the commercial."

"I don't know why you're so fascinated with this. It's macabre."

"Life's macabre."

"Death is, actually." Robert lifts the bowl to his lap. "You'll get nightmares."

"You're the one who gets nightmares."

"Then you won't sleep. It's like caffeine for you." He lobs himself a handful of popcorn, crunching absentmindedly. "I'd say the same if you were drinking coffee after seven."

"I do drink coffee after seven."

Robert plinks me in the side of the head with a flake of popcorn and it drops to a cushion. I flick it back at him. He pops it in his mouth, cushion fuzz and all, and smiles with his tongue sticking out between his lips.

On-screen, a slender, suited woman files her report in front of a line of palmettos and two-floor condos. Presidio Heights at night. It could be any Gulf Coast community, I suppose— we're all the same species of sunbird, sixty or seventy, each of us with absurdly expensive cars and a taste for nautical-themed toiletries—but over the woman's right shoulder is the ice cream stand Robert and I like to visit, the Balanced Diet. Its logo weighs two scoops on either side of a scale.

Robert stops his crunching. "That's our place."

"I know." To think we were there so recently, licking butterscotch and marshmallow confetti, imagining these headlines were so far away from us. Now we're both imagining that poor woman. That beautiful beach. An eight-year-old's life destroyed.

The news switches topics: we won't believe how high the Powerball has gotten. Yeah, that'll help us forget there's a killer stalking the Gulf Coast.

Robert sets his popcorn on the coffee table. "If you were defending this guy, how would you get him off the hook?"

"That's not how it works." I've told him as much a thousand times.

"C'mon. Indulge me."

I clear my throat, ready to indulge. My old life as a public defender is a constant fascination to him. My steel stomach. Before I knew Robert, I could take my work home with me, let crime-scene photographs flashbulb in my brain while other people, normal people, tried to sleep.

"Assuming there's no alibi? I'd need something else for reasonable doubt. As far as I can tell, there's no DNA evidence so far, not so much as a hangnail left behind at any of the scenes, not even a make or model on a car. Whatever the prosecution gets on him, I'd have to demonstrate it doesn't only apply to my client, but, say, one-fifth of the general population. Reasonable doubt. Now, if they had a single hair, or a phone location that puts my client at the scene . . ."

"Let's say he did leave some DNA behind."

"That's beyond a reasonable doubt, so I'd have to start digging. Is that evidence inadmissible for some reason? Mishandled, maybe? I'd ask for time stamps on everything, buy one of those giant calendars and start reconstructing. You wouldn't believe how incompetent some police are."

"You make it sound like his odds are fifty-fifty."

"Well, yeah, if he hired me." I shove my knuckles into his shoulder. "Don't ask if you don't want the answer."

"You wanna order a movie?"

"Sure. I'm just gonna wash my hands."

"Les, your hands are clean."

I look at my palms, spread my fingers wide. They are withered pink, knobby and thick, and technically clean. Robert doesn't understand that for people like me, *clean* is an emotion. "They're gonna feel gritty during the movie. I can't watch a movie with gritty—"

Robert captures my hands, brings them to his lips to kiss a fingertip. Then another. "If they're dirty, aren't I contaminated now? So we're in this together."

He smiles, and my lips can't help but mirror his. That is vintage Robert, the feeling of the screwy puzzle nubs of my personality snapping into the only other piece they'll ever fit. Something in his smile reminds me of why it was this man who convinced this old widow to remarry: he filled me up too happy to have room for anything else. And by the time the movie's on, I forget all about my hands.

I'm up first the next morning, whisking eggs and dicing Roma tomatoes at the kitchen counter. I stare at the weeping red mountain on the cutting board and decide the omelet needs more oomph. Goat cheese, if we have it. The saltier the better.

A little expensive for breakfast, and Robert has to watch his blood pressure, but the man deserves some oomph. He's been achy lately. The strain of our mortgage, maybe, the tightrope act of me paying for Steph's college out of my underfunded Roth IRA while we get by on his modest pension, of learning how expensive books and board are these days, of never quite broaching the subject that everything would be easier if I borrowed money from my sister or went back to work.

And on that unutterable thought—unutterable to Robert, anyway—I go for the omelet flip. A spongy streak of egg sticks to the pan. I stir, a little too angrily. Not an omelet now: a frittata. As intended.

I leave it on the stove to stay warm, then pour my coffee and head outside. This routine is the point of our whole retirement: sip coffee, let the salty sea breeze whisper through our hair. It's Saturday morning and the sky is already sparkling under the June sun.

Three years of routine in the condo we've named the Senectitude haven't erased the pleasure of the Gulf of Mexico.

At high tide, our beach doesn't go out far. There's a thin, pitted layer of sand dunes, then a lip where the beach goes smooth and wet as sealskin. Then the furry white foam, then the water: turquoise mixing to deep blue. The tide, now slipping away, has scattered peach-colored seaweed in its wake. A storm rolled through last night and scrubbed the sky clean. There's not a single cloud. Or a single person.

"Mornin'," Robert says. He closes the screen door behind him, coffee mug in hand. It's a collage of nineteenth-century impressionists like van Gogh and Monet with a caption underneath: I SEE DEAD PEOPLE. A retirement gift from the art department at Suncoast State University.

"Mornin'. High tide."

The thing about that salty sea breeze whispering through our hair: beach access like ours is expensive, which is why we had to settle for the side-by-side condo. Foolishly, Robert and I pictured more privacy in retirement, clinking champagne flutes in our hot tub, our lives a looping Cialis commercial. Instead we share deck space with the octogenarian next door. Steph got into Wharton, and when your daughter gets into Wharton, you don't say, "No, Steph, you can't attend your Ivy League school because your mom and stepdad had their hearts set on the full beach house with the private deck."

Maybe I retired too early. *Maybe* is a nice word. A fabric softener of language. Sussing out the *maybe*s made me a decent defense attorney. But I seem to have brought that work home with me, too: the reasonable doubts.

"A bit eerie out here," Robert says.

My fingers rise to guard my throat. For the past several weeks, the Gulf Coast Killer has been a story for the mainlanders. First the young man, age twenty-seven, a Walgreens worker from Marco Island, then slowly north as though the killer were hitchhiking his way up the coast. After Port Royal—about three murders in—local media started connecting dots. Victims always turned up *in a state of extreme dehydration*, according to the reports. When one reporter in Miami dubbed him the Gulf Coast Killer, the two hard *k* sounds were evidence enough for the public: we had a serial killer on our hands.

"I'd pick a different title," Robert says, sipping coffee. I blink, then realize he's talking about last night's movie. "It sounded like a comedy. And they needed different writers. Two stars. Maybe another half star for the performances."

"Mm-hmm."

"What are you going to do today? As little as possible?"

"I'm hoping to see someone."

He shoots me a startled look. "Who?"

"Patricia. Back from Santorini today. You all right?"

"Fine."

"It's not like I said *Wes*. Is he even in town?"

"I think so. I don't know." Squinting into the sun gives Robert a lemon-sucking look. He leans back and sighs into the breeze. Steadily, I rub my hands across his shoulder blades from behind and kiss the back of his head. Robert's a maze of a man—pointy elbows, Osgood-Schlatter in his knees—and it's not always easy to find the soft spots in his crevasses. But when he slides his hand up and takes mine, rubbing his thumb over my knuckles, I can feel him tremble.

Robert and I had only been on two dates when he confessed he had a son named Wes. He would wince like he was telling the story of an old war wound to explain the hitch in his stride. Their relationship teeter-totters. It's not as simple as checking the tide clock, in or out. It's impossible for me to picture a parent-child relationship so unlike mine and Steph's. How could Robert be anything but insatiably curious about what Wes is up to? How *couldn't* he want to sift through the notes in Wes's backpack, sort through his mail, scroll through his phone? But maybe that's my issue. Somewhere between Robert and me, there is one perfectly balanced parent.

The good news: it sounds like he and Wes are speaking again.

As I wonder how to nudge Robert on that, I head inside to wash my mug. The dishwasher is already open. Rudely, brazenly, the blades of the steak knives are facing up. I crouch down to remedy that. Face down might cut up the plastic, but if Robert trips and falls and lacerates a kidney, I won't have to blame myself for the dishwasher being an open spike pit. I snap the cutlery basket shut to finish, but a doubt snags in me. I unsnap it, try again. Snap. Not quite it, either. Still feels wrong. I know it's the obsessive-compulsive in me talking, but if I shut it when my mind isn't fixed on a perfectly clean thought, it will spray knives everywhere.

I try again.

Robert walks in and watches my whole routine with soft eyes. "Les. Let me clean those. Use the ones I got you."

I'd forgotten. A gag gift from our first Christmas. Plastic knives for kids: grippy handles, bright pastels. But they're serrated, so with just enough wiggle, you can slice oranges. Robert had noticed me nudging aside a steak knife on our first date and asked me about it. I confessed the red flags of my own, all my irrational fears, how they had gotten worse since my husband passed. Six months later, I had these knives. Robert had brought sliced fruit back into my life.

"I know." I snap the basket shut. "I know."

He licks his lips to say something, but the sound of rattling glass interrupts him. I'd left my phone on the coffee table in the living room.

CALL FROM: PATRICIA.

Wincing, I tap *Accept*. I already know what's coming. "Patreesh. Mea culpa."

"She *is* alive." Patricia's voice is shrill, blaring through a crowd somewhere. Even across telecommunication lines, I can tell how inappropriately loud she's being. "Do you know how distressing it is when you're an old lady and your ride doesn't show up? I feel like a lost toddler."

"I just woke up. I'll leave now."

"Too late. I'm going to the bar. I'll ask a strange man to drive me home."

"Not funny. There's a serial killer. Stay put!" I hang up.

Robert, still standing in the kitchen, shoos me. "Go, go."

"Her flight must have gotten in early." I pluck the keys from their wall hook and comb my fingers through my hair—the sea breeze whipped it into the texture of a Brillo pad—and blow Robert a goodbye kiss. I head out to the driveway leading out to our cul-de-sac. A full Florida day: swampy air, cicadas sizzling. I jangle my keys in my hand, pausing, spinning around aimlessly, before remembering my car's in the shop.

"Take mine," Robert shouts from inside.

I whirl around. The black Lincoln Aviator is sitting turtle head in the garage.

Robert's car it is.

ROBERT

A missed-call notification blips as I hop out of the shower. Still dewy, I step into my slip-ons and swipe the screen to find the tiny phone icon that always makes my guts swim these days. It isn't Wes's most recent number, or else the contact would have shown up DOMINO'S PIZZA, but the four-digit suffix is still a tad familiar.

A blow-dry and a polo shirt. Khaki shorts and a brown belt. Kind of a uniform at this stage in my life. I brush my hair back, glad to still have something to brush, white and willowy though it may be, and tip back a gargle of Listerine. It has alcohol, so I consider swallowing. Not that desperate, am I? I spit into the sink. A deep breath will have to do. Then I bring up the missed call and tap the green icon.

"Madre Island Police Department," a voice rings in my ear.

"I was returning a call? Robert Woodhouse."

"You've reached the main line, sir. Do you have an extension?"

"Sorry, no."

Without an extension, she says, I'll have to wait for a callback. Maybe someone left an extension in my voicemail inbox, but that's been full for months, and I'm a bit of a procrastinator with these things.

Still. Now a voice from Madre Island PD is probably in there. There is no amount of mouthwash that will clean the abscess of dread lodged in my gums.

After hanging up, I wipe the counter down—Leslie insists, lest we electrocute ourselves—and set the hair dryer back on her side of the his-and-hers countertop. We have an arrangement: I can use her hair dryer as long as I put it back in its place. It's a snug fit into its holder and always rests with a satisfying *click*. Of course. Everything about Leslie has always fit.

I'm in the living room thoughtlessly scrolling through Netflix when my phone rings again. Same four-digit suffix.

"Hello?"

"Mr. Woodhouse." The voice on the receiver is low, bellowy, and familiar. "Sergeant Clay Ingram, Madre Island PD. Can you come in today? We'd like you to participate in a witness lineup."

I should have chugged that Listerine.

"Now, I know it sounds scary," says Ingram, "but think of it this way: it would be a great way to rule yourself out."

"No. Yeah. Of course. It's just—my wife's car is in the shop, and she just took mine—"

Ingram's long, sighing *oh* sounds far more disappointed than the situation warrants. "We can send a cruiser. Now okay?"

"Now's . . . fine."

Then we exchange casual goodbyes as if arranging to pay a speeding ticket.

A cruiser. It's so important to have Robert Woodhouse at this lineup that a police officer will take time out of their busy day just to give me a lift.

I glance at one of Leslie's many legal pads strewn about the house and wonder about leaving a note for her, something about acupuncture or drinks with an old friend, but maybe it won't be necessary. Time bends around Leslie and Patricia when they get together. They'll go hours, sometimes overnight (I'll get the *Don't wait up* texts), the two of them stuck bingeing on some show they'll barely remember the next morning thanks to an empty bottle of chardonnay and the fact they talked over it the whole time.

I'll roll the dice: no note.

The cruiser pulls into our driveway a few minutes later. I'm already waiting by the door and beeline toward the police car as soon as it's there, eager to avoid a neighbor's glance, to keep things moving. I climb into the back seat and say hello politely, innocently, like I'm not one of five potential killers, like I'm not saying my hellos through a steel safety cage. To my great relief, the officer at the wheel is in the same hurry I am, all business and no chitchat, peeling out of our cul-de-sac with a firm start.

Maybe I'll beat Leslie home after all.

LESLIE

"Santorini was bleh," Patricia says halfway through a virgin margarita. "Don't get me wrong. I don't regret going. Lovely place, gorgeous people, sunsets, islands, blue water, all that. But just you try finding a steak. It's all fish and vegetables in oil. If I popped a zit right now, olive oil would come out."

"Sounds rough." I hide my smile behind the mimosa she's poured me. The complaints this woman has.

"The *worst*." Patricia laughs her spicy, five-alarm laugh. "Well, back to the salt mines."

Patricia's *salt mine* is a Mediterranean Revival home on the mainland. A palace, really. Beach access, like me and Robert, but her beach access is vast and private, bordered by a ferocious outgrowth of palms and privacy mangroves. She even has a lawn. We're sitting out on her deck, overlooking the Gulf and the channel between the mainland and Madre, toasting pleasantly in the sun.

Patricia winks at me. "You like that mimosa? Want more?" She leans in, whisper close. "I could put a little white rum in it. The white rum, she calls to you."

"Stop trying to get me drunk."

"Live a little."

"I drove, remember?"

"So stay over, sleep it off. I'll have Lucille fix you one. Lucille! Ah. She's not here. Gave her the full two weeks off. Remind me again why I travel?"

Patricia. Like *patrician*. Nobility, wealthy person, the cream of ancient Rome. She was the homecoming queen in Summerville, Wisconsin, a thousand years ago, and with me coming up two grades behind her, people would hear our long compound German last name and say, "Are you Patricia's little sister? Didn't know she had one."

My sister is still queenly. Long, fussy, sun-bleached hair drapes to her collarbones in a textured lob, and she wears gold bracelets around one of those thin watches that are too small to tell you the time but tell you plenty about the wealthy wrists wearing them. Papery folds of skin trace the mask of her face. If she looks straight at you, she's still the homecoming queen, but if you catch her from the side—ah, there's the wear and tear. I can imagine a police officer writing her description: *woman, blond hair, green eyes, approximately five foot ten.* Age? Either forty-five or seventy, and more than happy to keep you guessing.

Me, I don't even have to show ID for my senior discounts. Clerks only have to glance at me. That has its advantages, too.

"What did I miss while I was gone?" Patricia asks. "You seem a little—I don't know—down."

"Well, I told you about what happened on Madre."

"Awful. I remember hoping they'd catch him by the time I was back. Instead, he's right here." She reaches across the table for the pitcher. In her presence, there is always a mild scent of potpourri. The summer heat makes it sharper. "How's Bob?"

"Busy, lately."

"Oh? Golfing, painting?"

I sit back, thumbing my glass. "I've decided not to ask. I think it has to do with Wes."

"Oh yes, the estranged son."

"I don't remember if I told you, but our only big fight was about why he wouldn't let me meet him. Bob ended up in tears, so I dropped it."

"Did that ever happen with Saint Cal?"

Patricia's nickname for my first husband is a term of endearment, not irony. Cal Tressler. A brown-eyed, huggy, absolute plush toy of a man whose idea of four-letter words was to call someone "vile." He'd settle down with a cup of ginger tea and apologize, he'd say, *for flying off the handle like that.*

"Not really. But I'm not going to make the mistake of assuming he's Cal. He's Bob. We've both had entire lives before each other, and I decided it's not my place to push in."

"Look at you. Very worldly."

"Of course, maybe he's having an affair," I joke.

She's silent, nibbling her way through a handful of mixed nuts, her smile sloughing off. I rarely see my sister's face drop. It brings the gnarled memory from when she told me Dad had passed.

"I never told you this," she says, "but James cheated on me."

"*No.*"

"Uh-huh. James. My James."

"Why are you telling me this? I loved James."

"I know! I didn't want to think about it either—in fact, I'd go out of my way to avoid it—but there were all these little signs." On my crumpled, despondent look, she adds, "I mean, it was decades ago. Couples therapy, forgiven. We were even semi-young at the time."

"How'd you find out?"

"Slowly. But I should have known straightaway. There were all these little signs that flew under the radar. He'd insist we'd seen a movie together that I knew I never saw. He got a gym membership, out of the blue, years after I gave up on getting him to join me. You know what bugs me? Even with all the signs, I could explain them away. I thought, 'Hey Patricia—maybe you're not remembering right, or something else, this is just intimacy waning with age.' I figured eventually the warning signs would disappear and I'd think there was no reason to worry. Then one day when he didn't know I was home, I picked up our kitchen phone and heard them on the line. And there it was."

I shake my head. "James."

"Well, Bob's still with us. Do you really feel fine, leaving all this Wes stuff alone?"

"Of course not. But it's our only sticking point. Besides, I don't tell him everything about Steph. If I was feuding with her, the last thing I'd want is Robert inserting himself. If he's having some kind of argument with Wes, he probably figures I can't do much to help. And he's right. They're both adults. You realize how old we are, right?"

"No, I never admit defeat. But I get it. I'm just saying, it says a lot about a man."

"What?"

"How he treats his only son."

I shoot her my best *Drop it* look. The way she blows back in her chair suggests I might have overdone it.

"Okay." She tips back the last of her margarita with a sour wince and points the rim of the empty glass back at me. "Just don't keep looking away forever and then act surprised when we're talking about this again in a couple weeks. You know I can't resist a good I-told-you-so."

WESTON

It takes a while to find a side street, but when I find a service road behind a grocery store, I am beyond glad for the respite. Not much through traffic here. Florida folk are nice, but seeing a man with his hood open by the side of the road would look like an emergency and that sort of attention would bug me. Better to park five minutes out of my way than tell a helpful middle-aged man his help is unneeded.

Once the engine is off, I walk to the hood and prop it up. An ovenlike wave of heat wafts up. When you drive as much as a mobile locksmith does, your SUV becomes a whack-a-mole of problems, but today's mole to whack is only the fluid.

In Florida, I burn through washer fluid like gasoline. My windshield is always crisscrossed with gunky yellow streaks, a cemetery of all the mayflies and lovebugs I mashed on the way up I-75. Still, this excursion through Florida is proving worth the trip. I have already dropped by good old dad once or twice, and I hope to see Leslie and her sharp green eyes before all is said and done.

As I top off the fluid canister, a car pulls in front of me. Overflow from the parking lot around the way. A woman gets out, her door opening with a *ca-chunk*, followed by the soft *plop* of her wallet on asphalt. The woman tugs the leash of a frizzy brown Yorkie, shuts the door behind them, and the two walk off toward the store. I run up to pick up the wallet.

"Excuse me. Did you drop this?"

She turns. Her hazel eyes lock on it for a moment. She takes it and flips the plastic sleeve to pop a glance at her driver's license.

"Weird," she says. "Not sure how that happened."

"Must have happened when you got out. It was under one of your tires."

"Huh. I would have run right over it." And though I wait patiently for more, maybe two words specifically, that is all she says.

Her Yorkie is nipping pleasantly at my pant cuffs. After a

glance at hazel eyes for permission, I crouch down and pat its head. The poor thing is panting like a motor. My cooler has plenty to drink, but hazel eyes understandably declines my offer of stranger-danger water, and when she throws a thumb toward the grocery store and says she has to get going, I take the hint. Have a good day.

I watch the polite Yorkie trot excitedly by her side. *Hope she gets you that water soon.*

Most of my supplies are in my trunk, and though I do my best to keep them organized, the road has tossed everything together. It takes about thirty seconds to fish out the box cutter. I extend it two clicks—just enough to expose the blade—and hold it joystick-style, face down. Then I walk over to the tire where hazel eyes dropped her wallet. A glance at the store. She is well out of hearing distance. A glance the other way. A lonely road, black heat shimmering off the asphalt.

I plunge the box cutter into her tire. It blows out in a brief but satisfying bellow, then whistles to death with a *hisssssssssss* that makes me grin.

LESLIE

As I get fidgety on citrus and champagne, a bright idea occurs to me. "Let's call Steph."

"Won't she be working right now?"

"She can take a five-minute break for her mom and her favorite aunt," I say as the phone chirrs.

"Don't be so overbearing."

A second chirr, a third. "It's a phone call."

"I bet you ten thousand dollars she won't pick up."

The voicemail clicks. *The caller you have dialed* . . . I tap it dead with a desiccated feeling in my fingers.

Patricia flits her brows. "You can owe me."

My lips pinch. I'm picturing Patricia talking with her swanky friends, making five-figure wagers, clinking cocktails at the marina where she keeps her yacht, the *Gutted*. Its mooring fees are more than my mortgage. "Excuse me a moment."

Inside, her spotless house tingles with her potpourri scent, her open-concept kitchen exploding in whites, silvers, and creams. Someone—and probably not my jet-lagged sister—has laid fresh-cut hibiscus in a vase. Quite the touch. Mr. Fluffernutter, her elderly Pomeranian, greets me outside the bathroom door, and I give him a hello tap on the skull before he loses interest and totters away.

I freshen up. I wash with Patricia's hand soap, rinse with Patricia's water, press my face dry with Patricia's plush towels, apply some of Patricia's Ruby Woo lipstick as Patricia's mimosas ring seashells in my ears. This is even Patricia's state. She met James in college and followed him down here as his real estate development firm went gangbusters. My parents followed her soon after—already thinking about leaving those achy-jointed Wisconsin winters—and I wasted a good year back home trying to prove I could make it on my own. After an insufferable run of bad dates from a video matchmaking service, I took an extended Florida vacation to visit Patricia. Then, through Patricia, I met my first husband, Cal. And then, through Patricia, I had a place to stay while I studied for the Florida bar. And again, through Patricia, I had a start-up loan for an office and a new practice in Fort Myers. A two-week visit, I thought. It's going on thirty years now.

You can owe me, she said. That's putting it mildly.

Despite the lipstick, I look sloppy in the mirror. My hair never behaves. Unlike Patricia, I received the German Polish genes that favor our father, which means humidity fluffs me up like static shock. Growing up, I'd always feared I'd end up looking like my grandmother on my father's side. Yet here was the same boxy, rose-tinged hair. I'd even asked for this haircut. Why? I don't remember. It's strange how we pour ourselves into the molds of our fears.

I grab my purse and keys off her kitchen counter. Patricia is dozing when I step out to the deck. A thread of saliva unspools from her Ruby Woo lips. She was wearing a sun hat, but she's set it on the table, exposing her neck, making a brown spot I'd never noticed that much more obvious.

"Hey. What's that?" I flick my finger at her neck to see if the brown spot is just a glob of dust. Instead, my fingernail digs into skin.

"Ow!" Patricia chirps. "Is what new? I can't see."

"This." I snap a photo of it and text it to her.

She can only squint. The woman refuses to wear her glasses. "I don't know. Maybe."

"I haven't seen it. Maybe it's nothing, but get it checked out. Can't hurt."

She eyes it, clicking her tongue against her gums. "I can think of at least a dozen ways it can hurt."

I sit down with my purse still around my shoulder. "Does Steph think I'm overbearing?"

"She's nineteen, and you're a mother who cares. It would break the laws of physics if she didn't think you were overbearing."

"But am I? Really?"

"Well, yes." Patricia clears her throat. "But moderately. Just enough where it's a little endearing."

"She tells you more than she tells me. You knew she wouldn't pick up."

"A guess. And, yeah, sometimes she tells me things, sure."

"What's the secret?"

"What, like there's a book you can read? I'm a friendly older woman who's not her mom. That's the secret."

I stand. "All right, change of subject. I'm off, and you have homework. Have this thing checked out, stalk Steph a little—I grant you permission to violate all her personal boundaries—and let me handle Robert."

"Sure. Right after my seventy-two-hour nap. But thanks. This was fun."

"It was. Missed you, sissy."

"*Missed* me. You forgot I left!" She throws a theatrical hand on her forehead. "Stranded me, remember?"

"Oh, please." I shake my keys to jangle the point home. "You know I can't live without you."

WESTON

The flank steak is medium instead of crispy to burnt, the key lime pie is a little mealy, and I usually limit my tips to 30 percent, but I like the way the plump-cheeked waitress calls me Stringbean, so I pin a twenty under my coffee cup before I leave. I overheard that she was on hour ten of a scheduled eight-hour shift.

Poor thing. My mother was a waitress and I still remember the night she came home weeping because a patron burned his tongue sipping coffee, then waited until her shift was over so he could thump her into a wall. She swore she had warned him. I swore to be kind to servers for the rest of my life.

Next: the cabin. The place I found is a thirty-minute drive inland. After a quick drive through Immokalee, I pull onto a side road and onto a swampy private lot.

Cabin is a loose term. More of an aspiring fishing shack. The owner is so old he forgot he owns it, and squatting here leaves no paper trail, so the thing has been a real find. And it has a basement, which is rare and exactly what I need.

Tha-dump.

There is no refrigerator—no electricity at all—so I throw my water bottles into a cooler with the fresh bags of ice while I unload the rest of my supplies. High-SPF sunscreen: a few days of activity in Florida already has my neck crunchy and peeling. I am too salmony, too pink, too inflamed. Nothing like Robert's toasty shade of amber. Bug spray: for the flies. Disinfectant wipes: I go through them like toilet paper. Tallow soap and distilled water: ditto. Duct tape: well, you never know.

Tha-DUMP. Tha-DUMP.

When the supplies are in their places, I sit in my cutesy-local camping chair—SIEGE THE DAY, BUCCANEERS!—and flip on the radio. Even now, with local media hysterical over a killer on the loose, the Madre Island police scanner is not exactly Top 40 listening. Still, I like the radio's calm presence in the room, the oceany white noise of it. Occasional blips of static, mumbles, traffic blotter. Surprisingly few mentions of the *now-infamous Gulf Coast Killer.*

Tha-DUMP. Tha—

Silence.

"Water!"

Her voice is so pitiably hoarse. Something about that is either awful or endearing. There is an attic-style latch that muffles the steps below, the basement below, that whole *scene* below, and for that I am grateful. Lucky, even.

"Please! *Water!*"

A day or two always brings them beyond the point of fear and into raw animal thirst. At some point during my errands, Barbara Tiller apparently got there, too. I turn the radio up. The static seethes in a way that rattles my achy ossicles, but at least Tiller's voice is no longer there. I pull a chilled bottle of water from the cooler, disinfect its spout with a baby wipe, and bring it to my lips. Then I sip it down, long, cold, and clean.

LESLIE

Robert isn't home when I get in. Like his eyes, his personality is a slight mismatch. One side of him will leave the condo at random times; the other side is my favorite retirement companion and fellow movie critic. There's no telling what kind of side he'll land on today. But when I snap the door shut behind me, the TV's off, and when I walk to the kitchen, it's empty. The tide clock points to LOW.

But there is a clanging sound outside. I slide open the deck door and find Charlotte, our octogenarian neighbor in the side-by-side, hammering a hasp and staple padlock into our shared gate. Every *ting* of the hammer seems to surprise her. I'm not sure she's used one before.

"Leslie. Hello. I was gonna ask permission, but no one was home." *Ting*.

"Well, you should've waited."

"I know. I'm sorry. I got a battery-operated doohickey. We'll share a combination." *Ting, ting*. "But I'm sure you heard the news?"

"I did."

"Right up the way, Presidio Heights. Right here on Madre."

I'm leaning on the rail, standing on the side of Charlotte's bad ear. I step over it and onto the grassy dune, achy hips and all. "I did, Charlotte. But you know, a young man can hop this fence even when it's locked."

"You think?"

"I just stepped over it now. Look."

Charlotte stops her *ting, tinging*, pulls the nails from her lips, takes stock. "Well, it stops me."

I've seen tufts of Florida pusley growing in sidewalk cracks that have managed to stop women who were Charlotte's age. "Just promise me you'll pull these nails before Robert comes home. He's gonna hate this."

Charlotte looks at the hammer like she's just discovered it has a back side. Then she starts peeling nails out with the claw. The nails are small and smooth and come out without a fight. This padlock was never stopping a murderer.

"Well, joke's on me," Charlotte says, "because the idea was to do this for you, anyway. I'm not sure I wanna be here. I'm thinkin' of visiting my daughter. You know she's got that place on Jekyll Island, and it's not so important for me to be on Madre right now."

"That'll be fun. Maybe you'll get a vacation out of it."

"Not so much *vacation* if her husband's there." The thought cools her, but then she picks out the last nail and her mood brightens. "What about you—you got a daughter up in Pennsylvania, right? Maybe she can host you."

Sure, Steph would *love* that. Mom and stepdad so spooked by a killer in the news, they drive up the East Coast to sleep on their nineteen-year-old's pullout sofa. What will I say when we arrive? *Don't worry; we won't cramp your style, sweetie. By the way, lights out at nine p.m. And don't mind all the foot powder.*

"I don't think it's as serious as all that," I tell Charlotte. "You know, I've been following it. All of the victims were out in public someplace."

"That a fact?"

I think. "Well, he's probably an opportunist. There's no consistency to the dates. He's gone months between victims, then sometimes a couple of weeks. I think he's out in public a lot, completely anonymous, and he only strikes when he finds the right opportunity, someone alone, no one around—"

"Please. You'll give me nightmares."

"Sorry." Sometimes I forget that other people don't have the same calluses.

Back inside, I reset the kitchen back to homeostasis, dropping Robert's cups into the washer, re-rolling a loose flag of paper towels into their pin. The notepad on the counter is blank. A note—that's all I want. A normal, domestic, adult gesture.

I pull out a wineglass and consider a finger or two of rosé, but driving home after mimosas at Patricia's was already pushing my limits. The coatrack is missing Robert's newsboy cap. Good. At least I don't have to worry that a serial killer attacked him, which I know is a ridiculous, paranoid thought, but not more ridiculous than Robert being attacked and having the time to say, *Wait, let me get my favorite hat first.* No. Wherever Robert went, he's safe.

ROBERT

FBI Special Agent Teagan Cook looks ready to pop. Her belt is tight, the seam in her hair is down-the-middle precise, and the ponytail she clips at the base of her skull never swings.

"Lovely place to live," she says as she palms the steering wheel. Fontaneda Boulevard, the main thoroughfare of Madre: palm trees and ice cream shops.

I can't tell if there's a touch of envy in her voice, so I just whisper, "Thank you."

"You been retired long?" She does, of course, know my file—this is just small talk.

"About two years."

"You ever miss teaching?"

"Is it horrible if I say *not really*?"

A twinge of a smile. "I know the feeling."

My ride home. I pull off my cap and comb quivering fingers through my hair, still shaken from the lineup but loose with the postsauna feeling in the limbs that comes after great reliefs.

Being innocent is one thing. I walked through the metal detectors with my nerves finally calming, gave my driver's license to an attendant while making small talk about the Tampa Bay Rays, and then sat in a busy police hallway tapping my knees, hammering out the snares to Billy Joel's "Innocent Man."

On the way in, I looked up witness lineups on my phone. They're rare these days, and their usefulness is a matter of passionate debate, but they still exist. The idea isn't to gather a group of suspects but to confirm the confidence of an eyewitness. My question was, an eyewitness to what? This latest Madre Island abduction? Police never told me, and I never asked. I hoped I wasn't a suspect but a *filler*, like an extra in a movie, a man only there to round it out. There are plenty of reasons it would make sense if the killer looked like me. But it's not a crime to look like a killer.

If I was smart—and I never claimed to be—I would contact my lawyer. But isn't Leslie my lawyer? She'll tear me to shreds for letting it get this far without telling her. No. All I need to do is survive: get home, hold her hand, feel her fingers working my pressure points, the dip between my collarbone and my neck, prodding me to sleep.

But then they walked in. Four men, white haired like me, white skinned like me, about five-ten like me, all faintly waifish: like me. My stomach nearly fell out when I realized all of them made perfect *fillers* if the suspect was Robert Woodhouse.

None of them struck me as murderers. But neither did the man in the mirror, and here I was. One of them tried to make small talk: "Not how I wanted to spend a hot day. I have a pool." By the time we entered the sticky-aired room—reverse mirror on the wall, intercom, surveillance camera in the corner—I realized I'd forgotten to wear deodorant. A voice over the intercom told us to stay still. The man in the chambray shirt fidgeted, but I tightened, clenched every orifice.

Then we heard shuffling. Low voices. A witness, no doubt, being led in. The eight-year-old girl Leslie had gone on about?

A few minutes later, the intercom crackled.

"Number four, turn your face to the side, please."

I turned stiffly. A shiver at the corner of my lips threatened to bloom into a nervous smile. I bit it down. Thinking: *Not the killer, not the killer, not the killer.* Remembering my heterochromia. Was having one green eye and one blue one a disqualifier? Or was that exactly what they were looking for? And then, after a few excruciating ticks of silence, a voice announced that the session was over.

Now, Special Agent Cook points at a half-shaded street sign and asks, "Jefferson Lane, is it?"

"That's it."

After she pulls into our driveway, I throw out my hand to pick up the hat I'd left on her dash. "Oh. I brought my hat with me. Did you see that anywhere?"

"Hat?"

"Yeah. You know, a newsboy hat? Khaki colored, kind of flat? I just set it down."

She shakes her head, hands still on the wheel. "Didn't see it. I've got to get back."

"It's just that it's lucky. I was sure I had it with me when I got in—"

"I'll check the lost and found at the station."

"I don't think it's there."

"I'm in a bit of a hurry, Mr. Woodhouse."

"All right. Thanks."

Then I walk up the stoop as the SUV almost skids off the driveway. Maybe that's a good sign; she's in a hurry. Gotta catch the real Gulf Coast Killer somewhere. Before I open the door, I suck in a breath, collecting my story. I push in.

LESLIE

The door clicks and closes. I'm working on a jigsaw puzzle in the dining room, a Caravaggio print someone had gifted Robert. At this point I've only started fishing out the edge pieces for the frame. There's a rumbling outside, so I finger the shades open and watch a black SUV just as it pulls away. Robert walks through, mumbling.

"Where were you?" I ask, glancing up from the puzzle.

When I'd wriggle answers out of clients and witnesses, I learned it's best to state a question without context first. The evidence—the hat he's not wearing and didn't leave on the coatrack, the SUV without a Florida prefix or a Florida orange—can always come in the next line of questioning.

He turns with a bloodshot look. "Whoa. Didn't see you. The garage door was closed. Everything go well with Patricia?"

As he slides past, he plants a shaky peck on me. Old habit has me leaning into it. My hand rises to swipe my cheek clean. "The usual. But where are you coming from?"

"Lunch. Surprised you're back so soon—I know how it goes with Patricia. I'm gonna mix a drink. Want one?"

"Another?" I wave him off. "I thought you said you know how it goes with Patricia."

"It's not healthy for a man to drink alone, but if a man must . . ."

A wry smile tugs on my lips. Robert has a great skill for distraction; he's always been able to massage my worries until

I forget what I was going to say. Not this time. Patricia and all her warnings leave me with a phantom presence in the room. At least he's not doing his usual tell, not massaging his jaw like he does sometimes when I ask if he took the recycle bin out for the truck, when he says yes and then I look outside and only see empty curb. Still, I wonder. Was he at lunch? Alone? Or with Weston?

"So that's a yes? A no?" He grins at me, then heads for the kitchen.

I drop my puzzle pieces and follow his footsteps through the hall, glancing at the door, the empty coatrack. I find him clanking through collins glasses in the kitchen. "When I got home, Charlotte was nailing some kind of padlock into our gate," I tell him. "I convinced her it was pointless before she did any more damage."

"I've said a hundred times that we need to contact her family about her. She's too old to be living on her own."

"And Patricia was in a mood." Offering something to get something. "I suppose so was I. She'd had a long flight. Needed to pass out, I think."

"She shouldn't travel alone these days. It's dangerous."

"Where was lunch?"

"Gina's. The sandwich place."

"What'd you have?"

He pounds the glass he's holding onto our countertop. "Christ, Leslie—"

"You can tell me if it was with Wes. I know he's tough to talk about, but maybe I could help—"

"It's not that." His jaws pinch tight. "It's your tone. You're cross-examining."

When he says it out loud, it rings true. I swallow, stiffen, folding my inner attorney away somewhere murky and deep. "It's just I feel you've been gone, or more distant lately, and I'm never sure where. Or why."

"Then you're not listening to me. I told you acupuncture last week, lunch just now. It would be nice if you took my word for it once in a while."

Then he walks out, glass in hand, rubbing the ache out of his jaw.

That night we watch a movie on separate ends of the couch. But no matter how strange it feels, we still share our circadian bond, and we go to bed at the same time.

We whisper awhile, and as the night goes, the butterflies in my stomach start to shake free. Robert recounts his conversation with our favorite waiter; he ordered a Reuben sandwich. I still suspect that the lunch was with he-who-shall-not-be-discussed, but I leave it for now. The sleep that follows is my favorite kind, dumb and dreamless.

The next morning is a Sunday. I take Robert's car (sans Robert) to St. Anthony's, and when I come home, Robert isn't out at acupuncture or an impromptu lunch but happily scrolling through his tablet out on our deck. Comforted, I stay inside to puzzle. The Caravaggio is slow work. Too many brown shades. There are entire sections without reference clues, countless pieces cloaked in shadow. In that way, Caravaggio reminds me of Robert. When it's done, I stand over it and frown. "You didn't see a puzzle piece, did you?"

"What?"

I point. "I'm mostly done. But I need his eye."

Robert squeezes himself up from the sofa to have a look. The puzzle is *Narcissus*, a youth leaning over a black mirror of water. When Robert sees it, his face flushes.

"Are you all right?" I ask.

"Hunky-dory. I'll look in the cushions."

There are more questions I could ask—what happened to his newsboy hat? Why does a missing puzzle piece send shock waves through him?—but Robert whips up a delicious, oniony shrimp ceviche, which we eat outside until the evening light hits me like melatonin. Soon I'm ready to dip my head into his shoulder and numb myself with three episodes of a TV show I will forget by sunrise.

Which is when my phone rumbles on the glass of our coffee table.

Need you, baby sis

WESTON

Sunday is a tour of western Florida. A quick Craigslist job for a landlord who needed to change the locks of their apartment's upper level. Their very first tenant! Then picking up hair dye (my original color somewhere near 118 Off Onyx) and a clean, maintenance-grade bucket. Before dropping off the Aviator at Hertz—no need for that anymore—I stop at a gas station / car wash to sanitize my dashboard and vacuum out any tufts of DNA. I get a long look at myself in the rearview mirror. I am not even close to the face on my Colorado driver's license, but the woman at the Hertz only asks, "Fashion statement?" She means my white Robert Woodhouse hair.

"More like a failed fashion experiment." I smile.

She smiles back. Her coppery hair rolls like silk in the sunlight.

Then I take a rideshare inland and hop out for a sweaty evening stroll back to the cabin. Once "home," the man looking back at me in the hand mirror looks a tad disheveled. The bleached hair will meet its end today. Strange to think I might miss it a little. It gave Robert such a shock when I turned up at his condo all that time ago, my hair bleached as white as his. He stood there with two plump grocery bags. The apples shivered in the plastic.

Robert, I said.

Wes?

I bit down on my teeth and corrected him: Weston.

He cupped his lips and tongued his gums, question marks hovering in those mismatched eyes. Had I gone prematurely gray overnight? Did I somehow want to *be* him? What did I have planned, anyway? As to the specific question he wanted to ask—I have no idea. The lines of his face, of anyone's face, were like some illegible cursive I would have learned in fourth grade if anyone had had the patience to teach me. I muttered something about needing help.

Weston, he said, you know I don't have a lot of money.

Not help like that.

I told him about Marco Island. Sparing details, of course.

He set the grocery bags down on the ground, which was a terrible idea. (Once, when researchers put a slide of street-puddle water under a microscope, they found thirty-one thousand types of fecal bacteria.) And he offered to get me the help I needed, but his notions of help all involved police somehow, and besides, I told him, *we* were responsible.

We?

Yes, I said. We. We, the white-haired man with the same mismatched eyes and the same attached earlobes and the same sunken-in temples and the same approximate height, five-ten. We.

He invited me in—Leslie was away—and I felt so pleasant when I surveyed their home, so lived-in with its warm amber lamps and unfinished puzzles. At some point I excused myself to wash my hands. The guest faucet was broken, but I could use his.

His shavings were still left over from that morning. Clipped hair sticks to everything. His stubble rolled through the sink in the spots he had forgotten to rinse, spinning down in hairy ant-like veins.

A silent thrill washed through me. I had imagined possibly digging through a shower drain for the appropriate DNA, but he shared a shower with Leslie, too, so that was out. Saliva on his toothbrush might suffice, but there was no reliable way to leave that at a scene. Hair. It had to be hair. You can scatter hair like seeds. Well, here it was. Robert Woodhouse, in stubble form. I had a baggie on me, because baggies are always handy. The real trouble would be washing his stubble out of the webs of my fingers.

As I walked out, I stopped at the puzzle on the dining room table. A sunny-blue cross-section of the Amalfi Coast.

"If you really hurt someone," Robert said, "you have to tell someone."

"Tell," I echoed. "Tell who? The police?" The notes I had left in my phone were perfect for this exact moment. I pulled it out. "Patricia Colton lives at 33 Pheasant Crossing. Her home has a gate. The passcode is 1957. Stephanie Tressler, 2938 Seventy-First, apartment 7G. No code there. Place was built in the sixties. Probably has a dead bolt. Funny name, I always thought, for something meant to protect you." I worked the puzzle with my fingers. I picked up a piece—a roof one, rippling with terra-cotta tiles—and held it aloft for Robert to see. "Leslie."

The way Robert swallowed that, the pathetic click of his throat, told me the message was received.

Then I pocketed the piece.

Thump thump thump. Tha-DUMP.

The sound yanks me out of the memory. And now, thinking of my father, and my father's dumb, checkmated look, not to mention the baggie full of his stubble, my entire head itches something fierce. Time to wash out the dye. And rinse and wash. For the Off Onyx, the process is no trouble at all. Start conditioning two or three days before, the internet said, because if you bleached your hair recently, as I have, the whole thing might go limp. Cloak yourself in towels. To be truly careful, you can dab petroleum jelly on your hairline so as not to stain the skin.

Pa-dump-a-BOOM.

That noise from downstairs again. Still toweled, I tap my foot on the basement latch, two staccato notes. *Quiet, please.*

The 118 Off Onyx runs more like 148 Midnight Black as I brush it in, but my hair is wet, and the color will soften after I dry. The green contact lens will give me more trouble. Eyes are more than windows to the soul—they leak into the entire immune system. Every drop of saline, ostensibly straight from the factory, has had contact with the air. The pinch-and-pull method gets the lens out on the first try. Still, I feel it. A snag in my thoughts. A speckle on my fingertip. A parenthetical memory of one of Robert's gray stubbles sticking to my skin: that's all it takes to dirty the whole process. And in goes the saline, and the contact lens again, so I can pull it out—pure this time, pure thoughts only. Pinch and (Robert) pull and *No, I did it again.* Saline in. Eyes itchy and red. Contact back in. Pinch and (Robert) pull and "Will you get it together please," I say this aloud. Too aloud. I have company. Barbara will hear. I quiet myself. Will you get it together, please. Saline. Pinch and pull. My left eye is weeping and bloodshot and (Robert Alan Woodhouse) *AND THAT IS THE LAST TIME, THE VERY LAST TIME*, but it is eleven and eleven is an uneven number and three is a good number and saline—am I running out?—and again and again and (Robert) again.

This goes on into the night. Night three. That means The Big Day is tomorrow.

But all of it is worth it for the sake of a head of white hair, one seafoam-green eye. To have become *him*. To see the face Robert made on that first day after Marco Island when I told him *I* am not responsible for a single death, but *we* definitely are.

After I towel off, I am glad to see my hair dry to a fainter shade. I think I was right. Onyx, not black.

LESLIE

"Cancer." Patricia's voice quivers, stuffy through a tissue. "They don't know how long it's been there. But that's the word of the day—*cancerous*—and they want me in for more tests first thing."

I wrap a useless hand around hers. It doesn't feel like her to tell me news like this in the waiting room of some clinic. She called me direct after the news and didn't want to go home alone. It isn't how I would have pictured her. In my mind, Patricia would have waited to get home, poured us both a pinot gris, then broken the news once our stomachs were stuffed with French pork rillettes. Instead, we're sitting next to a humming Powerade machine and a HANG IN THERE! poster.

"It's so strange," Patricia says. "I was walking around Santorini that whole time, feeling more miserable than I deserved. Missing James, I guess. Or grumbling whenever a restaurant served squid instead of steak. All the time I was carrying this in me. I'm so . . . ungrateful. I was in the most beautiful place in the world."

"Did they give you any sort of prognosis?"

"Oh, you know doctors. Never want to get pinned down. They'll do some more tests to confirm it hasn't spread. Can't wait to find out myself." Her voice buckles.

"Hey. You're an otherwise healthy woman. There are all sorts of treatments now. People live for decades after their diagnosis." That's a guess. "But if you do kick the bucket, do you mind if we list you as *Patty* in the obituary?"

She nearly chokes on her tissue, which I can tell is a laugh.

I never gave any thought to the notion that my older sister might die one day. I know it as a general concept: we're all mortal, everyone eventually dies. But the thought was never specific to her. Patricia is the only person I've known my whole life, from the beginning until now. Mom went first, and dad would've been 102 last Wednesday. An older sibling is different; they're with you for the entire run. I do my best to share her laugh, pat her hand, show her I'm not worried. Somehow, I'm not. The spry confidence that usually belongs to her has leapt over to me.

I use that confidence to handle a few logistics. Will her son in Scottsdale come to support? She already told him no: she has plenty of support here. And I referred a lawyer to help her plan the estate one year ago, so paperwork is not an issue.

Later we walk to the parking lot, arm in arm, cheeks drying in the crisp evening wind. We say our goodbyes and get in our respective cars. I follow her for a few turns, skipping the exit onto Madre, and then the second-chance turn for the exit onto Madre. She throws her hazards on at an intersection and I pull up to her side.

"Stalker!" she teases through the windows.

"Oh, you thought that was goodbye for the night? No sister of mine is ending the day alone."

When we get back to Patricia's, Fluf greets me in the living room. He's freshly groomed and eager to lick my fingertips.

"That dog is so bizarre," Patricia says as she drills a wine opener into a bottle of pinot. "Barks at *everyone*. My neighbor—the one with the mastiff—crosses the street when she sees us."

"What can I say? I'm delicious."

Patricia brings over two glasses and we settle on her big sectional. "Okay, if you're here to distract me—I'm game. But you're going to have to come up with ideas. If it was just me, my ideas would end at wine."

"We could do some internet sleuthing."

"Now we're talking. Robert?"

I cough: a squirt of wine went down the wrong tube. "Steph would be more fun."

"Perfect. Five bucks she's got a boyfriend."

Out come the phones. Patricia keeps a more active Instagram account than I do—it's currently bright and beachy with seaside selfies and carousels of handmade jewelry from a shop in Oia, Greece. My profile stops at three pictures. The most recent is a month ago: a goofy POV of Robert sticking out a blueberry-purple tongue at the Balanced Diet. I can't help but smile. All the tiny, glorious nonsense he has brought into my life.

I tap over to Steph, who isn't hard to find because she's one of the seven people I follow. There's nothing new. Every post is already loaded with a full red heart from Mom. I recognize a study-group photo, a plaid shirtdress selfie, and—my favorite—a soft black-and-white mirror portrait. The top she's wearing in her last story shows a little too much navel for me, so I leave that unliked. She's an adult now, but I still have my protests.

"Boyfriend!" Patricia shouts. "Boyfriend, boyfriend! That was easy."

She flashes me the picture I blew right past: the study group. White chicklet Ivy League smiles, pressed shirts, trestle table, a big Philadelphia balcony. In her Penn crewneck, Steph looks like a lithe, young, brown-haired Patricia. Four women and two men. One is tall and oafish with more gums than lips, and the wispy one isn't Steph's type at all—she has him by a solid six inches. "That's not worth five bucks. Steph would have told me."

"You *think* she would."

"You can't assume anything from that. That's a group picture."

"The tall one is kinda cute. They're standing next to each other."

I study it and pinch to zoom. "Okay, so only four of them are tagged and he's not one of 'em. She's leaning away. He has his hands folded. He's nervous. A guy isn't nervous around his girlfriend. And he's wearing Polo. You remember Steph's high school boyfriends? One was Gothy and the other was a theater kid. She likes alternative and offbeat. If she starts posting backstage pictures at some tattooed guy's *gigs*, then, yes, I'll give you your five bucks. But this guy—I remember her making a joke about how she'd never run with 'the Ivy League crowd.' This guy looks like he was born in Allen Edmonds. He's a prep. He's an anti-Steph."

Patricia is staring at me. "Yeesh. Does the defense rest, Ms. Woodhouse?"

"Defense rests."

Later we stream trashy island-dating shows and eat crackers on her sectional, splaying out like we're still college students with big limbs and screaming-hot metabolisms. That's what it reminds me of: coming home in the summers when Patricia and I were in college. We both worked at a frozen-custard stand in the evenings, leaving us nothing to do in the mornings. We'd sit on the couch and make fun of all the dating-game shows and cheesy soaps the world had to offer. We were immortal then. If there is no Patricia, there is no one who has an answer for my remember-when questions. To lose a person is to lose the corroboration of your memories, which is the same as losing the memories. The same as losing everything.

Between episodes, I grab the remote to turn the TV off, thinking Patricia is asleep. Instead she leans over and sets her fingers on my wrist. "Les. What's that thing you always say about heaven?"

"That life is to heaven as dreams are to life. One day, we'll wake up, and we won't mind the bad stuff. We'll be glad it wasn't real."

"That's it. You think I'm going there?"

"What, heaven?"

"Yes, heaven. You're stalling."

"When's the last time you went to confession?"

She pricks my shoulder. "I'm serious."

"So am I." But I'm a hypocrite: it's been too long since my last confession, too. "I'd say yes. But you shouldn't think about heaven. I think the people who think about death are always inviting it in."

"I don't know." Her green eyes hold to mine for a beat, and hers are always so mysterious, bright and vague like soda glass in sunlight. "Some things we gotta face, Les."

We watch another half episode. Patricia is sleeping by the time the screen dips black and asks if we're still watching. I click off the TV, peel off all three rows of her necklaces as she mumbles a complaint, then parachute a blanket over her legs. Before I go, I watch her chest rise and fall. I don't leave until I see her make three good, healthy breaths.

ROBERT

When you get home I'd like to talk about Wes

The cursor blinks on the *s* in my son's name. My thumb hangs over the arrow. Once tapped, it'll instruct the app to convert *Wes* and all my other words into a series of ones and zeroes, pop them to a nearby cell tower, and transmit them to Leslie, where her phone will decode all that black-and-white data into these words of infinite meaning. Texting is strange like that: a single slip of the thumb can cut through your entire life. One tap.

Leslie won't let a text like that go, though, even if I rethink it later—she'd come in asking five piercing and perfect questions I can no longer avoid.

I clamp my thumb over the text and hold tight. *Select all.*

I go to the cupboard and pour a quarter cup of popcorn kernels into the coconut oil I've melted over the stove. They *ting* pleasantly into the pot. A Pavlovian response warms my insides: first the popcorn, then the *pfffff* of a can of sugar-free Sprite, and soon the percussive *ka-chunggg* of Netflix. Tonight I will miss Leslie's murmur as she reads every title I scroll through—I don't think she knows she does it—and when I grab the potassium salt, I will start to feel the circadian hug of bedtime.

The kernels are heating as I grab the Sprite and look out toward the ocean. Charlotte is out sweeping the sand off her deck. She sees me and waves; I smile, flick up a hand. She goes back to sweeping, *whish-whish*. A Sisyphean effort, of course, but I understand why she does it. One sandy misstep could change everything for a woman her age.

A single slip.

But it never feels like a *single* slip, does it? Looking back, I see all my missteps came in bunches. Wes's mother, one mistake. Wes, another mistake. Then the thousand mistakes she made rearing him, and my mistakes, all leading up to that day he showed up in the driveway with his hair bleached white.

Maybe that was the slip. Everything before then had some element of plausible deniability attached to it. *I was young, I wasn't ready, I didn't know how to be a father.* But when he comes to you and tells you he killed someone when he's dressed like you, and then threatens your wife, picking up her loose puzzle pieces when no one's home—what then?

The afternoon tattooed itself into my memory. I sat on the love seat on our porch with my hands folded, lungs heaving, checking my watch so I could tell the police exactly when he had visited: 1:02 p.m. But the afternoon melted out of my hands. Every minute would be another tick of embarrassment if I had to answer awkward police questions: *If it was three hours ago, sir, why didn't you report it right away?* Would they start suspecting *me*? A man with similar hair, similar build, similar eyes? I woke up the next morning with a wood-chipped texture inside my cheeks and knew it had become official: I had let a night pass. It might as well have been a year. Now, every time I feel as though I'm finally gathering the courage, Wes goes and does something. It's like he knows. A puzzle piece missing. A blank envelope dropped in our mailbox.

That woman at Presidio Heights.

The soda almost makes me gag. The lemon is too fake, too medicinal. Leslie never buys the full-sugar ones, and I'm not supposed to have full-sugar ones, but I like the full-sugar ones. Sometimes she keeps them in the back, behind a bag of celery or leftover chopped onions.

Thump-thump.

I stand and clamp the refrigerator shut. Hover in the darkness, soda bubbling in my hands. Waiting to hear if the sound will repeat.

It came from the front yard. Charlotte, maybe? Leslie said she'd been outdoors trying to install some lock. Charlotte is sharp most days, but sometimes she looks at you from those foggy eyes for so long, you start wondering if you'll have to plug her back in.

As I approach the front door, the plumbing gives a squeak. The thin walls of Senectitude have made this a routine sound. That's Charlotte back indoors and safe in her bathroom, then.

Leslie's most recent text said don't wait up, so I'm still not expecting her for a while. Maybe it's another neighbor having an episode; Leslie and I are spring chickens in this neighborhood. I walk on light heels to the dining room window, then pull the curtain back. The palm trees are dim in the queasy yellow light of Jefferson Lane.

Thump-da-dump.

Footsteps. Undeniably. The wooden stomps of someone climbing up the stairs to the deck. I rush to go lock up, but before I make it through the kitchen, the wall darkens. I spin around in time to see a figure clouding the beveled glass of our front door.

LESLIE

The drive back onto Madre takes me past St. Anthony's. CONFESSIONS TONIGHT a reader board announces. That's a thought. How long has it been? Patricia's news left a heaving slice somewhere under my heart, but the idea of finally gaining the courage to tell a priest all my troubles might suture me up. A tiny accomplishment.

I click on the blinker and pull in.

Incense. An old woman mumbling prayers in Spanish. The altarpiece glowing in golden light. I cross myself with a dab of holy water and kneel somewhere near the back, the usual corner, and pull my rosary out of my purse.

None of the words come. I can only think about Patricia.

As I work the beads, hoping to at least mime myself into a sense of peace, I hear whispers in the confessionals. A classic Florida sunbird in a tea-length skirt pops out of one, kneels in a pew, and starts praying her penance. Five Hail Marys, I think. A light penance, the kind of woman who confesses mildly impolite thoughts about her daughter-in-law, no doubt. When she's done, I envy the easy smile on her face.

In the other booth, the line has dwindled. A young priest with thinning hair walks out. "Ma'am? Are you here for confessions?"

I smile. *Just a tiny accomplishment,* I'd thought.

"Thank you," I whisper. Meaning *no thank you.*

He returns the smile and retreats inside. A few minutes later, skipping a decade or two of the rosary, I drop a premature *Amen.* Once I'm out of the parking lot and back onto the bridge, I realize I've been holding my breath. That old superstition. But that was for cemeteries, not confessions, and certainly not churches.

At the protected left onto Fontaneda Boulevard, my phone buzzes. Steph, finally getting back? Patricia, awake and needing something? Nope. Unknown caller. I screen it. A car behind me beeps—the protected left is green—and I toss up an apology wave.

Almost home.

My stomach sinks when I turn onto Jefferson Lane.

Every dark corner of the cul-de-sac is rippling in red and blue. Another ambulance? They're too frequent around here. Maybe it's here for Charlotte. The lights are certainly close enough to our condo. But as I pull closer, I see an entire ring of cars around the cul-de-sac. I was wrong; there isn't an ambulance here. Every car, every SUV, is police.

They're right outside our door.

The officer who waves me down near my driveway is familiar. Sergeant Clay Ingram knows me from his prior years as the Madre PD records custodian. Not as a friend, exactly, but a constant source of small talk before I retired. The back of my throat goes dry as I recognize the heaviness behind his eyes.

I kill the engine and stand out in the road, but my legs go wobbly.

The police. The headlines. Presidio Heights, just up the beach.

I'm certain Robert is dead.

"Leslie Woodhouse?"

I nod, dumbly, and as Ingram catches me with his knuckly bear-claw of a handshake, my hand goes stiff inside his.

I can only scream.

And scream. And scream. The images come flooding. Is he splayed in the bathtub? Leaning against a spray of blood all over the brocade?

"Leslie, that's not it." Ingram's look is a wet mush of empathy and confusion. He holds me up under the armpits, pops me up, wipes the dust off my arms. "Your husband is under arrest. I'd like to discuss it somewhere else, if we can."

Ingram leads me down to one of the squad cars and hands me a copy of the search warrant. One of his gloved partners walks through, holding Robert's tablet under his arm. In the driveway, a woman in an FBI vest is collecting samples of an oil stain I've never been able to fully wash out of the concrete. Thorough.

When I speak, my throat is still achy from screaming. "You said arrested?"

Ingram leans into his car, pulls out a thermos of coffee. Sweat has matted his curly black hair to his forehead. It looks like it's painted on, the way children get when they've been playing too long outside. "We suspect your husband is responsible for a string of murders along the coast—"

"*Murders?*"

"Yes. He's been charged with six. Now, I don't know if you've heard—"

"You think he's the Gulf Coast Killer."

He only looks at me, lost for words.

My gutted breath spills out of me in a wheezing, restless sigh. Ingram doesn't seem to notice I don't want to hear the rest. "Stop. Please. Just take me down to see him."

"I'd really feel better asking you a few questions—"

"This is your car, right?" I point. "Has he spoken to you? Is there anyone advocating for him at *all*?"

"Leslie, please—"

"I'd like you to drive me down to see him."

As Ingram looks down, I imagine taking me in: this tiny woman, her rocket-fuel adrenaline. "All right then, Leslie." He catches himself. "Ma'am. Seat belts, please." And then he drives me back up Jefferson Lane, past the Lincoln Aviator—*the Aviator*, is that why they think it?—and past St. Anthony's, where evening confessions, I see, have ended.

ROBERT

"Leslie. Woodhouse." In just two words, the muted trumpet of Leslie's voice soothes me. And then the voicemail bot takes over: " . . . is not available. At the tone . . ."

My phone call. Special Agent Cook flips open a metal tray so I can slide the mobile to her without any risk of flesh-to-flesh contact.

I'm the only one sitting inside Madre Island PD's complete overkill of a holding cell. The thing could fit maybe half a dozen drunk drivers, with room enough to sleep off their buzz. But there's no one else here, no one else even on the same floor except the officers at their cubicles, each in different stages of filing, calling, or staring. *Six victims, some of whom were completely overpowered. By this old guy?* Well, I hope me and my liver spots are a disappointment. In a half-hour or so, they'll have the pleasure of witnessing how often I pee.

"Was that your wife or your lawyer?" Cook asks.

"Both, I hope."

"Both?"

I don't reply. Leslie told me never to talk to the police. Or at least she shouted as much at her favorite crime shows—*Never talk to the police, you idiot, no, no, noooo*—and I knew she meant it in a deep, cold Wisconsin corner of her soul. The elongated *o*'s from her youth sprang thick from the back of her tongue.

Cook holds the mobile in her hand, her nose wrinkled. "Really? Nothing?"

After an offer of water or food, which I decline, she walks off to talk to some of her dark-suited FBI colleagues. They shoot me stares of caffeinated frustration. As if I'm the one holding them up, as if I'm holding back some key piece of information that will save Barbara Tiller.

Maybe they have a point.

My head went fizzy as they read the charges, even if my worst fears were coalescing into a blinding and unbearable focus. Six counts of first-degree homicide. The Gulf Coast Killer. There was no more pretending I'd heard Wes wrong, that our conversation from months back had just been another one of his spastic, meaningless ramblings. He did this. He really did this.

Which means the threats are just as real. The incomplete Caravaggio flashes in my mind.

Cook walks over with an impatient look in her eyes. "I'll try again. If there's anything you know about Barbara Tiller, you could help us save a life."

I pluck at the cage with a fingernail, feeling trapped. But a small wave of relief washes over me: Wes can't hurt Barbara Tiller if he's trying to frame me.

"I know," Cook says as she walks away. "Lawyer, lawyer . . ."

Yes. Leslie is my way through this. She's been my way through everything.

These last few years—before Wes came back to Florida, anyway—have been my favorite. My absolute favorite. Meeting Leslie made me feel like I'd been married for decades. We bit off more than we could chew with the seaside condo, that much was true, but still I thought, *I made it. I found peace.* Before Leslie,

I'd settled into a routine. Being a lifelong bachelor wouldn't be so bad. And as soon as I accepted that, there she was one day at the farmers market, all of five-foot-five, with blushy skin and a bronze pixie cut she was letting gray. I remember thinking, *A woman like that would be exactly what I need*, then leaving to sniff some heirloom tomatoes. Life had given me better luck with tomatoes.

Then she stood next to me, searching, and picked up a Cherokee Purple. "Reminds me of a Jackson Pollock," she said.

"I'm an art professor. That's more of an Elaine de Kooning."

She scrunched her nose at me, then off we went.

At our age, baggage was a given. She had a daughter approaching high school age, a saintly late husband named Cal, and if I searched for her online, the first ten headlines were about a killer she'd once defended. She had a fear of glass and open blades and had to "correct" them if they pointed at anyone in the room. I remembered that and, for our first Christmas, bought her a set of plastic children's knives. Her eyes welled up. I was about to apologize—*No, no, it's a gag gift, not a women-belong-in-the-kitchen gift*—when she wrapped her arms around me and confessed that she hadn't done any cutting since Cal had passed. Later, she told me that was the moment she knew I was her "second One."

And all I'd really done was make a bad joke. *Remember? Knives? Ha ha.*

But I didn't correct her. The gift brought her too much joy. And I knew I was the one dragging the real baggage into our relationship. She asked constant questions about my estranged son: What is he like? What does he do? Did you spend time with him growing up?

No. Not really. Wes had become a child to me the way an old house becomes a money pit—first a bright hope, then a steady grind of reality, then an everlasting obligation. There's no kinder way to put it. Leslie would probably never have married me if I'd spelled out the whole story. It was much easier to pretend his mother and I had ended things badly and maintained a respectful, distant arrangement. Ending things badly—that much was true. Which explained why I was estranged from my son. She'd raised him. Poisoned him against me. Made me the source of all that had ever gone wrong in their lives.

But none of it really matters. The sickness was in him from the start. I'm just his excuse.

And now I've waited too long.

My first step: Not guilty. For that, I need Leslie on board.

I should've taken the water because I feel a headache coming on and I have to piss anyway. I turn away, unzip, and barely manage a trickle. An old man's prostate and a room full of cops—not a prescription for flow. I zip up. I fall to the bench, tired, thirsty, raw. The inside of my cheek is still scraped from Cook's hard DNA swab.

What I really need is an Ambien, my wife, and the perfectly firm king-size mattress that took me sixty-odd years to pin down. But of the three, I'd pick my wife.

WESTON

Radio off.

All right, then. Time to move.

For the past few days, I've slowly hacked away at my un-essentials. Now my life can fit in a backpack: wallet, tablet, burner, universal chargers, rakes, hooks, ball picks, bump keys, pick gun—all the tools of the trade, really—box cutter, sanitizing wipes, hand soap, gardening gloves (who questions a gardener?), plastic baggies, and the aforementioned radio. All of it takes about a minute to clump into my rucksack. Easy-peasy.

Thankfully, the radio started crackling with activity early in the evening, which gave me the most important gift: time. *Suspect in custody.* Now I could clean. Truly clean. A rag, a bottle of bleach, and one solid hour of work should do it. Call it a form of procrastination. If not for the whole scene downstairs, I might have done this sooner.

When the hour is done and I have no more procrastinating to do, I snap on an N95 mask and kick the latch open with the blunt tip of my sneaker. The way the hinge whines announces years of rust. I have opened it exactly twice before this: once to test, second for the real thing. This third time, a new scent burns under my eyelids: urine and feces.

Regrettable, but ultimately unavoidable.

I snap on a headlamp and work my rag and bleach up to down, ignoring the mass of flesh on the floor that sometimes catches the light. Ignoring all her simpering, broken-puppy noises. Dropping a few of Robert's leftover whiskers on the floor makes me want to wash my hands. I am positive a few whiskers caught in the webs of my fingers. Maybe one in a knuckle crinkle. The light makes it impossible to tell.

"Please . . ." she whispers. "Please . . . don't . . ."

The poor thing. Her voice is down to a shallow croak.

And then I have to do what I came for. I flash the light on her, careful to keep my face behind its glare. It catches her soiled legs, the soft peak of her hips. She lies side face just as I left her, her feet still chained to the utility pole, still blindfolded. Her wrists are bound to the leg of a utility sink. A simple bump key unshackles her ankles. The irony of that: any old key would have set her free, if only someone knew where to find her.

I thumb the box cutter, extending it three clicks.

"No." She wiggles out of my grip. She swallows a dry click of air. Her cheeks are flushed, almost pretty. "Please."

"This will be very quick. I promise."

"No!"

She kicks herself across the floor as far as she can, all knuckles and knees. Poor woman. But to do the gentlemanly thing, if you can call it gentlemanly, I have to force the issue. I work the cutter into the lashes and yank.

There is an animal instinct in the way she kicks at me, which startles me and pushes me upright. And she goes on kicking air, as if expecting to bleed out. It may be hours before she realizes I have cut her loose. Fear has that paralytic effect. But even so, I am better off gone.

I toss the cutter in my backpack and leap to the stairs before she realizes something in her lashes has come loose. Ideally, she'll think she escaped by herself somehow, and no police officer or lawyer will ever wonder why I—why *Robert*—might have cut her free.

Once outside, I finally breathe.

The air outside is much cleaner, thick and heady. The sun bleeds red. A fine late evening. I pull out a bottle of hand sanitizer and wet myself clean. I quiver despite the heat, shaking out all her unpleasantness, trying to stir myself into a smile. Robert Woodhouse is in custody. Barbara Tiller is free, or will be, once her fear washes off.

I tighten my backpack straps around my shoulders and make for the road, walking through a womb of palm and tupelo trees until I am born again near a busy gas station.

A bottle of Coke from inside their big reach-in cooler sounds pretty nice right now, but for the surveillance cameras. Instead, I stuff some cash into a vending machine, settle for a can, and sip it while doing a little people watching. Their own lives are so absorbing: their fascinating phones and their wailing toddlers and their pump TV screens fretting about chances of rain. No one has any reason to look at me, unremarkable as I am, my homochromatic eyes, my 118 Off Onyx hair, my "Hello, nice weather tonight."

I ask a passing man if he can believe how much a can of Coke is now. He whistles and says, "Rip-off," without breaking stride. I love the invisible rhythm of it. By the time he walks inside and I walk a few yards up the road, the conversation is already forgotten. I am safe and invisible and free to do as I please.

PART
TWO

LESLIE

When Ingram walks me into a conference room, I think about Robert in big red words. *Arrested. Suspect. Murder.* I sit. And as I do, my loafers catch on the spine of the table, exposing heel. Now that I'm alone and waiting by the windows, I can't seem to slip it on again. Not in a way that satisfies me. Not until my foot clicks in as I'm thinking pure, green words.

That's how it is for me. Some people wash and wash; others can't leave the kitchen until they've checked the stove light five times. Mine is about timing. Correcting the snag in my thoughts. If I say *good night* as I flick the light off, a good night it will be. When I sit down at restaurants, I turn the steak knives blades-out so I won't suffer an accidental stabbing. As I hop from the last step of the Jetway to the plane, I have to be thinking *good flight*—green words—or else the blood of a hundred passengers will be on my hands. A therapist once tried to pinpoint the source of these compulsions. A controlling mother? An absent father? No and no. It simply sprang out of me, dry and itchy and bleeding, an unpredictable rash of the mind.

It doesn't help that the red words sometimes come true. These compulsions tend to kick in at the worst times: first when my mother was in the hospital, then when I was opening application replies from law schools. Now I'm in a police conference room, streetlights shanking in through the blinds, wondering at my husband, working and reworking my loafers until I think good green thoughts about Robert. There's rustling outside the door; police headed in. I slip the shoe back on, *Robert is innocent.* This time it takes.

FBI Special Agent Teagan Cook introduces herself along with Ingram, and we sit at the head of the conference table. Cook offers a cardboard smile. Am I comfortable? Would I like water, coffee, something from the vending machine? It always irked me when police would go overboard on these offers with my clients, creating the effect that we were all on one big team. I tell her no, no, and no.

Cook flips through a folder and reads the charges, six counts of first-degree homicide, without dancing around the fact that my husband is accused of being the Gulf Coast Killer. She watches my reaction; I give her none. She opens a fresh legal pad. "Were you ever witness to anything your husband did in relation to these murders?"

"I'll stop you there," I reply. "I'm not going to say anything until I can speak to my husband."

This makes Ingram squirm. His eyes are hazy and bright, almost ghosty. "Leslie, we have a potential victim out there by the name of Barbara Tiller. We might be able to help her. Anything you can do to help *us* would be much appreciated."

As if I know, as if I've been reading Robert's *how I murder* diaries, as if there are any such diaries to begin with. "And, as I said, I can't help you until I speak to my husband."

"You'll have plenty of time to speak to him," Cook assures me. "If we can just ask—"

"I'm sorry," I start again. I can go all night. I've had decades to develop the thick husk of a lawyer who's spoken to countless police. "I can't help you until I speak to my husband."

Cook shoots Ingram a questioning look.

"She was a criminal defense lawyer," he replies.

"Still licensed," I note.

"Forgive me. Still licensed." A beat, then a whisper to Cook: "She defended Cokie Dean."

Blood roils in my jaw. Cokie Dean. That name again, twenty years on. The way people talked about that case, you'd think I was some sort of magician. Truth is, I got lucky. And I'd had more glorious moments in criminal defense than Cokie Dean.

Ingram sighs. "You're speaking as his lawyer, then?"

"What I said was that I can't help you until I—"

"I did catch that much." Ingram sits up, twiddles his pen between his fingers. "Agent Cook, can I see you in the hall?"

Cook is writing something. I don't know what. She's already halfway down the front page of her notes despite getting nothing out of me. "I'm not finished here."

"Just for a moment?"

She gives him a huff, tosses her pen so it clatters noisily on the table, then follows him out. I tuck a mental note about Cook for later: it's late; they'll have worked at least a ten-hour day, but nothing satisfies her. She wants to keep asking questions. When Ingram asked for a break, blood bloomed in her cheeks. In the hundreds of law enforcement personnel I've dealt with over the years, anxious and ambitious are fraternal twins.

The heel of my loafer pinches. I've been slipping my shoe on and off ever since she mentioned Cokie Dean.

My most infamous client. Google me and you'll get two headlines about him. Go to the images and you'll see a mug shot of Cokie, a forty-three-year-old man with neck tattoos, a red ducktail beard, and tracky, pumped-up arms betraying years of steroid abuse. The name used to follow me everywhere. I hoped an early retirement might put it past me, yet here we are. Again.

When I asked him what happened the night his wife died, he kept rubbing his arms into his nose. We only got fifteen minutes in before I begged him not to testify. It would've ruined him. He never blinked, he spoke in a stuttering Morse code of f-bombs, and he had a habit of sucking up saliva every time there was a question that pricked him. He denied the accusations to my face, even after I gave him the spiel about attorney-client privilege. I told him I chose to believe him. He smiled at that. I saw the silver in his teeth.

In Cokie's version of the night in question, he had been drunk but innocent. Went to a dive bar, downed too many vodka Red Bulls, and drove back to his RV park with a buddy to plink beer bottles with bows and arrows. Conveniently so, because this same friend turned out to be his alibi. Sometime around 10:30 p.m., a neighbor near Cokie's old house—where his wife was staying—testified to hearing a loud noise and seeing a man of Cokie's swollen silhouette limping down the block. When I invited the alibi down to the courthouse, he took one look at the media camped out front and decided to recant his story. Suddenly, he'd been too drunk to say what Cokie did that night.

That's when the case grabbed headlines. Cokie's wife was a grocery cashier, one with a smile everybody loved, and far too pretty for him. Every time they showed her photo on the news, side by side with Mr. Neck Tattoo, the injustice of it all whipped people into a frenzy. Everyone assumed he was guilty. I would have. But then fate threw me a lifeline: for some reason, two young cops claiming exigent circumstances that didn't exist raided his RV. They found a T-shirt of Cokie's they later ran for his wife's blood. Positive. It seemed like the case should have ended there, but my defense attorney instincts kicked in: Cokie still had rights. Maybe the T-shirt was from another night, maybe the police had no right to search his RV. I grilled the two cops on the stand, one right after the other, and nailed them on what they thought *exigent circumstances* really meant.

They were wrong. The jury agreed. Without the T-shirt, Cokie's case never rose to anything close to the reasonable doubt barrier, and now, with the exigent circumstances thrown out, jurors started wondering what else was wrong with the investigation. We'd all seen the blood results; we could all see the guilt written on Cokie Dean as clear as the Gothic-print HELLBOUND tattoo above his collarbone. Yet because of me, he went free. When I shook his hand—at minimum, a wife-beater's hand—I remember how his smile gave me all sorts of red-worded thoughts.

Later he moved to Alaska, where he beat his twenty-two-year-old girlfriend to death.

After that, the community now had its proof: Cokie had always been guilty, I was the one who got him off, and now an innocent woman was dead thanks to his sharky lawyer. And I remembered those thoughts—our handshake, his smile rotten with silver bicuspids—knowing for certain the whole thing had been my fault. In thought, in legal action, in everything but the deed itself: it was my fault.

Hence my loafer. I can't get it to rest comfortably on my heel. *Innocent, innocent, innocent—Robert is innocent.* Still red thoughts. The Gulf Coast Killer wouldn't be as obvious as Dean was. Dean's crime was a drunken passion killing of the woman he knew most; the Gulf Coast Killer chooses at random. The frustrating lack of evidence means the killer must be precise. Maybe even obsessively clean. Unlike Cokie, he's probably average size, no kitschy tattoo, no obvious silhouette. Robert fits that bill. Even so, what sexagenarian is powerful enough to commit a series of gunless murders? Not the slender, achy-kneed man I married.

That thought swallows pleasantly into my stomach. But by the time it does, my heel is starting to blister.

Good Cop and Bad Cop walk in again, Ingram wearing an apologetic look. "Before you speak to him, I'd be an idiot if I didn't try one more time," he says. "Is there really nothing you can give us?"

"Nothing."

"What about time frames? Could you tell us *anything* about his movement?"

I think of acupuncture. "No." I think of his Reuben sandwich. "Nothing." My shoe refuses to slip onto my heel. "I want to speak—"

"We know," Cook mumbles. "Follow me."

ROBERT

As they lead me into an interrogation room—bare Berber carpet, desk bolted into the floor—I recall an odd piece of advice from my grandmother. *Always wear fresh underwear in case the police pick you up.* I don't know what police would ever have taken grandma in for, or why a thought like that was banging around in her head, but as I sit wearing cuffs, a faded Beach Boys '83 tour tee, plaid pajama pants, and a pair of ungodly briefs thonging into me, I can't help but think she was right.

There's barely a moment to breathe before the door opens. Leslie walks in. The humidity got its fingers into her hair and her smudgy lipstick makes her mouth look swollen, but, thank God, she smiles when she sees me.

"You don't have to ask," I say as we sit, "because I'll just tell you. I didn't do it."

And the smile vanishes. Only when her lips go soft do I realize how much I'd been counting on her: the thin, gummy smile, maybe a friendly squint of those pea-green eyes. The adult reassurance of her approval. The comfort when someone far more perceptive than you gazes into your soul and sees good things.

"You didn't—" She clears her throat. "You didn't say anything, did you?"

"No. Nothing. It wasn't easy. It made me feel guilty as hell."

"They count on that. Feel however you like, as long as you don't talk."

"I don't like feeling guilty. Does Florida have the death penalty?"

She squints, possibly hurt: *You've lived with a lawyer all this time and you don't know?* Or maybe something more serious: that the possibilities of Florida's death penalty laws had never once traipsed through her mind. "They have to convict you first."

"Okay? And if they do? Because I definitely didn't do any of it, yet here I am."

"But why did this land on you? What did they tell you?"

"Well, you know about the Lincoln Aviator, I assume. It's what the killer drove. And apparently, I fit the description. The hair. The eyes."

"Eyes? The killer has heterochromia, too?"

"You ignored my question about the death penalty."

She picks at the table with a pearly fingernail and avoids eye contact. She's cringing with her face tipped ever so slightly away, nose-first, almost like the secrets I keep are giving off fumes. Like my presence is something to be endured and not enjoyed. As if at any moment the Gulf Coast Killer in me—this monster I am not and have not ever been—might burst across the table and lunge for her throat. There is a brief moment when I consider confessing everything I know, if it would have us back together in the small, tidy, gloriously monotonous normality of our lives. But then I remember Wes reading off the addresses of the people we love, and a nerve in my stomach pins me to the chair.

After a while, I can't stand her silence. "I told you I didn't do it, Les."

"I know. Of course." She drums her nails into the table, rat-a-tat.

"Then what is it?"

"Yes, we have the death penalty. That lethal injection last year."

"Christ. How many people have heterochromia?"

"Not many. But they won't execute you for having different-colored eyes."

"Is that my lawyer talking? Or my wife?"

"Your wife." Leslie's voice falters. She'd cupped one of my hands in hers. Now she lets it slide free in one slick, sweaty motion. Without her hand on my skin, the air bites especially cold. "Just your wife."

That startles me. I had simply assumed: my wife was something of a notorious defense lawyer, and I needed defense. What else was there to think about?

"They could force me off the case if I'm a witness," Leslie continues. "And then you'll need another lawyer anyway."

"That's good, right? You know perfectly well there was nothing to witness."

"*They* don't know that. If they want, they can list me as a witness just to make our lives difficult. At the very least, we need someone else. A backup plan. Someone we choose."

"We can't afford someone else."

"I could ask June, my old paralegal."

"The one in Miami?"

Leslie nods. "Even if the prosecutor is feeling generous, the media will take two seconds to find out who I am. The Gulf

Coast Killer case is going to be famous. Infamous. And then it turns out *I'm* the one defending you? Everyone's going to assume you're guilty."

That shouldn't irk me. I'd rather be a free man with a murderer's reputation than an imprisoned man who inspires a "Free Robert Woodhouse" trend online, but still. It irks me.

"And before you ask," Leslie says, "perception does matter. It matters to the jury. And the judge, and the prosecution, and the public—"

"As long as we *win*, right?"

Something in the plastic of the table breaks. Leslie shakes the pain from her thumb and runs her palm against the plastic, smoothing it out, wiping and wiping, never satisfied that she's removed the threat of something loose and jagged. What is she thinking? She has that gormless look in her eyes that people get when big-picture thoughts carry them away. "It's not enough that you're innocent. We have to get you to *not guilty*. And that's not remotely the same thing."

"'We'? Does that mean . . . ?"

I don't finish the sentence. Leslie is smart, and like all the smart people I've known, she likes to make decisions herself. The choice can hang awhile.

As long as she's no longer against the idea.

LESLIE

The stupid thing won't snap back into *place*. A hangnail of plastic on the table's edge, scissor sharp. I hate the obscenity of it pointing into open air. No matter how much I run my thumb over it to click it into place, it twangs back to position. Robert should know why this bothers me, why it all bothers me, how little I can do to change anything, anything at all about this world, plastic and table shards and everything else—

"Les. You okay?" Robert's mouth is a soft line.

"These cheap tables. It's nothing."

"It's not. Gimme those." He scooches his chair forward, throws out his cuffed hands, and unpeels his fingers.

I stare at them, then fold mine into his.

"Sorry," he says. "My hands are cold. Feels like all the blood is in my stomach somewhere."

That nearly makes me smile. Even staring down the full barrel of the law, his first thought is my comfort. This is the Robert Woodhouse I married. I think of when we were dating, when my thermostat went hyperactive and I couldn't get my apartment above sixty-five degrees, how he came over and tinkered with it all night, canceled our dinner, ordered in, kissed my tight temples, fired a teapot on the stove so he could warm my cup of chamomile that'd gone cold. The thermostat, the company, the splash of hot water: he had topped up my life. I still remember how he hugged me goodbye that night, his hands crimping into me like a weighted blanket.

When had I become, to quote my daughter, such a *stone cold adult*? Sometime after Cal passed, no doubt. Widowhood has that flash-aging effect. My life unfolded on dotted lines: transfer deeds and creditor notices for Cal, fill out financial aid applications for Steph, review my taxes as a newly single filer. The full weight of my grief felt manageable as long as I could busy myself. The repetition of it soothed me. If I was lost in some document's befuddling legalese, at least I wasn't staring out windows and contemplating the Cal-size void in my life.

Still. There are questions.

Something has been shaking my unshakable husband for months.

Pulling my fingers out of Robert's, I settle back in my chair, this time regarding the broken plastic in the table with utter indifference.

"How truthful have you been about where you've gone lately?" I ask. "And why did you leave the house, when you had no car, just to get yourself a sandwich?"

ROBERT

The silence between us makes every numb sound in the room come alive. Fuzzy fluorescent lights. Air whirring through the ducts.

If only Leslie knew what she was *really* asking me.

An image sparks in my eyes. Walking through my front door, safe and free, having told the police all I know, only to find streaks of blood tentacling down the edges of the hardwood floors. Leslie, slumped against the wall, throat open, pupils fixed.

Me, collapsing at the sight of her, crunching on my old and worthless knees, wondering for the rest of my life if I could have made it to *not guilty* without putting her life at risk.

Wes is out there somewhere. We're safe as long as Wes—modern-day Wes, the Wes I know now—thinks he's in control. It might have been different before his mother died. He stuck to her like he was leashed, some toy breed in the yard that had atrophied from too much shade and too little exercise. But she died. When she did, the Wes I knew—toy-breed Wes with his tiny eyes and pinprick mouth—finally slipped the leash. The few times I saw him, the changes were obvious. The chains had clinked to the ground behind him and now he was a different Wes, hungrier, angrier, more volatile. He was no longer the creature I knew but some sort of ticking bomb, full of interloping wires impossible to cut without setting off. Why risk it? Even if I told police everything I knew, where will he explode? Will they arrive at Patricia's one day and find her missing, only to uncover her body four days later in some sewer, chewed up and dehydrated? Would Leslie be comforted by the fact that at least I'd *done the right thing* and *eventually* they caught him?

Call me a coward, but I'm not going to bet against Wes with people's lives at stake.

I can bet on Leslie, though.

"All right," I reply. "It was a witness lineup. I didn't want to alarm you, and I'm innocent, so I didn't think much would come of it."

Leslie huffs. "Why couldn't you just tell me that?"

"It isn't easy to talk about."

"Even so," Leslie mutters, "why would it kill you to share something like that?"

My throat snicks, nearly enough to laugh. Nearly.

LESLIE

After I find Cook for a quick check-in (no, I'm not being detained; no, I have nothing more to say), I make for the lobby in search of a ride home, hoping to find Ingram and his kind, ghosty eyes. Instead, he finds me first, stopping me near the metal detectors with a meaty tap on the shoulder. "Ma'am. Let me lead you out."

"I just need a lift—"

"Okay, but word of warning. There's press."

"Already?"

He just shrugs: *Already.*

Outside, beyond the all-glass doors and the row of police cruisers, a few news vans have pulled in. One crew is setting up lights and clamping down a divider while a photogenic woman checks her blowout hairdo in her phone camera. I can't read the tongue twisters she's warming herself up with, but it's probably rich in hard *c* and *k* sounds. *Gulf Coast Killer. Criminal defense attorney.*

Cokie.

"All right," I tell Ingram. "Give me a minute?"

He looks at his watch. "One minute. It'll only get worse."

I find the bathroom. Moment of truth. And no matter how you think you look, no matter how ready you think you are to encounter the woman in the mirror, you'll never find any lighting as unforgiving as that in the police station bathroom at ten at night. The humidity has scattered my pixie cut into a rosy-gray storm, my lips are parched and pale, my left eye is veiny and pink. A living, breathing mug shot of a person.

But I have my purse, and in my purse I still carry my lawyer's uniform by habit. A wide-tooth comb and a spritz of argan oil for the hair, a drop of Visine for the eyes. Never look at a jury with pink eyes. Both juries and the media know that eyes are the windows to the soul. You want them crisp and bloodless. Foundation. Lipstick. Stud earrings: professional, pinned together. There's nothing I can do about the pallid smock shirt I'm wearing, but I can throw on a collar bib. I scratch gunk out of my eye; I rub a dab of lipstick out of my teeth.

And there she is, even if she's a little weather-beaten and worn-out:

Leslie Robin Woodhouse, Esq.

Ingram has one of his burly partners waiting with him in the lobby. We head out. There's a steady sting to the wind, a feeling of wetness without any rain. Behind where they've chained off the media vans out near the boulevard, the trees are swaying.

Then the hounds catch my scent. Ingram's almost got me to his squad car when a reporter sees my obvious-civilian smock top and points at me. This sets them all in a tizzy. Shouts. Questions.

"Mrs. Woodhouse! Mrs. Woodhouse!" Names already. That's how it's going to be.

The photogenic woman stuffs the microphone in my face as we amble closer to Ingram's cruiser.

"No comment," I say. "No comment." And I stop. "Except this: my husband, Robert Woodhouse, is not the Gulf Coast Killer. And we're going to prove his innocence in court."

Monday morning. A strange dream—I'm picking grasshoppers out of the dunes and eating them by the gobful—smacks me out of sleep at sunrise. Being awake doesn't feel any less strange. Robert's absence and the low tide make the world feel quiet and dried out. I make myself a coffee, steeling myself for a big day, and sit on the porch waiting for signs of Charlotte on her morning walk. She never turns up.

It's early, but there's also no point in putting it off. I pick out my phone and thumb my way to Steph. She picks up after one ring.

"Mom!" That lovely, froggy voice. "Jesus. I saw you on the news. What is *happening*?"

"Well, first—Robert's okay. Shaken, obviously, but okay."

"But they think he's a murderer."

"There's a lot to unravel. I don't have a full picture of the charges; I don't even know who the judge is yet." I swallow. "And since when do you say 'Jesus'?"

"You're going to defend him?"

"If I can. I don't trust a court-appointed defender, and it's not like we can afford anyone—"

"I could take a semester off if it would help."

"What? No."

"Being this far away just feels so wrong right now."

"You have your own life to worry about. And Aunt Patricia's here." My hand shoots up to cover the wide cringe of my mouth. Aunt Patricia, I said, the uncouth implication being *Aunt Patricia's money*, and I almost let something else slip I wasn't supposed to let slip. Nothing about the cancer until the scans come in and confirm they've caught everything early enough—and what if they haven't, what happens then, one disaster after another? My hand drops to my chin. It sounds ridiculous to pretend everything is under control, but I'll keep the bluff going. "I just wanted to call and let you know not to change anything, not to worry, and remind you about my two favorite words . . ."

"*No comment.* Okay. But who was that I saw on the news last night again, saying all those words that weren't *no comment*?"

"I don't know. A lawyer doing her best."

"You sound tired already, Mom. Seriously, let me come down and help."

Help. Help who? This call is for her. It should have been last night, would have been last night if I hadn't fallen asleep while putting it off. "No," I say. "Don't jilt your roommates. Keep your summer going like you planned. You can always change your mind if we need you later."

"And Bob—he's going to stay in jail until the thing's done?"

I meant *we* as in *Patricia and I*. "Yeah. There's no bail home release for cases like this one, sweetie."

"Well. Shit."

"Just try to keep your head down if you can. Don't be surprised if journalists start digging around. It's always 'No comment,' all right? Nothing but 'No comment.' Reply to nothing, no voicemails, no emails."

"Of course."

"And since when do you say 'shit'?"

"Just remember to get your rest, Mom. You never sleep."

After our goodbyes, I hang up, never telling her about the dream with the grasshoppers.

The courthouse is on the mainland, a white-and-brick Colonial Revival that looks completely out of place, like someone plopped Independence Hall between a Dunkin' and a twenty-four-hour fitness center. Walking through the metal detector and onto the sticky tap-dancing floors, I recall the feeling of searching for classes on the first day of school. I am lost in a familiar place.

But at least I am dressed, I am suited, and my hair is brushed flat. That fills my sails some. After filing the paperwork I came for, I check with the clerk to find out which judge we've been assigned. The sooner I know, the better. A good lawyer works the law; a great lawyer works the judges.

I know the clerk, too. Plump, old Felicia, a woman I've known for years but have never seen standing up. She keeps a bowl of Smarties on her desk, even though kids rarely come through here. I organize it for her while she's clicking away on her mouse. That soothes me. The twist ties on the candy wrappers have to align with north and south. I'm getting back in the swing of setting things right.

Felicia's smile dissolves when she finds the name. Robert's going to have to appear in front of the Honorable Christopher S. Bates. No-Gates Bates. Friend of prosecutors. Fond of obscenely high bails. Thirty years on the bench, frequent guest at police pancake fundraisers, the most warrant-happy judge in the entire Sunshine State. Once, at a charity golf outing, I accidentally stepped on his shoe and made his blister bleed through his socks.

Already reeling, I walk through the lobby to the old coffee machine. It's still there. The coffee always tastes like hot pennies, but it'll give me something to do with my hands.

And of course I forgot it only takes cash.

"I got it."

Someone at least a foot taller than me snakes his hand past me and slips in a crisp dollar bill. I see his suit before I see him. Crisp charcoal, Italian, glossy. The fabric swallows a young man with oil-slick hair and a square jaw, though I wouldn't call him handsome exactly. His forehead is winning a war of attrition against his hairline.

"Half caf," I say. "Thank you."

"Not the adventurous type." He pushes the button. The machine starts sputtering. "Leslie Woodhouse, right?"

I look at him sideways.

"Sorry. Randy Freeland."

He sticks out a sinewy hand. By the time I shake it, my palms are sweating. I know him by name only. I have extensive theories about how hair is the true window into the soul. It's not what happens to it—you can't help that—but more about if one accepts a receding hairline with grace. Back in the old Wisconsin days we once had a priest named Father Harlan who combed up several foot-long strands from the back of his head like we wouldn't notice the mealy scalp between them. Why should a man consumed with the spiritual world need a comb-over? After taking a vow of celibacy, there should be no one on earth worth keeping hair for. Sure enough, it turned out he was having a fling with one of the parish's widows. With Freeland, I see an inability to know when he's losing the battle.

"Randy Freeland," I echo. "How soon before we see charges?"

"Filed this morning."

"You work fast."

"Well, it's the Gulf Coast Killer, isn't it?"

"Is it?"

Something about his crinkly paper-bag smile makes me wonder how old he is, or how young. I can't tell. His musk is funerary, like hairspray at a wake. My eyes burn when he gets close. "I don't want to get off on the wrong foot. There are a thousand ways we can work together on this."

"I only count one. Plea bargain. And seeing as my husband's completely innocent, we're not interested."

"I know I'm new, but there's always interest, isn't there?"

"I don't see what I could give you." I sip the coffee he bought me. Yep, hot pennies.

"North Naples. No death penalty, life in prison. Which at his age—"

"Are you a man who has trouble with the word *no*?"

He shrugs. "I just think it's easier. For both of us. There aren't a lot of cases like this anymore. People don't have the patience for something drawn out. They'll want something quick and clean."

His genial tone echoes that of some of my first cases, when older DAs with obscene mustaches thought they could charm their way to a plea deal. The routine was tired even back then; now I just find it impudent. Still, the claim is true enough—psychological profiling and the DNA era have mostly wiped out cases like these.

"Saw you on TV," Freeland offers when I don't respond. One advantage to being Leslie Woodhouse: when I lose my train of thought and stare at you, it makes you want to talk. "You're planning on representing him yourself?"

"Yes."

"That's a big—excuse me—that's a big mistake."

"Well, you're the prosecution. Feel free to raise it with Bates. Or list me as a witness and get me booted off the case so I can testify about how little I know and how upstanding my husband's character is. I have this old assistant, June Daswell—she works at a firm called Williams and Moore now—she might be able to take on the defense pro bono—"

"All right. Point taken. If there's any stink about you defending Robert, it'll come from Bates, not me."

"Thanks."

"Can I get something in return?"

"Really? We're back to life in prison?"

"Just that you think about it."

I'd sooner jump into a steaming hurricane of Randy Free-land's hairspray than think about it even for a moment, but this is a negotiation, and I can buy myself more time on Robert's case for the cost of nothing. I pick at my lip, *deep in thought*, to show him how hard a bargain he drives. "Okay. Under consideration. I'm gonna need a copy of the charges—"

"Got one right here." He pulls it out of his folio, the top sheets, already handy—such a coincidence. "Paper-clipped my card to it. If you ever want to chat."

I thank him for the coffee. He gives me a little salute as he walks off, practically skipping, so pleased with himself. Maybe I could've asked for more concessions. He's so certain he's going to win, that this case is going to springboard him to greater things, mayoral races and mai tais at the yacht clubs, but I think his happiness is more than that: he's so certain he's going to be famous.

Six counts of first-degree homicide, Marco Island up to Estero, plus the abduction of Barbara Tiller on Madre Island.

Once home, I roll up the Caravaggio puzzle into a mat and set up my new home headquarters in the dining room. Charges go in the center. I bring a magnetic whiteboard out of the garage, wipe it clean, and draw boxes for every count: Marco Island, Port Royal, Naples, Golden Gate, North Naples, Estero, Madre Island. I print out a map of the central Gulf Coast, draw the path in red marker, popping thumbtacks into each location a victim was last seen.

I let out a puff of air when I see the jagged scar it leaves in the paper. Robert may have been flaky lately, but he hasn't been *busy*. Not like this.

My hope is that Randy Freeland is stacking his case like dominoes. If I can knock one over—an alibi at Estero, North Naples maybe—then we have a chance. The jury can always convict Robert for just one or two charges if they want, but the central question (Is this man the Gulf Coast Killer?) still needs to haunt them when they enter deliberations. Freeland will play on that uncertainty—he might say that we don't know who this killer is at heart, if he works alone, et cetera, et cetera—but how can he prove Robert was at Port Royal if he wasn't at Estero?

Which brings me to the charges. I have yet to read those in detail. I don't know that I'm ready; I need support, both legal and moral. But I liked the way Freeland's face sagged when I mentioned I knew someone at Williams and Moore.

Monday morning. She'd be in the office right now.

June answers on the first ring. Her voice crackles like a bright neon sign. "Leslie. Thought you might call. I'm so sorry."

"Thank you." I make the words as nonchalant as I can, even if I'm not sure what she's sorry for. "Do you have a sec? I just wanted to bounce some ideas off you."

There's always time for me, June says. The paychecks she made as my paralegal helped her pay off law school, so even if she doesn't have time, she'll make room for me.

"First point," she says. "Don't rep him yourself. What if you need to testify to give Robert an alibi?"

"If it comes to that, I will."

"It's easier to hire someone now."

"Okay—how much do you cost?"

"Four-fifty, and I round up to the nearest hour." I don't respond. "Okay. Point taken."

"I'm going to start with my own memory," I tell her. "See if there are alibis there, if I remember what I was doing on each day. If Robert was out, I can also check a few with his son, Wes. I think they spent a little time together. So that might plug some gaps."

"Great. If you're really doing this on your own, I'd start easy, work your way up. What are we dealing with, exactly? Do you have a copy of the charges?"

"Right here. I haven't read through it completely."

June takes a second and understands that to mean I haven't *been able to* read through it completely. "All right. Imagine I'm holding your hand and whispering very supportive things."

And, with her very supportive things in my speakerphone, I slide open the folder, reading aloud, wincing at my husband's name next to those red words, *with malice aforethought, unlawfully, willfully,* and *did deliberately cause the death,* chewing the inside of my cheek as I read through the *deliberate torture, starvation, and dehydration for a period of no less than ninety-six hours,* the victims always *cut* to death, never *stabbed,* never in vague terms like *the gut* or *the neck* but the *jugular vein,* always the *jugular,* whether Estero or North Naples or Marco Island—*jugular jugular jugular—with small incisions marking a common knife or box cutter,* this sixty-two-year-old husband of mine who could not have been there, would not have been there, yet—

I stop.

"Leslie? You there?"

"DNA. They found Robert's DNA in the North Naples case. Hair."

Concrete hardens in my temples. Panicking, I squeeze the paper with the thumbtacks in it so I can ball it up and throw it away, but one of them pricks me through the paper. I run my finger under the faucet and tighten a bandage around it, then drop the phone on the way back to the dining room. When I pick it up, June's voice is distant.

"Leslie? You there?"

I pick up. "Sorry," I say, reading. "And they're saying Robert was on their radar once they got an anonymous tip, just after the Estero murder."

"Leslie," June hums. "DNA . . ."

"I know. But it's impossible."

We're silent awhile. There is the faint *swish, swish* of the tide closing in.

"Well, you know his heart," June says. "Start there and build up. He's not the first innocent man accused of horrible things, and DNA isn't an automatic win." It's reassuring coming from June. She's met Robert, knows Robert.

I force out a breath and relax: my husband's hair is in North Naples, we never go to Naples, we are not Naples people. Yet even if the puzzle pieces don't fit, they are all the perfect shade of dark, bleak, and color matched, as though they belong in the same corner of my skull.

"All right," I say. "I won't bother you until I know more. I'll start with what I can find and work my way up. You ever have any other thoughts, you've got an open invite. Drive up, maybe. Eat all my cereal like in the good old days."

"Anytime." Then her voice gets pitchy with sarcasm. "You can afford four-fifty an hour, right? Let's call this an hour."

"Very funny. Thanks, June." And even with my mind on alibis and DNA and the thousand cuts of a serial murder case, I can't help but slip into our old routine. That's the other half of the reason I called her. "Check's in the mail."

WESTON

Vacancies must be high at the Seaside Paradise RV Park, because when I walk half a mile down the road to apply for a month-to-month lease, the attendant hands me a key that only reads NUMBER THREE. I walk the half mile again, and sure enough, the place is mostly empty, save for a smattering of trailer hovels. *Recreational* vehicle indeed. I unlock Number Three and sniff first. The air is yeasty. There is a wardrobe full of springtails and a sink crusted with what I hope is toothpaste.

I will have to clean.

Inside my bag, next to a pile of nitrile gloves, is my laptop. As the laptop boots, I think of how convenient it would be to rig a Flipper Zero and clone the tiny signal from the Woodhouses' video doorbell. Convenient and fun. But, no: too complicated. Too many neighbors, too high a likelihood of being spotted when I install it, and even if I did, the police would probably pull it, run it for DNA, and come bumbling after me.

And look at me. Look at these thoughts. Fantasizing. Daydreaming about pushing the envelope. What is it that gets people like me caught? Not lack of intelligence but lack of humility; the hubris of forgetting that the longer you go, the more the evidence stacks against you. Not quitting while ahead.

If I left Florida right now, if I found a quiet place in, say, Montana, would anyone ever find me?

Montana. I should be there. Instead, I am wiping down a stranger's toothpaste, spreading spackles of it into the air, developing an unbearable itch above the wrist.

I have no shame about trailers. Most of my childhood, with Caroline Adekins, was in a trailer. Sleeping bags and sheeted couch. Funny. These days, I rarely think about Caroline. The trailer brings it out of me. The yeasty air, the musk of particleboard. If there is a heaven, I wonder what thoughts are skittering through her head, seeing me here.

"Look at us now," I say aloud. "So close to pulling it off."

Caroline does not answer. She never does. She is not haunting me. If she were here, her presence would be obvious. Rattling chains, knocking pictures off the walls: *Your father, Weston, he never answers, he never helps us.*

The sink is clean. I pull off my gloves and stuff them into my pockets so I can wash my hands, which sends a cardboard softness poking into my thigh. A puzzle piece from Robert's home. An eyeball from an old painting.

I pull it out, rolling it in my fingertips. The eye seems to prism in the sunlight. And as I set it aside to wash my hands in that public water, coating my palms in that tacky, mineral smell, part of me does feel her presence in the room.

You might think my mother, Caroline Adekins, was abusive. Not in the traditional sense. She never raised a hand to me. She never raised a hand to defend me, either, but then, they were such small hands. Even well into her middle age she seemed frozen in the same petite body of her youth: boney, mousey, with hair the color of Italian-roast espresso. Her mother—herself single—died young, T-boned at an intersection near Samoset. At seventeen, Caroline lived in her car. The only job she knew was waiting tables at Denny's, and someone there must have told her that college was her way forward in the world, because she put in for student aid, and who else should take pity on her but that Harvard of the upper-central western coast of Florida: Suncoast State. Go Fighting Seagulls.

Things were probably looking up for a while. Then she had me, which put everything on pause. Her schooling. Her career plans. The full ripening of her prefrontal cortex. She had to drop out, so she had no degree. She had no degree, so she had no way to pay for the semesters she had already taken. How could she know better? She was barely a woman and barely a mile from her hometown. She measured her universe by the inch. Even when we made it out of the trailer and into one of her boyfriend's shotgun bungalows, she had no concept of ambition beyond whether a restaurant manager might grant her more shifts. Blaming her for these failings always felt wrong, like blaming a bird's egg pecked to bits by some predator for the fact that it made a damned yolky mess.

Robert had really been the sum of her ambitions, anyway.

She mostly called him *your daddy*—she always said it with bright eyes, her voice hushed and delicate—man of brilliance and art and history and culture who might one day save us. He had to be. If not, it was like admitting her life had been a disappointment.

In my youngest days, there was no Robert. Just a vague, trim-bearded phantom who loomed in the same plasma of consciousness in which I placed the Easter Bunny. But there were times he dropped in. On the occasion Caroline had been incapacitated (the brandy or, later, the injectables), he might occasionally agree to pick me up. He never liked to take me to his house, but he once took me out to a museum so he could tell me about all the painters' lives, their broken families, their secret miseries. One series in particular spoke to me. *The Sick Child*. Robert went on about how Edvard Munch's poor fifteen-year-old sister died of tuberculosis and how this single event wrought pain into forty years of his art. But you see, Robert lectured: that is *exactly* what made him great. The hard things either kill you or become the whole reason you live.

I burst out crying.

Robert gaped and whirled around as if there were some emergency in-case-of-crying glass he could smash, then slung me over his shoulder and walked me outside. He waited until I calmed. He should have taken me to the Cretaceous exhibit, he admitted. That was his mistake. Then he dropped me off and patted me on the head and waved at my mother as she stood at the trailer door, her eyes still full of fantasies. She could not *wait* to begin our new life.

Which is probably why when she opened his envelope one morning soon after, she gushed over it like she had received an invitation from Buckingham Palace. She read parts of it aloud.

> *Dear Caroline . . .*
>> *Will be the last time I write to you . . .*
>> *This last trip taught me I am not cut out to be a father . . .*
>> *I do not have the temperament . . .*
>> *How sorry I am . . .*
>> *Enclosed is a check . . .*

She stopped reading.

"This last trip." The museum? With me? Was it my fault? Had I made the wrong face as I listened to his macabre stories about some painter's dead sister? Should I have insisted on dinosaurs instead? That was the first time I saw Caroline pour a tall glass of Bertoux and suck it dry. It was no longer her secret drink. I might have wanted some myself if I had ever seen it make her happy.

The letter was full of hedging language. That gave us, not knowing Robert well enough, some hope. At least he had promised to rethink everything in a few years. The one thing he was clear about was that his fatherhood would now be in the margins. The milestones. Should I ever graduate college, the old man would be there. Huzzah. The occasional checks kept us stocked in Bertoux, but Caroline stopped fantasizing aloud about our plans with Robert. And that was when the boyfriends began in earnest.

These men were hit-or-miss. Often literally. Dommy was a hitter, Travis was a miss, but Conlan—the really formative one, the one I would always remember—he changed my world when I was about fifteen.

Like in the painting.

LESLIE

The gas station is a wide, fifteen-pump convenience store on the way into Fort Myers, with a food mart in the middle that's only a hair bigger than the icebox out front. If a place like this keeps security footage for more than twenty-four hours, it will be a miracle.

The clerk barely registers me as I walk in. Is it too much to hope for, I wonder, that they keep security footage from last Friday?

The man clicks to life. "Oh, sure. It's all cloud based now." The zoned-out smile he shoots me is delighted and, I suspect, slightly medicated. "What do you wanna see?"

Like June said: start with the easy bits.

The easiest bit so far has been running Robert's credit card statements in search of alibis. There aren't many, but at least the acupuncture had proven to be true. If a side trip to a gas station bears out, I can punch a jury-size hole in the testimony of Randy

Freeland's star witness, Sarah Tiller. She's seen the Gulf Coast Killer more clearly than anyone else. Allegedly. Yet an eight-year-old can see all the wrong things, misremember events, maybe even peg a thirty-year-old man as sixty. Every adult looks old at her age.

The clerk lets me behind the counter, dropping a thumb on the green button on his keyboard to approve customers at the card readers, then logs in. "Police related?"

"You've heard of the Gulf Coast Killer?"

His stare is long and ruminant. Then he kicks his roller chair away from the computer. "Then have at it, lady."

The footage is sorted by date, and I have Robert's credit card history with me, a $56.57 charge at 2:51 p.m. on June 27—not precisely when Barbara Tiller was being abducted, though far enough of a drive that if he was busy fiddling with the pump instructions or fretting over a flavor of Coke, he couldn't have driven down to Presidio Heights in time. But a credit card by itself isn't enough. Without physical proof, it may as well have been me running Robert's card.

The security footage is organized by the hour. A click on two o'clock brings up all five cameras. I scroll the time cursor forward. And scroll and scroll, until it's about 2:45, which would be the perfect time to place Robert here, and I try to have a green-colored thought (*innocent, innocent, Robert is innocent*) when I release the cursor and let it play. Nothing quite yet; a single sedan out at the pumps.

Then, at 2:48, there is his Aviator at Pump Three. And there is Robert, tumbling out of it with his achy knees. A tank of gas on his way home from the acupuncturist. As he said.

Maybe it isn't the healthiest thing for me that the green thoughts occasionally seem to come true.

"Guessing that's what you wanted?" the clerk asks.

"It's perfect. Can I email this file to myself?"

"If it helps prove a man innocent? Hell, you can have that, a Coke, and your choice of scratch-off."

"Thanks." But given my luck recently, I only grab the Coke.

Acupuncture wasn't enough of an alibi on its own—Robert could have gotten home in time for Presidio Heights if he'd had a full tank of gas already—but now I have him on video. He was on the mainland and nowhere near the dunes where Barbara Tiller was abducted. I drive home with a soothing antacid feeling in my stomach.

Later, I pull into our driveway in my own sedan, finally home from the shop. I walk into my dining room headquarters. The opening hearing is tomorrow, and there are still six murders to contend with. And despite the consistency of the killings, the Gulf Coast Killer has a commitment to randomness that makes each crime feel like a separate category. The first (Marco Island) has a witness who might have seen a man stalking the single white male victim, age twenty-seven. DNA only started turning up at the fifth killing, North Naples. Something about that pricks at me. The killer had gotten more careful over time, yet on the fifth killing, Robert's DNA suddenly appears?

The police would have noticed the same. And what do they think about that? My own brief interrogation told me so little.

Cook was tightly suited, belted, buttoned-up, and ponytailed; press-conference ready. A living embodiment of *dress for the job you want, not the job you have.* A future somebody in DC. If I'm starting with the easy bits, as June said, cracking the diamond hardness of Cook's façade goes at the bottom of my list.

On the other hand, there's always Ingram.

There aren't many bars on Madre Island, so I choose the only one close by, the one Robert joked would have been the worst place to catch a venereal disease: the Thirsty Crab. I deposit myself at a stool and order a tonic water to pace myself.

As I sip it down to ice pebbles, I wonder about the entropy of murder. Most serial killers get caught because they develop patterns. The longer they go, the more likely police are to catch on to those patterns. Ours isn't like that. Up until North Naples, the Gulf Coast Killer was getting stronger, tighter, more police-paranoid. Then it all fell off a cliff. There's something askew about that.

Sergeant Ingram sinks into the stool next to me. He's wearing street clothes: cargo shorts and a tan polo so crumpled it looks like his skin is sloughing off in the heat.

"Fair warning," he says as the bartender brings an IPA from the tap, "I can't give you anything I haven't already given Freeland."

"That's all I want."

It's not all I want. But it's like starting with tonic water: a matter of pacing.

"Reading the charges," I continue, "especially North Naples, it sounds like you've got a lot on my husband. Especially the DNA."

A sloppy sip of the beer. "I can say yes to that."

"But DNA takes time."

"It can. And?"

"Those charges came quick." Absurdly so. Barbara Tiller is still missing, though we've already well overclocked the usual Gulf Coast Killer timeline of ninety-six hours. "So quick that I want to ask some questions."

"I read about you, Leslie."

I slide my phone away. "My least favorite words."

Even though we've met, we only know each other enough to have had the same isn't-it-hot-out conversation a thousand times. So I did a little reading on him, too, piecing together what I could from our conversations, an old Facebook account, and the public record. Ingram is Florida-born. He's only a year or two removed from the desk job he knows me from, got himself his own patrol car. He was probably sitting on a speed trap in that car when he got the call about Barbara Tiller's abduction. He's a widower—about three years back, he had a successful GoFundMe to pay the bills after his wife died of pancreatic cancer—and now he's raising their only daughter by himself. Evie, age twelve. Brown hair and brown eyes. Plays softball and oboe.

"Police get it wrong sometimes," I continue. My usual response to the aren't-you-Leslie-Woodhouse questions. "And everyone has rights. I don't see what's so controversial about that."

"Nothing at all. I know plenty of good defenders. Matter of fact, you're one of 'em. But when I saw your name on my phone, I only thought, 'Here we go.'" Ingram is a bear of a man, the kind to make quick work of a pint glass. He clinks it on the countertop, suds melting down the insides, and looks at me for permission before ordering another. "You should ask the FBI if you're wondering about the speed. Once Cook came down, things kinda got expedited."

"Cook." That registers. I can already imagine the scene: Cook flying down from Quantico, ears ringing with her supervisor's expectations, hating the humid speed of Florida locals. "And when did Cook come down?"

"I dunno. Recently. The days are running together."

"It's the timeline that bugs me. Cook comes down, and suddenly you have a suspect in custody?"

"Something like that. Don't forget Presidio Heights happened, which changed things. And when it did, I was glad for Cook. The FBI has a lot of resources we don't. National resources. CODIS, fingerprints, labs. That's how things happen quickly. The only thing with Cook is, she's a little—"

"Twitchy?"

"I was gonna say ambitious. But *twitchy* works."

"How ambitious?"

"If this is going to turn into a shit-on-Cook session, I'm sorry, I can't. I can drink your beer and tell you about procedures. That's it."

All right. He's a little reticent about sharing secrets. Not unusual. But there are other ways to connect with him. I pull up my phone like someone's just texted me, start typing a heap of nonsense autosuggested words to Steph I'll have to save as a draft. Her most recent text is from last night.

"Sorry," I say. "My daughter goes to college in Pennsylvania. Anytime she texts, I'm on high alert."

"She doesn't text much, huh?"

I bring up Steph's photo—the balcony one, zoomed in to crop out the man Patricia claimed was her boyfriend. Steph is so bright faced and pretty, she should be a model for Ralph Lauren. "I miss her like crazy, I don't mind telling you."

Ingram nods. "I know the feeling. I ever tell you I have a daughter?"

I coo, as one must. "What's her name?" Evie, age twelve.

"Evie. Younger than yours. So she goes to Penn? I won't ask how you swung that, but that couldn't have been easy to get into. Any advice?"

"Yeah: don't let her. Hold on to her. Suffocate her in hugs and don't let her go. Make her go to a local college."

That startles him. He shows a pair of chalky-white buckteeth that pinch over his bottom lip. "You think so?"

"My daughter's all I have, too, and my life was so boring without her. Pleasant, but boring. Before all this, I mean."

"Well, it's not boring anymore."

"That's the beauty of life. It can always get worse."

Finally a chuckle. I can almost hear the ice cracking in his façade. "All right. Well, seeing as I owe you for the beer, and you're Robert's defense, I do have something I can give you now instead of later. You know we have his phone. Didn't find much in it. But the night he was arrested, there was a message to you."

"He never sent me anything that night."

"Saved as a draft. It said he wanted to talk to you about his son. Not sure what that means to you."

"Neither am I."

Then his posture straightens as if someone flicked him on the back with a wet T-shirt. He shoots out of his chair. He pulls out his phone and reads, an eye flick. "Whoa. I . . . have to go."

I whip up a smile, but it's an eyeless one. I can feel the disappointment in my cheeks. "One more beer?"

"No." He slaps on a Rays hat, then stops, thinks. "Might as well tell you, since you're gonna hear. Barbara Tiller just turned up."

An hour later, Robert is waiting for me in a consultation room. He's wearing an oversized orange jumper that swallows him. His face is frosty white with a five-o'clock shadow. I wish it would age him forward. What jury would believe a man so visibly in his sixties could overpower Barbara Tiller? Instead, there's something handsome and young in the way his beard slices new shades into his cheekbones. He looks healthy and vital and strong enough to be deadly.

Tenderly, and just for a moment, we hold each other's hands. And then we're conscious of the omnipresent camera on the wall. I take a seat to his side, brush my pants, set out his case folder.

"A guard told me they found Barbara Tiller," Robert says.

"It's true. I was talking to Ingram when he found out."

"That's great news, right? She'll confirm it wasn't me."

"Could be." I pull out a pen and write *BARBARA TILLER* at the top of a fresh page. It occurs to me, suddenly, how many lines there are to fill under that name. If he wasn't my husband, I might have asked these questions already. "So we're clear. You never spoke to Barbara Tiller?"

"Never saw her in my life until that night on TV."

"But I read a report that her daughter picked you out of a lineup, only to change her mind at the last second. Any ideas why?"

"I don't know. The colors of my eyes, probably. She's what, eight? That could explain it." Robert chews a dry wad of air. "Is this a problem?"

"Just something to prepare for." *Uncertain re: lineup* goes into my notes. That word—*uncertain*—is fast becoming load bearing. "Robert, I told you I was talking to Clay Ingram. He said that the night you were arrested, there was a draft in your phone for a message you never sent me. Apparently, you wanted to talk about Wes."

Robert's eyes flash, veiny and sharp. "That's . . . right. You'd been asking about him."

"So let's talk about it. There's always the potential Randy Freeland brings him on as a character witness." I flip a sheet of paper over and scrawl *WESTON* at the top. The pen goes dry on the *N*, so I have to force it in. Underneath it, so much empty space on the paper. Thin blue lines over a yellowy, nauseating void. "So. Tell me."

"What are you asking?"

"Let's start here. What were you going to text me that night?"

"I don't remember."

"Then what don't I know about you and him? Your lives. Your whole lives."

He swallows. "Where do I begin?"

"Is it that bad?"

"No," he says quickly. "No. Just—that hard to explain. Complicated."

The chisel sound of a fingernail scraping plastic fills the air. Only when the grinding sends a sharp streak of pain up my thumb do I realize the sound is me, grating the table again. I shake the tenderness out of my thumb and fold my hands in my lap.

"Robert, you're not talking to your wife right now. Imagine you were talking to your doctor. Would you really want to change the subject? Or would you just tell me where it hurts so I can cut out the tumor?"

His body trembles. Half a head shake, half a shrug.

My fingernail snicks the table. I had been digging into it until the nail broke free and clicked, one of my many bad habits. This time I catch myself, smooth the nail out with my thumb, sweeping away imaginary dust and brushing these thoughts aside. Too many wife thoughts, not enough lawyer ones.

"Well," I say finally, "think of it this way. As uncomfortable as it is now, at least it will be *less* uncomfortable if Wes ever has to testify because I'll already be out of the dark."

"If I had anything worth saying, don't you think I'd say it?"

"Would you?"

"Christ, Leslie . . ."

Heat pounds in my cheeks. "Stop making me beg for answers—"

Snap.

My fingernail catches on the table and cracks. It's an awful, bone-rattling feeling that startles me, sending a shock wave of pain so stinging I check to see if I've tugged out a clump of nerves. I fold my throbbing hand under my arm, guarding. "I just mean that I've had a hundred clients who withheld information from me. And every time they did, it always hurt their case. So tell me something. Anything. Even if you don't think it's relevant, maybe I can find a way it will help."

His sigh is long and shallow, full of distant pains. "All right. Buckle up."

ROBERT

Leslie makes a long scratch in her notebook, opens up a fresh page, and telescopes her beany eyes on me.

So I tell her.

I tell her the first and only time I slept with a student was in a particularly broiling summer. A lot like this one, in fact. Leaf scorch on the trees, itchy-crotch heat. I don't tell Leslie that sometimes when I see Wes on a hot day, it puts me right back there, the way old songs tag us to the places we heard them. The summer he was conceived, the radios constantly blasted Sinéad

O'Connor at the peak of her tinny, deep-throated powers, so whenever I hear her, I want to drive the car into oncoming traffic. "Nothing Compares 2 U."

Wes doesn't have my surname. He's an Adekins, like his mother, Caroline, the eighteen-year-old student who had me in spring semester. The May heat kept her in sundresses. I remember her poofy black hair, cut shoulder length like a pyramid, and I remember the way she'd always finger her necklaces up and down as they dangled between her perfectly symmetrical collarbones. I probably stared. I was twenty-seven, practically late puberty, and I was still noticing eighteen-year-old collarbones.

She had me in a 100-level class, which meant I taught the things we all know: the *Mona Lisa*, Rodin's *Thinker*, the *David*. The textbook wasn't much and I didn't add much to it. But I was single and I was her professor and I was kind of her age, so every Tuesday and Thursday, Caroline would throw her chin on a fist and flutter her eyes at me like I was speaking in sonnets. She let out an audible *whoaaaa* when I told the class how to interpret Michelangelo's panel *The Fall of Man*. (The fig tree, the fig leaves—the symbolism of the fruit. Groundbreaking.)

A man doesn't always know when he's imagining a flirtation. We've been tricked by too many waitresses for that. But the closer we got to June, I didn't think I was imagining anything about Caroline Adekins. One day she lingered after class. Could I help her before the final exam? Just fifteen minutes of my time? This was Suncoast State: there was barely an art department, let alone a teaching assistant. Sure, I said. Meet me outside the library at seven. We met out in the parking lot, me with my briefcase and her with her backpack, fingering the straps. We stared at each other. The air was fizzy. Heat lightning blinked on the horizon. I hadn't eaten. Had she? No. Biting her lip raw. I had food at my house. Well, I didn't, but we didn't make it to my house; I pulled over in an alley and idled the engine and looked at her chewed-up lips until she had to ask me, *What?* And then we made the suspension of my '82 Ford Escort sing.

I don't tell Leslie that last part. Not in any great detail.

Her notes are scant. Just a few words, the Morse code of an odd dash or two. "I know the broad strokes. You didn't tell me she was that young."

"I told you she was a college student, didn't I?"

"I guess I assumed a senior. And even then—she was *your* student."

"If we're going to relitigate this, Leslie, don't ask me to tell you—"

"All right." She shakes the thought away. "Keep going."

Caroline and I fizzled. I regretted it by July. I'd plucked the fig off the tree and eaten, tasting my own nakedness, and finally made a few never-again promises in the mirror like a man nursing a monthlong hangover. But still, I swore it. Never again.

Then one day in the fall semester, she turned up in the fine arts building. Caroline was such a skinny little thing, she was already showing through her Seagulls sweatshirt. I knew it right as I saw her, so I tried to duck into the bathroom. She walked in after me. Yes, the child was mine, and what was she going to do?

I made the mistake of asking about her parents: they were both dead. Good time to find that out. She kept turning her head to the side, giving me wet looks like she was waiting for something.

You want me to marry you, I realized aloud.

Her wet look congealed into something hopeful. And I had to let her down. How would it look if a professor married the student he'd been teaching a semester ago? Would she be late-stage pregnant by the wedding? I'd be fired. Maybe I would be with her eventually, but, no, not now. She was struggling with tuition already and constantly on the verge of tears, so I wrote her my first check. In the memo, I wrote *future home down payment.* I knew it was a mistake when I saw her practically skipping away with it down the hall.

By October, nothing had happened. No letters. No phone calls. I wondered if I had somehow gotten away with it: if by some sweet miracle, Caroline had decided she hated the idea of me and moved to Siberia.

"So you were embarrassed." Leslie's tone is deadpan. "Embarrassment is an emotion. Emotions subside. I want to know why this enmity between you and Caroline lasted so long." Interrogation mode.

"I don't know."

Caroline worked as a waitress right up until the birth. Truthfully, I didn't know she lived in a trailer until one of her neighbors called me to tell me she was in the hospital. It was weeks ahead of her due date. And maybe I didn't want to get married—or even be *seen* together, depending on who was looking—but there were some things I wasn't going to miss. I arrived late, I remember.

The baby had already been born, and a friendly, red-cheeked nurse told me it was a boy. Born a little early, but healthy.

"And?" Leslie asks, pen tipping down at me.

And? What else? I suppose my heart swelled with a strange potion of pride and apology. I'd been so uncertain about her. Now, I could see myself throwing away all my cautions and starting a life with Caroline. She could sell her trailer, maybe. We would figure out all the rest. In my head, it was always possible I might do the right thing—eventually. I had just been waiting on the timing of it all.

Caroline's face had been pale. But she brightened when she saw me—we even hugged, I think—and I felt my eyes go heavy at this absurdly fresh idea that I was now a family man.

Then the nurse tapped me on the shoulder and handed me a child.

His eyes were pinched shut, his fingers were curling little beans. I swallowed. Waited. When was it supposed to hit me? Maybe it was my fault. What had I expected? The same eyes? The same nose? The very image of me? This was a premature infant wrapped in cotton flannel.

He could have been anyone's son.

He's Wes, Caroline whispered. *Weston. Like that movie,* Princess Bride.

The character was actually *Westley.* I should have told her that while the ink was still wet. I should have done a lot of things differently. I never had the heart.

"The heart," Leslie echoes. "The heart to what? Tell her you didn't love your son the instant you held him?"

"The heart to correct her on the name, actually. But I suppose the two amounted to the same thing. I wanted to care, I was aching to care, and I couldn't. I wasn't a member of their family."

Leslie chews her pen. Most of the page is still empty. "There isn't anything else? Some deeper reason your relationship went sour? Something you did to him, maybe? Or didn't do? Something he'd be angry about?"

Something hideously adolescent within me wells up. I just told her so much. And it was true. It all started with my sins. If she doesn't understand something so small, how will she understand anything about the decades in between?

And I tell her, "No."

Her face dims. "Then think on it, at least. For me. I need time to think through our response."

"All right. Will do."

Suddenly uncomfortable with the idea that she's assigned me homework, I lean away. She grabs her pad, pushes out of her chair. We look at each other. Does she want me to stand with her, maybe? Take her by her hands, whisper sweet nothings? My life is on the line, and even the truth doesn't win me any prizes.

She is standing tall, soldierly, and, after a long minute, flashes me a nod. *This concludes our meeting.* Then she opens the door and walks into the hallway.

LESLIE

On the day of the first hearing, I walk into Courtroom Three wearing an old uniform: a crisp linen shirt, a navy blazer, and silk trousers. It's always those three in some variation. It was Patricia who first helped me with that. In my baby-lawyer days in Milwaukee, no one looked twice at my off-the-rack public defender frocks, but down here, I had a chance for a fresh start at a Real Lawyer look. Naturally, I turned to Patricia.

She took stock. What colors did I like? What fabrics kept me cool when courtrooms got suffocating? She returned a day later with a full Monday-through-Friday wardrobe in her car, a list of piece names if they ever needed replacing, and a note: *Pay me back anytime*. When I tried to, she wouldn't hear of it.

Most pieces still fit. It hasn't been *that* long, really.

Courtroom Three is empty and familiar: the tangy carpet-cleaner smell, the oily polish of the wood. I always used to come early to run through mental flash cards and size up the terrain. What I was really doing was marking my territory. I hate walking into crowds, but getting in early makes me feel like everyone else is here at my invitation. I can't remember why I stopped the habit as I approached retirement.

"Hey."

A pinch in my blazer. I turn and there's Patricia, wearing a floral square neck and a head full of fresh blond hair. That's new. She told me she didn't want to sit around waiting for her hair to fall out; first she'd shave it all off and *get it over with*, and here it is, like nothing has changed. Even her taste in wigs is impeccable.

Patricia swallows me in a hug and then points at the public gallery. "I always forget. Is there assigned seating?"

There isn't, but I don't blame her for forgetting. I forgot so much about this place. I forgot how the nerves start to pile up as people file in, all the pieces stacking on the chessboard: the stenographer running practice pages; the bailiff walking through on his security check; an assistant of Freeland's pouring water into a glass; Felicia asking me what days will work for jury selection; the defendant, my husband, my Robert, led in by the handcuffs, in his orange jumpsuit and nearly a week's worth of beard scruff. There's something slow in every hitch of his knees now—those bad knees, now bearing so much unseen weight. I go to squeeze his hands and get a fingerful of cool metal, but I keep fishing, and there he is, the hot flesh of him, the battery-charging shock his touch sends through me. Then the media files in and I feel self-conscious. Our hands uncord from each other. Now there is a sketch artist, a reporter I recognize from cable news, countless curious members of the public. My nerves flare up as the ambient temperature rises, all this new body heat.

Now I remember why I stopped coming early.

"All rise."

Benches creak, chairs shuffle, knees crackle. Courtroom Three is as packed as I've ever seen for an arraignment. The back benches are full: journalists, assistants, young lawyers in pressed pantsuits hoping to learn the ropes. Everyone thinks they're here to see the Gulf Coast Killer on trial.

The Honorable Christopher Bates waddles up to the bench. No-Gates Bates with his Sicilian tan, tight forehead, and wings of silvery hair. When he sits, he always winces like someone left out thumbtacks. The national reporters and everyone else new to Madre will think he's in a bad mood. I've known him for fifteen-odd years, long enough to know this is simply his default setting.

"Thank you, be seated," he says with utter routine.

He pinches on a pair of rimless glasses. It's a casual touch, as though he's settling in with a good book. I'll give him this: he is undaunted by the moment. Bates barely reacts as he runs through the charges, all six Gulf Coast Killer murders plus the abduction of Barbara Tiller, and, by extension, attempted abduction of Sarah Tiller. The prosecution is carpet-bombing us, knowing full well I don't have the resources to fight a war on multiple fronts.

"My understanding is that Barbara Tiller has been found and is currently recovering in the hospital," Bates sniffs. "I'll thank you for your patience. I know the prosecution and the defense will be keen on interviewing her."

"We're submitting a request for a protective order, Your Honor," Freeland says. "She's been cut off from food and water and is clearly going to be extremely traumatized. There's a lot of media attention—"

"Very good. I'll take a look at that."

"I'd like to see it, too," I say, "Your Honor."

"Of course." Bates studies me. "Allow me to finish with the charges."

My mistake. Freeland was the one who interrupted him, but by jumping in, I'm the one leaving the sour aftertaste. Finally, Bates clears his throat. "Mr. Robert Alan Woodhouse, please rise."

I rise with him.

"Mr. Woodhouse, do you understand the charges against you?"

Robert, bowed in his orange romper, gives a faint nod. "I do, Your Honor."

"How do you plead, Mr. Woodhouse: guilty, not guilty, or no contest?"

"Not guilty, Your Honor."

A murmur sighs through the crowd, but Bates only has to glance at his gavel to quiet the room. He hates delays. One of the reasons everyone calls him No-Gates is because he thinks slow justice counts as cruel and unusual. Back in my practicing days, I noticed he overruled most objections late in the morning, when he'd gone the longest without eating. Sometimes justice really does hinge upon how cranky the judge is.

Within a few minutes we have a date for jury selection. Though it feels slightly rushed, I raise no objection. My schedule has never been so clear.

Bates's eyes settle on me. "Am I to take it you'll be permanently representing your husband, Ms. Woodhouse?"

"With the court's permission, Your Honor."

"We have no objections," Freeland puts in.

Bates scowls at the interruption. Maybe he's already developed a distaste for Freeland. Mental note.

"Your Honor," I say, "if I can raise another issue to this court, we believe my client's right to a speedy trial precludes courtroom cameras. They're a logistical nightmare—one hour in, one hour out. And that's every day."

"Mr. Freeland?"

"As long as the cameras don't interrupt the flow of the courtroom, we have no objections, Your Honor."

"I'm going to deny it, Ms. Woodhouse. I don't think it's as bad as all that, and the public deserves transparency on this case. Now, on to the flight risk and request for bail. You have anything else to add to your earlier arguments?"

"Yes." I shift through my notes, stalling. The chance for a yes from Bates on this next one is remote. But Robert asked me, and sometimes that's what the job is: putting up the embarrassing questions so your client doesn't have to. "Mr. Woodhouse is a man with no priors, no strong connections out of the state—or even out of the Madre Island area. Keeping him on house arrest won't pose major logistical challenges to the state."

"That's very good for the state, but given the heinous nature of these crimes and the exceptionally high profile of this case, this court is forced to rule on the side of public safety. Request for bail is denied. Mr. Woodhouse will remain in custody for the duration of the trial."

Two quick losses for me, hammer-drop speed. Bates is a slightly different man with a camera on him. After setting the schedule for more hearings and the beginning of jury selection, he drops the gavel and the opening hearing is over.

* * *

I don't offer Robert a hug goodbye. Nor does he reach for one. Cameras are always on us now and we are married across a chasm, living in parallel universes that only intersect in the public eye. It aches to see the dip in his shoulders as he's escorted through the side entrance. The torture he must be going through.

It's a media frenzy in the hallways. After repeating *No comment* to a throng of reporters and catching up with Patricia, I notice a woman waiting for me next to the water fountains.

"June," I say. "Sweet June."

Short, smiley, with dark hair that shows the Vietnamese influence of her mother's side, June Daswell throws her arms out for a hug.

I embrace her. "What are you doing here?"

"I'm asking the questions, counsel. You didn't bring an outside lawyer? Even for appearances?"

"Can't afford one."

"I'm cheap."

"Ha, right. I especially can't afford you."

"I think you can afford pro bono. You still have a spare bedroom?"

I coil back, dumbstruck. "What about Williams and Moore?"

"This is an emergency. I asked and they said yes. Enthusiastic yeses, too. They loved the idea of a lawyer from Williams and Moore on the most high-profile case in the country."

"They *loved* the idea of you defending Robert?"

"All right. They didn't hate it."

June was the only assistant I'd hired who ever stuck. I had hired enough students to know that most people study for the

LSAT because they have to. They have no appetite for flash cards or conditional-logic formulas; they just want to get into law school. But the truly frightening ones enjoy it. June was one of those: flash cards on her dashboard, legal biographies in her gym bag, looking up old precedents I'd never asked for in lieu of her morning crossword. Ever meet someone whose destiny was obvious from the start? She can't be older than thirty-five now, yet she's already made a junior partner at Williams and Moore, charging more per hour than I used to earn in a day.

We take our reunion outside, but the colonnade is bursting with reporters, so we drive across the bridge to Madre and head back to my condo. It's quiet there, except for the foamy hiss of the beach. Charlotte's gone. She abandoned our cul-de-sac as soon as she heard Robert had been arrested. Now she probably thinks she was living next to a monster all this time.

I mention this to June, who shakes her head. "You know better than anyone that the public constantly gets it wrong. How are you holding up otherwise?"

"You know." The words burst out of some macabre, misguided instinct for small talk. Always a weak point of mine. Of course June won't know what it means to have a husband accused of murder, of *serial* murder, or for our eccentric neighbor to think she's lived next to a murderer and his enabler all these years, and then there's Patricia, and Steph thousands of miles away, and me, acting out that enabler's role, trying to sweep it so casually aside—*You know how it is in these situations.* As if Robert needs something simple, like foot surgery. My limbs go shaky when I realize I have no way to finish the sentence without it coming out so morbidly absurd.

"Hey." June grabs my hands. "If this needs to wait, it can. You can rest. You can go for a walk, take a nap, do whatever. That's why I'm here."

"No. No, it'll do me good. Especially with you here." I suck in a long, energizing breath. "It just hit me that our weird old neighbor thinks we're the strange ones."

"Well, let's start convincing everyone otherwise."

I get the coffee maker rumbling while we talk over our jury selection strategy in the living room. June's come prepared, setting up a makeshift office by spreading papers in Williams and Moore stationery on the coffee table. We'll want anyone with gray hair on the jury if we can get them. Robert's peers, people who know how difficult it is to overpower someone half your age when you've got a bum hip or an achy knee. There's no shortage of them in Florida. It is, of course, technically against the rules to discriminate on jurors based on age. We just have to find legitimate reasons to disqualify the young jurors Freeland will want. That's what the work is, mostly: wading knee-deep through the swamp of technicalities. Welcome to criminal defense.

Then it's down to the case. "Wonder what Barbara Tiller will say," June says.

"I'm not too worried. I already have an alibi for Presidio Heights, rock-solid."

"You do?" She sets down her coffee, jots it down. "That's a hell of a start."

"Credit card swipe and gas station footage. But we're still missing North Naples and Estero. Both cases where they found DNA."

"Even so. That opens so much." June pulls out a grip of papers from a new section of her case. "I've been doing my own research on the Gulf Coast Killer. Every little quirk I can find. Everyone knows about the ninety-six-hour thing. No one knows why, but we do know the autopsies give us completely dehydrated bodies, no food in their systems, no drinking water for days. At that point, they're all cut in the jugular vein. Sometimes other places as well, but always the jugular." She stops. "You all right?"

I must have turned white. Where's my iron stomach now? "Go on."

"What I didn't know was how clean he keeps things. They found the Marco Island body dumped beside a trash can. The victim had his fingertips burned off and there were traces of acid on his skin. It was as if the Gulf Coast Killer was killing people specifically for headlines while still avoiding detection. So we're supposed to figure that when he comes north, he starts getting lazy, leaving DNA behind?"

This is one of the many reasons I love June. We're of one mind. "I was wondering the same. The first few murders were utterly mysterious and random. Then it was like he wanted people to catch up."

"Do you have any reason to believe they'd have Robert's DNA on file?"

"Nope. No priors. For sixty-two years on earth."

June clicks her tongue. "There aren't a ton of late-bloomer serial killers. Usually young men."

"Do we know that for certain, or is that a myth?"

"Do we even *want* to focus on alternative theories yet?"

"No. Not unless there are ten more of you."

We go quiet. I can hear the metronome of the battery-powered clock above the mantel as June jots that in her notes. Then she changes the subject. "And what is Barbara Tiller saying?"

"She's still recovering, last I heard. They aren't letting her talk to me. To anyone. The news said she saw the killer, though, heard his voice. If Freeland puts her on the stand—"

"It means they're confident they've got Robert."

"Which they shouldn't be, because I've got evidence he didn't do Presidio Heights, where Barbara Tiller was taken."

June taps the keyboard of her tablet. "We'll prep for that cross-examination. Oh yeah—and we need to talk about Weston. Randy Freeland's going to go after Robert's character, and when it turns out he's got an estranged son, it doesn't help. Where does he live?"

"All over. He's kind of a wanderer, never had a steady job."

June raises her eyebrows.

"And far away, Colorado, I think, when the murders started." I place a hand on the ball of nerves tightening in my stomach. Trying to remember how I know that. From Robert? Do I now have reasonable doubt hanging over every last thing he ever told me?

"Just being thorough," June says. "But we should talk to him."

"He's in Florida now, so maybe I can dig him up. And while we're on it, let's draw up a big list of everyone else who's a potential witness or has a potential grievance. I mean massive. Put your mom on it if you think she can help." An old habit with every case—start wide, then zoom in. You never know where the first cracks will show. "I've been talking to a Madre Island police officer. I'll see what I can find out about Tiller and the DNA. I need you to pretend you're Randy Freeland, come up with every point he can possibly make so we have three rebuttals to each." I shoot off a text to Clay Ingram, though I keep the screen tilted my way. Can I ask what Barbara Tiller is saying? Is she saying anything? An answer dings back within a few seconds: Gotta leave that for the stand. but if you have any questions I can answer . . .

June's too busy nodding, furiously punching notes into an app.

"And don't let that thing out of your sight," I say.

"What thing?"

"Tablets. Phones. Yesterday morning, I saw a reporter going through our recycling."

"Right," June says. "You really don't mind me staying?"

"You kidding? You're an angel from above."

"Just one thing."

"Name it."

She puts the tablet on standby, turns her knees to me. "I won't lie. I only got the okay from Williams and Moore to be here because they want to go regional one day, and they'd love it if I could raise the firm's profile. But if we're banking on Robert's case, there's always the potential downside."

"What's that?"

"That things go poorly. That all we do is find the best possible deal for a guilty man."

"Robert didn't do it, June, if that's what you're asking." I lick my lips. That bile taste again. "I can promise that: Robert did not do any of it."

"Of course. I just mean Williams and Moore want me to prove it as cleanly as I can. Alibis, if we can get them. Their worst nightmare is a mistrial. Or that the case gets bogged down in procedural gunk that doesn't make any sense to the public."

That almost makes me laugh. "*Their* worst nightmare?"

"And mine."

"They really gave you the time off? This could take months."

"I'm a partner there, and now I'll be on camera for the biggest case in the country. They're just hoping it's worth it."

"It will be," I say unsteadily.

"I imagine they're hoping I come across clean and competent. So am I."

"Well, competent I can guarantee."

"But not clean?"

I only shrug. Fair or unfair, we both know what my reputation is. "The only option for me is *not guilty*."

June pings her tablet back to life. "That's what they're afraid of."

WESTON

Fixing smart doorbells and changing out apartment locks is not what you might call a salaried job, so I arrive "home" to my new trailer with nothing but a can of tuna fish and rice to boil. The trailer is barely better than a tent. It has a foldout single bed and an awning for sitting out on the "porch," though these days the heat is all swampy mess, so the most important piece is the AC unit I duct-taped to the window.

The phrase *trailer trash* is unfair. Some of the finest people I ever met lived in trailers. When Caroline was late coming home from the bars, a neighbor—a bachelor who liked to smoke unfiltered cigarettes—brought me into his and taught me how to play gin rummy until Mom came home stinking a different kind of gin rummy.

My trailer is toward the back of the lot. The walk takes me through a handful of people sweating in lawn chairs. Close to mine, a woman sucking on a tinny e-cig is watching TV on an exterior plug. She turns up her volume when the news comes on. A reporter outside the Madre County courthouse is spelling out how many life sentences might stack up for Robert Woodhouse, not to mention the mystery of whether Barbara Tiller will testify and identify her white-haired assailant.

That pulls a starter cord inside me, revs up my nerves. Have I done all I can? Was I thorough? I tried to be. The contact lens, the hair dye, even putting on a couple of pounds to give myself the look of a slowing metabolism.

Still, the beach was an awkward place to do it. A lone woman on the beach so close to Robert's house was perfect, I thought, but then I saw her daughter playing in the sand and nearly changed my mind. I had to fake that heart attack just to get Barbara alone. It was more face-to-face time than I had planned on. Say Tiller points Robert out in the courtroom and still says, *No, too old*? What then?

"Somethin', ain't it?" The woman waves a hand at the TV, then puffs out a fat cloud of vapor.

"Absolutely something."

"Awful. I hope he gets the chair. Or whatcha call it—" She mimes a syringe into her arm, pushes her thumb in slow.

"Me, too."

The tuna fish and rice go into the pantry. I slip on a latex glove so I can pocket my baggie of Robert's shavings, trash the glove, and once my phone is charged and tells me I have twenty-four hours of battery, I start walking.

And walking.

And calling a cab. Small talk with the driver. The Rays, they're breaking our hearts.

And walking some more.

Night falls. The salty wind gets crisp, then cool. I arrive at Presidio Heights and its beehivey apartment complexes, then the parking lot, the hairy dunes, the snaky private beach. South of that is where the boomer cul-de-sacs begin. The island is so thickly wooded I can walk the beach in secret. Hands in my pockets, whistling *Götterdämmerung* into the wind. Most of the windows are dark. In my efforts this year, I have learned that boomer bedtime averages about nine, depending on the quality of the TV news that day. And it is easy to remember which street is hers: just the presidents running north to south. Washington, Adams . . .

Hello, hello.

One condo still has its lights on. Leslie's. She might have had a few sleepless nights recently. Stressing out, pulling her short hair into nibs, *working the case.* Hopefully she's still chewing over that basic question: *Did he do it?* How well can a woman know her husband, anyway? One might think the possibility that Robert was a murderer would be too much to bear, that she could never stay with him, let alone defend him. But no. Here she is, helping. No woman ever left a man because he *might* be a monster. The happy privilege of being Robert Woodhouse.

A narrow, fluffy-sanded trail leads through the oaks in their neighbor's section of the yard. As good a place to wait as any.

From here, I can see the kitchen. Leslie and someone with very dark hair file in and out of it, flicking yogurt lids into the trash, unspooling paper towels to wipe their hands. After a few moments, the small woman with the very dark hair steps out onto the deck with a phone pressed to her ear.

"She's hopeful," the woman is saying. "I don't know. She's going to want a not-guilty verdict at all costs. But she promised to let me take the public lead and we'll try to make it as clean as we can."

Case talk. Leslie has a friend.

My fingers wrap around the bulge in my pocket where the box cutter is. I slide it up through the fabric, almost jerking. The plastic is cool and familiar on my fingertips. How much time has it been between victims now? A long, stressful, itchy time. Maybe the longest since the first. I never count Barbara Tiller; she was more of a catch and release. I work my wrists, rub my watch into the skin, then force myself to stop. All I need is a photograph.

"There's a promising lead on an alibi," the woman continues. "They can't possibly have any new evidence on the first few, so my hope is one alibi will bring the whole thing down." A pause. "Yeah. Nice and clean."

Clean. I bite the word into my tongue as I extend the box cutter a click or two. The wind hides the sound.

Oh, it would be such a rush.

She is *right there.*

And I snap the box cutter shut.

I look at my watch, count my pulse against the clicks. One-forty. Jogging levels.

A second voice breaks in. Leslie's trumpety contralto, something underneath my hearing. And in the middle of their eye contact, I pull up my phone, pinch the zoom to 1.5x, and snap a shot of Leslie through a windowpane.

They walk inside to work Robert's alibis, not alternative theories. Good. I pocket my phone and the cutter and fall back into the sand, almost laughing, practically giddy. The wind. The sea. The prickly-pear stars above me. Everything about this is perfect. Absolutely perfect.

LESLIE

"Ms. Tiller," I say, "would you say your abductor was approximately the age of the defendant? Seventy years old? Sixty? Somewhere in that range?"

June clears her throat and shifts high in her seat, one of the barstools I nicked from the kitchen. We've set it up in the living room next to the flat-screen, mock-courtroom. The house is now a cityscape of papers and folders and printed-off notes that covered us through jury selection and opening statements. "Yes. If I had to guess, then yes."

"If you had to guess. So, there's uncertainty in your mind?"

"No."

"But you said you had to guess."

June's mouth flattens. "Les. I was trying to give you a positive ID. That was just a turn of phrase."

"Good. Those are the little cracks of daylight I want to exploit." That's something else my mock-trial-practicum professor hammered in my head. A certain answer stated uncertainly can be as good as a *maybe*. Sometimes as good as a *no*. "And stop being June. You're Barbara Tiller and you're terrified."

"Because I see the killer in the room?"

"No. The lights and cameras. You, Barbara Tiller, don't recognize Robert."

June wiggles and flicks her shoulders straight, donning the mask. She's a surprisingly good actress. "I meant that I don't know his age, but he was certainly in that range."

"And how do you know that?"

"Leslie," June interrupts. "June again. None of our assumptions make sense if Freeland pulls a positive ID out of her. The courtroom would be reeling over the fact that she just pointed at Robert. We should be on offense. *How* could she remember? Is she pointing at Robert because he fits the general description, or because she *recognizes* him? How many people have heterochromia? What are the odds? What's the population of Madre?"

"Let me develop my way to the point."

"Maybe you can't. Maybe Bates gets impatient, Freeland objects, and Bates sustains. *Move it along, Ms. Woodhouse.* Because the problem with all your arguments is that you're planning on Barbara Tiller giving you some sort of *maybe*, but we *have* to take into account if *maybe* never comes. What if she's certain Robert did it? What if she points at Robert and says, 'There he is'?"

I melt into the sofa and let the tablet slip from my hands. I can feel my veins constricting, my skin seizing like a wet suit. A headache is coming. I whisper something to June about taking a break and walk to the kitchen with her sharp what-if questions still plucking at my nerves.

The plastic knives aren't in the drawer. I'm not hungry, exactly, and a couple of orange slices won't dissolve my headache, but it'd be nice to have something of Robert's inside my palms. He should be here. He should be home. It's wrong, it's all wrong, and I'm wrong, too. The wrong lawyer who couldn't see that maybe Barbara Tiller could end our case with a single wrong word.

"Sorry," June says under the archway. "You told me to get on the stand and be hard on you. That's me being hard on you."

"No. You're right. You're absolutely right. Have you seen the good knives?"

"You're looking at them. I just don't want you to prepare a hundred scenarios for *No* and *Maybe I didn't see him* when we need to prepare for *Yes, that was your husband, your husband tried to kill me.*"

"I was thinking of the witness lineup. Sarah didn't ID him exactly." I shuffle through a jumble of clinking steak knives. They're all so recklessly unsheathed. "And I'm *not* looking at them. I meant the plastic ones. The ones with pastel handles."

"Oh, those kids' ones? I moved them to the back. I thought they were for Patricia's grandkids or something." June shrugs.

"You're right about Sarah, but Barbara is an adult with a clear memory. She's someone who *spoke* to him. Are you afraid of what she's going to say?"

The silverware tray is catching against the wood, so I try to cram it in. My fingers are mashing and clumsy. Then the drawer shudders and the tray gives way in a splash of dancing metal. I yelp. And of course I've drawn blood on my pointer finger, of course I've managed to cut myself in the search for the *safety* knives, Robert's safety knives, the soothing feeling of his fingers puzzling into mine. I suck at the wound and dig out a bandage from my purse.

"You okay?" June wonders.

I don't answer. I wrap the bandage and walk out the front door.

I'm halfway across the bridge to the mainland before I know where I'm driving. With Robert gone, only one person can heal me. Patricia. She will answer her door smiling. She will already be coiffed and spotlessly rouged. She will make a joke about how she didn't see my heads-up text; that's simply how she always looks at eight o'clock. Then she'll mix me a virgin piña colada and we'll sit at her coffee table while she tells me how all her friends believe Robert is innocent and I'm fretting over nothing, *absolutely nothing*, and by the way, is it okay that she splashed a little rum in there?

I ring her bell with my tongue working, already tasting pine-apple. The door opens a smidge.

The face peeking through is not my sister's. It looks more like Patricia through one of Steph's Snapchat aging filters. Cheeks parched, skin wan and limp.

"Pat?"

Patricia shuts the door. "You could've sent a text."

"I did. Tomorrow is our first witness, and I just thought—"

"Hold on." A pause. "I was asleep. One sec."

The porch light stings. I thumb at my watch, which feels suddenly and heavily wrong, and utter a prayer that what I just saw was some sort of optical illusion. But no: chemotherapy has plainly spun its cobwebs, haunting all the hollows of her face. How long has it been since I last saw Patricia? Days? Weeks? She'd had the wig on, but that had been her decision. She still looked like herself.

The person I just saw was someone else.

Patricia opens the door. "Before you get all worried, just know I'm in the thick of it," she says as I step inside and head for the living room. "Nurses say it's one of those things. Gets worse before it gets better."

"You look beautiful." I hear the words crackle in my throat. "I should be with you. Every session. What kind of sister am I?"

"A busy one. Your priority is Robert. Do you want something? I have that weirdo Fresca you like."

"No, thanks."

We settle into her satiny cushions as I tell her what's going on in Robert's case, about Barbara Tiller, about June and me rehearsing the testimony. I stop just short of telling her why I drove over because, at that point, Patricia's eyes are starting to lava-lamp into her lids. "Pat, if it's a bad time, I can come over tomorrow."

She starts. "No. Never a bad time. Just—another sec."

And off to the bathroom. The fan clicks to a whir and the faucet runs.

I stand, wanting nothing between me and her sounds, feeling the same helpless pit in my throat as I did when Steph became a teenager and started taking her phone calls in another room. But that's not whom Patricia reminds me of. Someone close, like Steph. Someone far, like Steph. Just not Steph.

Patricia shuts off the faucet and walks out. I prepare myself for the perfume dump of that potpourri she usually carries in whenever she enters a room, but instead, I smell nothing but a plasticky petroleum burn. Something medical. A skin cream, maybe.

Her eyes are small, funneled in soft lines. The tendons in her neck are loose. Her lips are crackled white. It's just a glance, a flash of eye contact, but I finally see whom she reminds me of. Mom. I have to sit down. I have to wonder why I'm even here. For comfort? *My* comfort? To have her comfort *me* while she's left to face cancer alone? To have her tell me what a great job I'm doing on Robert's case, even though there's a chance Barbara Tiller will point her finger and declare to the world, *Yes, it was him, he is a monster,* shattering the fragile glass I'd built my life upon?

And the thought shreds me from the inside out.

Tearing her pillows from the couch, I squeeze and squeeze until the cases rip and my tears fly out of me and I bite my teeth into powder.

"Hey," Patricia barks. "Hey. Les!"

She rushes over. Throws her scrawny arms around me, wraps me in her bones. And I throw myself back into her, screaming some foghorn wail as we fall into her sofa.

I find myself thinking of the biopsy my mother had to get when I was a child. Some dark cloud on her breast scan. I hadn't thought much of it—Mom told us over a dinner of hamburger hot dish with Tater Tots like she was dropping news about having to winterize the Chevy—until I woke up, randomly, at 10:00 p.m. A low, soft heaving was coming from the other room. I thought maybe the dog was sick, so I tiptoed out, went to tell Dad.

And the sound rose up, gathering vibrato as I approached his door.

It was Dad. The idea of it being a human sound simply never registered to me because I'd never heard my father cry. And I'm glad for that. Somewhere below the most awful, horrifying sounds in recorded history, there is a void, then a few steps down, and then, only if you're brave enough to venture into the dark and listen, you get to the bottom of the universe and hear the sound of a father's weeping.

My young head was whirring in that hallway as I finally put the pieces together. The dark cloud, the scan, hamburger hot dish—my favorite, mom still putting me first—and now Dad. The biopsy was life-or-death. I ran back to my bed, pulled out my rosary, holding it fiercely, praying until my palms sweat. *Please*, I said. *Please let this be a dream. Let life be just a dream.*

Sometime later, I came home from school to see Dad

tinkering with pots and peeling potatoes. He never cooked, but he was making Mom's favorite to celebrate. Celebrate what?

And there Mom was, beaming under the arch.

"The biopsy came back clear," Mom said. "These last few weeks—turns out it was just some bad nightmare. That's how it is, right?" Then she let out a glorious sigh. "Sometimes I think life is just a dream."

I stood there, still backpacked and weary from school, utterly frozen. Hearing the words pulled out of my prayer and slammed back to earth had a permanent effect on me. It was the day I knew for certain that someone was listening.

Now, Patricia takes me in another thin-wristed clutch, comforting her stupid baby sister, rocking me, the proud thudding of her heart obvious against mine. But I can't help my weeping. Because I've prayed and prayed for Patricia—for Robert—and where has it gotten me? I'm not a kid anymore, when hope was big and solid, an easy thing to grip. Most of life is behind me. All the miracles of my life feel like I was just wrapping my child's mind around coincidences I didn't understand.

And I think, squeezing Patricia's shoulder blades, *What if this nightmare never ends?*

The next morning, I meet Robert early for prep work. June has done her usual overpreparing and brought her own printer in from Miami, so I have entire armfuls of paper, folio after folio filled with worksheets and flowcharts. I slide one of them across the table for Robert. His mouth cinches with a tart fold.

"June pointed out," I say, having practiced this little preamble on the drive in, "that we have to be ready for the possibility Barbara claims you were the man who tried to abduct her."

"Why do we have to be ready for that?"

"Because that's the worst-case scenario."

"Not because you suspect I'm lying."

No reply of mine could be productive. I lay out another worksheet for him, this one written exclusively for him. Robert is not a quick study. I told June he'd need it condensed to one worksheet cut into big-picture bullets. *Remain composed at all times. No eye-rolling, no scoffing. When in doubt, take five plunging breaths, then decide how to react.*

"I thought I didn't have to do anything," Robert says.

"Meaning you don't have to say anything. But being mindful of how you react will feel like doing something. The cameras are always on, and you have to assume the jury's always watching. Even if it feels like they're not."

"What's wrong with how I react?"

I turn my palm up and make a *behold* motion.

"All right." He picks up one of the sheets, eyeing it blindly. "But is this really what swings cases? If Barbara Tiller says something sweet and then I scowl or something, that's it? 'Guilty'?"

"Not in so many words."

"Then how would you put it?"

I want to say that if Barbara Tiller buries us, there's no reason to hand Randy Freeland another shovel. But it's better for us if Robert is in a good mood.

* * *

Barbara Tiller swears in on the witness stand, sweeps her dress under her knees, and sits up straight. She's pristine and made-up: brunette with tight lip-wrinkles and a birthmark above her collarbone vaguely in the shape of Madagascar. She's doing her best to remain poised, but the poor thing is too willowy for that. The tremor in her fingers is obvious.

Randy Freeland has no tremor; he's all sugar and caffeine this morning. He stands slowly, deliberately. A little over-rehearsed, but the jury may disagree. He settles near a lectern, his shoulders back, hips out. The steady smile he wears suggests he's sitting on twenty-four-karat gold. "Ms. Tiller, I'd like you to describe the events of that Friday. You were with your daughter at the beach?"

"Yes."

"Tell us what happened."

Tiller takes us through the context: the divorce, the shared custody, the last day she had with her daughter. The storm-cloudy day, the man in the black SUV—Lincoln Aviator, just like Robert's—and when they tried to get away from the rain, the killer made his move with a blade in his hand.

"Any distinctive features?" Freeland wonders. "Behaviors you noticed?"

Barbara lifts a wrist above the lectern and works it, half scratching and half jerking, with the opposite hand. "He scratched himself through his shirt. Like this."

The air in the courtroom seems to cool. Freeland rubs his nose. A few eyes fall on Robert, whose hands are folded calmly in his lap. A minor victory. Hopefully, we're all asking ourselves why we haven't seen Robert do that.

Freeland can't wait to move on. "Please continue."

I watch the jury as Barbara recounts that day. Trying to see if anything sets off their internal red flags. A man Robert's age, overpowering a forty-year-old woman? Maybe. She's young, but she's birdy and thin boned, and Robert is, after all, still a man. But I sense nothing from the jury in either direction.

Juror Number Three is my target. My barometer. The middle-aged trucker with a mullet, the one June and I can only guess is our best shot at the government-overreach argument, gives me nothing. He's Robert's age and I've noticed he always crosses his arms when Randy Freeland stands up. Three is wearing a button-up now, but he showed up to jury selection in all denim. During selection, as I asked questions around his politics—those questions are always like needling your way through a game of Operation—I got the vivid impression from his long hair and DON'T TREAD ON ME shirt that he might be one of those sovereign-citizen types who loves to argue about his rights whenever police pull him over for a broken taillight.

All guesses, though. Such is jury selection. Now, he might as well be a marble sculpture with his eyes painted on.

Freeland glances at his notes. "Now this next part may be a little uncomfortable for you to relive, Ms. Tiller, and for that I apologize. But I need you to describe your final conversation with your abductor."

Barbara's eyes flit side to side, reading the memory. She takes a swallow so loud it clicks on the microphone.

"He came downstairs for the first time. I heard him click something open. Then he said, 'This will be very quick. I promise.'"

"What then?"

"I don't know. I was panicking. I thought he was going to kill me."

"Did you try to get loose, maybe fight back?"

"No."

"Did you see him?"

"I couldn't see. He cut something, hovered there for a minute, then ran upstairs. I was too scared to move. When I finally did, when I heard he was gone, I was finally able to get free."

"Ms. Tiller, you saw him earlier when he attempted to abduct you near the apartment complexes at Presidio Heights."

"Yes. Clear as day."

"Can you describe the man you encountered that day?"

"He was . . . medium build, on the slighter side." Barbara's lips pulse, an involuntary flick. "His hair was gray. He wore a button-down, I think, I don't remember, something thick with sleeves, which struck me because it was so hot. But it was black. Black denim."

"Would you say you felt the defendant matched the description of the Gulf Coast Killer?"

"Objection," I say. "Leading the witness."

"Sustained." Bates flicks his hand. "Rephrase, Mr. Freeland."

"Would you share any additional details you recall?"

"He was thirty, maybe older. One of those faces where it's hard to guess. And the color of his eyes didn't match exactly."

"How so?"

"One was a little more green than blue."

Freeland leans on the lectern, opening himself to the jury. "To summarize, your abductor drove a black Lincoln Aviator, wore black clothing, can be described as a male aged thirty or older, slight-to-medium build, with two different-colored eyes—a condition known as heterochromia. Ms. Tiller, am I accurate in describing your abductor?"

"Yes."

"And then, when he had you tied down in a basement in Immokalee, you say you never saw him except that once. But you spoke to him again. Was it the same voice, both times?"

"Yes."

"And can you describe your abductor's voice?"

"High. Soft. Very deliberate."

"In the course of this trial, you've heard the defendant's voice. Is it similar?"

"Objection. Leading."

"Overruled." Even Bates is leaning in now. "Ms. Tiller, please answer the question."

Tiller's eyes flicker, then stare down the gullet of the microphone. "Yes. Yes, he sounds like that. A little. Maybe not so—I don't know—raspy. It was a while ago now."

"And how old would you say your abductor was?"

"Objection," I say. "Asked and answered."

"Overruled. Witness will answer."

"I don't know," Tiller says. "It surprised me to see how old the defendant was. I'll say that."

I shoot a look at my juror. He's up in his seat.

"Well, why don't we just get down to it?" Freeland asks. He opens his hips directly to the jury now, playing to the crowd behind us. "The man who tried to abduct you. Is he with us in the courtroom today?"

Barbara squints at Robert. Raises quivering fingers, as if she means to point, then folds them under her chin. I can feel Robert shrink away. I'm tempted to put my hand on his, to buttress him, to share body heat—anything to give him strength. *Stand strong, honey, if you really didn't do it.* Because *you really didn't do it.*

Barbara Tiller's stare goes on. And on. Batteries will die. Digital recorders will meet their maximum. The sun will rise and set, the moon waxing and waning, eons passing and glaciers melting, and Barbara Tiller will still be there on the stand, staring at my husband and squinting through her indecision.

"Maybe," Tiller says. "I'm sorry. I just can't say for certain."

June's hand tightens on my thigh. *Yes!*

"But you said you *saw* your abductor, Ms. Tiller."

"I was protecting my daughter." A spark in Tiller's throat now—even I can tell Freeland's pressed too hard. "I thought I was about to die. I'm sorry I can't be more specific. He had white hair. Different-colored eyes. Yes."

Nothing to rule Robert out, then. Freeland turns—I think he smiles at me as he does—so he can pull up a new folder. I'd advise against that. He's done enough. Any more questions and he risks looking like the bad guy. You'd be surprised how quickly a jury can turn on the prosecution. Even if the defendant looks guilty, if they see too much of the prosecutor—slicked-back hair, silky button-down, fresh haircut every two weeks—they start to root against him. Before he dips into his notes, these thoughts seem to dawn on him. "No further questions."

"Ms. Tiller," Bates says, blocking the microphone with his palm, "we can recess before cross-examination if you feel you can't go on."

"No." Tiller's voice goes whispery. "No, I'd like to keep going."

"Defense's witness."

I stand at the lectern. Between my fingers, I've got a stapled list of questions June and I had gone through after collapsing on the sofa together. Counterattacks to everything. Fifteen follow-ups if Barbara gave us a *maybe*. Rebuttals. Highly logical defenses, arguments that it could have been any older man of medium build. First, I lift my face and try to make eye contact, try to make myself as warm as possible.

"Ms. Tiller—just to confirm. You can't say, with a hundred percent confidence, that it was my client who tried to abduct you?"

"Not with a hundred percent confidence, no. It was all a blur. I was terrified."

"Yet you got a clean look at your abductor?"

"I did."

"And you have a clear memory of him?"

"I do."

"But Robert Alan Woodhouse does not give you that same clarity?"

"Objection," Freeland says, "leading."

"I'll withdraw," I say. "No further questions, Your Honor."

I could ask more. Poke and prod her all day, find some weakness in her testimony. But that paints me as the bad guy, abusing an innocent woman for any slight advantage. I want the jury to sense that I'm insulted by the idea she even came close to identifying my husband. I want them to smell my confidence: that with a single question I can cast her entire testimony in doubt. At this point, it's all I can hope for.

WESTON

From inside the trailer I can hear the nightly news squawking about Barbara Tiller. All those overenunciated, full-throated reporter phrases—*stalemate in court today, failed to identify*—are so achingly loud they make me want to turn up at the courthouse and open a few arteries. This urge beats through me until it settles into an itch in my own veins. The ones I can see in my wrist are soft and blue. There is no good way to scratch them clean, so I rub them up and down, massaging, working them through the skin. Hopeless.

Perhaps setting Barbara Tiller free was hoping for too much. Try as I might, I am not my father, look *nothing like him*, whatever people told me as a child. When I look in the mirror, I never see Robert. I see soft cheeks and an underbite. Just a composite of all the men I knew growing up.

Men like Conlan.

Conlan was a former Division I tight end who got addicted to painkillers after tearing his ACL his junior year. When he met my mother, he was making good money in a construction crew, but the job kept murdering his knee, kept him blowing that good money on pills, so he was treading water just like us.

I liked Conlan at first. Even with one bad knee, he could lift me over his head like I was nothing but a milk crate. He would ruffle my hair and call me "Wes." He would take me outside the trailer, shake the ash out of the grill, and teach me how to grill a pack of precooked hot dogs. He would drink fat beers and tell me about how Big Pharma screwed him and how he should be on his second contract with the Buccaneers. He would plink empty bottles with dead-eyed accuracy and, when I asked his secret, tell me that practice makes perfect. Then, at the appointed hour, he would glance at his watch.

"You wanna get lost now?" he asked.

"Why?"

"Me and your mom need the trailer. You got a dad? Call him maybe."

I nearly asked if he knew my dad. I'd met so few adult men I wondered if they all somehow knew each other, herding together in a secret cigar club.

Conlan stuck around longer than most of Caroline's boyfriends. Maybe because in his hands, she felt like a milk crate, too. Things went well if I avoided him (kick rocks, drop in on a neighbor playing Nintendo, hunt for alligators down by the creek), but eventually, things *never* went well because he started mixing pills with all that beer. His nightly cocktail: Percocet Genuine Draft. He used to joke about pulling my pants down and spanking me. I think they were jokes, but he only made them when Caroline was at work. He liked putting out his cigarettes on my arm, too, when I was the only one home because that meant *my mom was at the bar getting piped down*, and though I barely knew what he meant, I could tell from my burns and the way he flicked the word in his bicuspids that it was not something a man like Conlan wanted a woman to be doing.

One night I asked Caroline what I should do about him. She smiled drowsily and said, "Just be nice. Everyone likes a nice boy."

That struck me as insufficient. I consulted the great wild internet. *How to deal with a bully*. Stock photos of out-of-focus schoolyards, lots of mollifying advice that made no sense. *Step one: reach a common understanding*. Again, insufficient. So I gave up and watched leaked CCTV footage instead, saw my first video of a gunshot victim bleeding out by a curb. That did something for me. Improved my circulation, maybe, worked some heat into my fingertips.

Robberies, street brawls, prison shankings. I especially liked the latter because it never mattered how big you were: cut a man in the right spot and he would fall down.

One night, with Conlan passed out on the couch and me eating mac and cheese again, Caroline came home in a cloud of her sweet rummy scent. Conlan swore he could smell *men* on her—and as she approached him to explain, his face went cold and he shoved her into the wall.

I jumped up. Something at the top of my stomach burned, some fuel moving my limbs without any help from my brain. I had said *please* to Conlan, like Caroline said. My brain regained control. Calmly, steadily, I picked up my bowl and threw it on the ground so hard it shattered. I picked up one of the shards, held it like I meant to carve a pumpkin, then jammed it into Conlan's shoulder blade.

He screamed, turned, shot me a wild, doe-eyed look of stun.

But practice makes perfect. I reeled the shard in a high arc and jabbed it into his thigh. Conlan shot me an electrified look and picked up his hand to strike back, but I kept ripping out the shard and shoving in again, the way I had once seen my neighbor's mother bone a chicken. Then Conlan, all six foot five of him, went stumbling out of the trailer on his one good ACL and never came back.

I stood there with the shard dripping in my hand. My lungs were pumping, but my heart was steady. A storm surge was rising in my head, lifting everything, relief and control and fear and rage and regret and a giddy, opiate power. *No, Conlan. I will not get lost. I will stand up, I will take back what little territory I have, and through it all, I will never lose my cool.*

Caroline did, though. She slapped the shard out of my hands and cuffed me by the wrists and shook.

"What is *wrong* with you?" she asked. Again and again, in every variation. "What is *wrong*, what is *wrong with you*, what is wrong with *you*?"

Then she wrapped me in her noodly arms and hushed her voice so she could whisper a dirty secret into my ear: "Thank you."

Now, scratching my wrists with that same hot feeling in my fingertips, I breath until I calm myself. Imagining Robert convicted is a salve better than any anti-itch cream I can find over the counter. All that work—the dyed hair, the weight, the contact lens I can still feel scraping my cornea—for nothing. It may all come down to the DNA. There is no way for him to escape his own DNA. They have to get him. It has to work.

And then, like Conlan, Robert will finally have been bled out of my life.

LESLIE

The number you have dialed is not available. At the tone . . .

"Hi, Weston? It's Leslie. Sounds like you're between phones right now, but if you get this, I was wondering if we could connect—I'll leave you my number. Two three nine . . ."

I tap *End* and set my phone on the coffee table, feeling a rare and earthbound kind of feckless. Is Wes screening me? He's not on Freeland's witness list, but maybe he hopes he is. Maybe he can't wait to get on the stand and excoriate his father. Or, glass half full now, maybe he's got a few surefire alibis that he wouldn't mind making me work for. Still. To be so hard to reach when you could tip a murder case in either direction? Maybe the wounds between him and Robert go deeper than I imagined, all the way to bone.

But it's a fresh morning and June is grunting in the kitchen nook. When I walk in, she tears up a piece of paper before tossing it.

"Still here?" I ask.

"Still here."

Our old repartee. Some days, when we'd stayed too late working some case, I was sure she hated me and hated the work and was fantasizing about quitting. Especially moving somewhere far away, even though I had already moved to my *far away*.

It became a tongue-in-cheek daily routine: *Still here?* It's a half joke really. Most of the time I'd expect her to up and leave me, move on to greener pastures. Eventually, she did. Plenty of people dream of retiring here; if you're born here, you sometimes dream about leaving.

"I keep trying to get some of the police paperwork," June says. "Are they always this slow?"

"I'll try my source."

June knocks an eyebrow. "'Source'?"

"Aspiring source."

I walk back for my phone. I can't tell if the seed I planted with Sergeant Ingram is germinating. We've gone back and forth about what it's like raising daughters. Evie is entering *that* age, the preteen years, and he's terrified of the looming boyfriends and pressure of high school. Any advice? Just that if he ever gets lost, he can always drop a question my way.

His most recent text is still that GIF of Keanu Reeves making a bursting-heart gesture: *Thank you.*

Cute, this chemistry of ours. Though not fruitful quite yet.

Back in the kitchen, I pull up a wicker basket for Patricia. I'm going to make her a care package. Lots of little things, lip balms and travel shampoo—that's to hear her say *hardy har*—plus wool socks and hotel bottles of booze. I fight off tears as I do it. The doctors tell her she's responding well, but they won't know for a while, not until it's time for the update scans. They just mean she can handle chemo without losing her appetite. She still has her eyebrows, which makes her furiously proud. I wish I could spend every night at her house instead of mine, every morning checking up on her, making sure she got up that morning, that she's feeling well, that she's breathing, three solid breaths, that she's well stocked with all the things she's not supposed to have, the wine and marzipan and those Bit-O-Honeys she likes so she can joke, *It's Bits-O-Honey when it's in the plural, Leslie.* This afternoon, I decide, June and I will pay her a proper visit. It's not as if there's been any helpful break in the case.

And as that hopeless thought slices through me, my phone buzzes on the glass of the coffee table.

CALL FROM: RESTRICTED.

"Leslie!" The voice is soft and fluty. "Weston Adekins. Returning your call."

"Oh!"

"Been a while. Is this a bad time?"

"Not at all, not at all—" I drag out the entire word *alllll* as I fumble through my things and grab a notepad. "I was just wondering if I could talk to you a little bit about—I mean, I'm sure you've heard—of course you've heard—your father's case—"

"Heard a lot. Not exactly sure what to believe, to be honest."

"Could I just ask you a few questions about it?"

"Sure. Now?"

"If you have—"

"How about this?" A pause. I think I hear water swishing. "Maybe we can speak in person. Kind of sensitive stuff, you know, and with phones these days—"

Though I don't, I say, "I understand completely—"

"So can I text you the address? I am currently kind of . . . in between homes. There. Let me know if you have it."

A new alert from Weston's unrecognized number. He wants to meet in Fort Myers. "Meet you in a half hour?"

"Looking forward to it," he says.

June is standing in the kitchen entryway. "Did I hear right? Wes Adekins?"

"You heard right."

"See if he's got alibis!"

"I know."

"And double-check our timeline." *Our timeline*, sourced from Robert, is that Wes returned from Colorado sometime between the second and third murders. And since we're confident Robert never committed the first two, there's a chance an alibi from Wes could change things.

"Am I dressed okay?" I throw a glance at the hallway mirror. The answer is mixed: gingham smock shirt, white shorts. There's nothing lawyerly about it, but it'll do for a lunch chat. I pluck a pair of buggy black sunglasses out of my purse and imagine myself making catch-up small talk with Robert's son.

"Remember, we need North Naples and Estero," June says as she picks lint off my shoulder. "I'll text dates and times in case you forget."

"Purse, phone, wallet," I announce, tapping each as I go. Outside, the day is steamy and cloudy white, the sun diffusing into a spirit presence. I turn back to gush at June, who's watching from the threshold, "Wes! We got Weston!"

"Go! Go!" she prods. "Break a leg."

* * *

A few minutes later I'm driving up 75 to Fort Myers, lead footed and doing fifteen over.

Why am I so nervous? Robert likes to say I get nervous over nothing, and maybe that's true now. Or maybe because talking to Weston is a rare and unpredictable thing, something to gear up for, the way the Death Valley superbloom only happens every decade or so when there's been enough rain.

I gather—mostly through Holmesian inference and the way Robert winces every time I ask—that Robert regrets his relationship with Weston's mother. I also can't imagine Weston enjoys feeling like a sour reminder. He came to our wedding—at my insistence—and there was a brief period when he and Robert would chat on the phone maybe once a season. Then Caroline Adekins died of lymphoma. That snipped the only link between them. Wes moved out of state in search of more stable work and Robert gave me that air-sucking look so often I stopped asking altogether. It's a long story, I suppose, like a three-hour movie I'd seen flashes of but never all the way through to the end credits.

It's been easy enough to toss this all aside for years, to tell myself that "someday" I'd finally uncover every answer, maybe even somehow manufacture a surprise dinner together. Hugs, breakthroughs, reconciliation. It was on my to-do list. My *someday* list. But "someday" is a papier-mâché word that only gives the appearance of patching. The truth is, I didn't always want to know what Weston had to say about his father.

Now, I need to know.

A huff of lemony, shrimpy air blankets the Riverside Café when I arrive. The Caloosahatchee River must be blooming with algae because it throws off an earthy funk. No one seems to mind. Half the crowd is alfresco, and it's noon, so there's not a free chair in sight. It all feels too public for the conversation I'm about to have, but I can handle that. Totally crowded is the same kind of intimate as totally empty.

I'm about to approach the hostess by the door when a man in a white seersucker shirt waves me down from a table next to the window. "Leslie," he says as we shake hands. He's thinner than I remember. His wrists are crisscrossed with red streaks. "I apologize it took these kinds of circumstances for us to get together."

"I feel the same way. I'm sorry. This has been a long time coming, and I haven't been much help on that front." We sit, and when the waiter comes, I order a scallop dish I'm sure I'll be too sour stomached to eat, plus a cup of tea in case I need something to do with my hands. "Robert always had a tough time when it came to the two of you. Anything I ever did always felt like butting in."

"I understand. The one good thing about this situation is it makes everything else seem so small in comparison."

The words are soft from his mousy underbite. Soft and careful, syllable by syllable, almost like a child learning phonics. His eyes are tart blue, a pair of robin's eggs set close together. He's around thirty-five, I think, but I wouldn't be able to guess by looking at him. His skin is going papery in spots, around the eyes, the lips—just like Robert's. The irony of their relationship is that they might as well have popped out of the same mold.

He's left the bread basket untouched. Now he's scraping the webs of his fingers with wet wipes he must have brought from home. As the waitress drops a steaming cup of tea in front of me, he eyes me with a searching look.

"You're in town for work?" I ask.

"Seeking it. Between jobs. This economy . . ."

"Remind me what you do? Robert never made it clear."

"Well, locksmithing gets me by."

"What got you into that?"

"Not sure. I always liked puzzles, I suppose. And every lock is a puzzle."

"Funny. Me, too. Not locks. Puzzles. You should see my house. I still find old puzzle pieces under cushions."

"Heh. You probably know I was in Colorado for a while, and since then, everywhere in between. Kind of a nomad. I think I always expect to find the perfect spot to plant my flag, and then some big apartment complex two towns over will call me in. And there I go again."

A little while later, the waitress sets a bed of herby scallops in front of me. I'm a little suspicious how fast it came, especially with seafood, but I'm relieved to find my appetite. The hard tangle of nerves in my stomach during the drive up has loosened its grip on me. "Robert told me that you'd seen each other. Before all this, I mean."

"Once or twice, yeah."

Twice, I hope. "How recently?"

"You mean, as recently as the murders in Estero and North Naples?"

I gape at him.

"I follow the case on TV," he says. "When I saw your number pop up on my phone, I figured you might ask."

"And? Do you remember?"

"Is it okay that you and I talk through this before I get called as a witness?"

"Of course. Wouldn't be here if it wasn't."

"Oh." He scowls. "I just worry about tampering."

Tampering is one of those legal-drama words people have heard enough to think they understand it. But it's really a word of many colors. A wad of cash to keep a future witness's mouth shut? Tampering. Lunch with my stepson? No.

I've been playing with my tea bag. It's been in the water long enough. I take it out, dabbing it against the rim of the mug, then slide over a saucer so I can set it down without staining the tablecloth. There's a chip in the side of the saucer about the size of a toenail. I twist the whole thing around until the chip faces where it should: northeast. Equilibrium.

Weston watches this with his mouth open. "What is that you just did?"

"Oh. Sometimes I like to straighten out objects, even if they don't have corners."

"Straighten. Why?"

"Oh, I don't know. A superstition. Silly stuff."

"Is a superstition silly if it works? I have a few of my own."

His words slur at the end, as though there are miles of conversation to slide down there if we wanted. Better to keep it light. "You think this is bad, you should see me at tax time. It's hell. I always think I'm going to miss checking some box and wind up in prison."

"I do the same thing when I spot smudges. I turn the plate around and eat off the clean side. You?"

"I never think about smudges. It's just—what feels right. Northeast."

"I never imagined you were the sort of person who had compulsions."

"Not terrible. When I was in high school, I had it bad. Now I'd say it's mostly . . . well, it's what you just saw." Robert, with his gifts of safety knives and knack for warming my hands in his, might argue otherwise. But he's the primary reason I can say *not terrible* with a straight face.

"How did you get rid of it?"

"Before your father?" I think back a bit. "My sister was the one who first helped."

"Your sister? How?"

"Back in my Wisconsin days. There was this bowl I could never eat out of. Because if I did, I had this horrible feeling my family would suddenly become violently ill and die. I know. Makes loads of sense. My older sister, Patricia, gave me a sort of ad hoc exposure therapy. She poured popcorn into the bowl and wouldn't let me out of a chair until I had a handful out of it."

"Did you?"

I nod. "Felt like I was going to vomit, but then I didn't. I didn't the next time, either."

His mouth is still open. An escarpment of clean white teeth shows under his tongue. "Sounds a little cruel, if you ask me."

"It's like she pushed me into a cold pool. But she saw I needed a push. After a few weeks, when I realized no one got ill or died because I ate from the cursed bowl, I forgot which one it was. It's not like these things totally heal, but from then on, there was no chance it was ever going to completely run my life."

He flicks the balled-up wet wipe onto the table, watches it bounce and settle back to center. "Maybe one day I can try what your sister did with you."

"Start small. Let a tiny smudge sit for a minute. Then practice two minutes. That sort of thing." I turn the plate so the chip is facing me. It's unsettling how much that feels like a thorn in my flesh, but it's for his sake.

"I feel funny about how you and I never connected. Maybe after the trial—impossible to say when, really—we could do this again?"

"I'd like that." The warm mint of the tea settles me. Why *had* I always deferred to Robert when it came to all matters Wes? There was nothing preventing me from reaching out. A thawing of relations would have saved years of bouncing around the issue, wondering when to ask about it, when not to ask about it. But no meeting after the trial will work unless Robert is a free man. And so far, I don't have a straight answer. Better to ease into it. "You know, you're not quite how I remembered."

"Oh? How so?"

I remember him at my wedding, standing alone next to the DJ booth with a drugged look on his face, bobbing slightly, never moving his shoulders, nursing a bottle of beer like it was a prop. But this man is someone I can talk to. "I don't know," I tell him. "You seem more . . . settled."

"Thank you."

"While I have you—let's say Randy Freeland called you as a witness tomorrow. What would you tell him?"

"Character stuff, I assume. What kind of man my father is."

"Do you think he's capable of killing anyone?"

Weston doesn't answer. As he looks off at the Caloosahatchee, I turn the plate until the chip faces out.

"What about times you were with Robert?" I ask. "Any alibi you could provide—"

"I went through my work calendar. During the Estero murder I was changing locks, and during North Naples I was out of town. Not with Robert, sorry."

And there it is. The nerves in my stomach re-tangle with fury. June wants to build the case off any alibi we can find ("We have him on tape and it's a serial case, for crying out loud, that's your reasonable doubt"), but that still leaves the two first-degree murder charges open for Randy Freeland. He hasn't even had Cook on the stand yet, and she's the one who found the DNA. My mind spins through the case as Wes goes on—something about what he was doing out of town. I set the fork down, prongs out or in, it doesn't really matter. "I'm going to use the restroom. Don't grab the check. I'm the lawyer; this is my treat."

"Oh. Well, thank you."

After I'm done, I splash water on my face and dab myself with a towel. I pull out a stick of gum and chew it into oblivion. I scratch off the herb stuck under my lips. I wonder if all my instincts have always been wrong. I towel off my hands.

Wes is standing outside the bathroom when I walk out, his fingers wrapped around my phone. "Sorry, Leslie, I saw you drop this."

"Good catch." I smile. I don't know what I expected out of Weston. From what I heard about his upbringing, he would have every right to hate Robert, maybe even hate me by extension. He could be a resentful man who spit anytime he heard the name *Robert*, someone who pounds his fist and makes grand declarations like *I'll never help that man, not as long as I live*. This is the Weston Robert's been hiding from me? This polite man who waits for me, holding my germy phone with his clean hands so no one else picks it up? "Thank you."

The startled, blushing, almost euphoric expression that flowers on his cheeks makes me wonder if I'm the first one to ever say the words to him. "You're very welcome."

WESTON

Leslie makes good on her promise and picks up the check. When we part ways, I stick out my hand—conscious not to press my luck with a terrible hug—but she pulls it in and wraps me in an embrace. Afterward, I head to the riverwalk near Lofton's Island, hoping the sunshine will help me process what I just experienced. The heat gloves me, fleshy and familiar, the way I imagine a mother's hug.

Next is a coffee shop in the river district. I walk inside and order something milky with ice, then unfold my laptop. I looked up *Leslie Woodhouse* before, but only casually. There was a lot to read about a man named Cokie Dean, now serving time at a federal prison in Sheridan, Oregon.

Now every headline screams "Suspected Gulf Coast Killer Robert Alan Woodhouse," and there are dozens of fuzzy street-level shots of Leslie walking into the courthouse. Lots of *No comment*s and YouTube clips of the trial. These are already familiar, mostly because I was extracting pleasure from Robert's seasick facial expressions.

Leslie had been so kind. So polite. Not just the check—the *consideration* of it all, sharing little secrets, making little encouragements. I had known she was a good egg since the first impression. Come to think of it, she was the reason I was even invited to Robert's wedding. That was a uniquely human experience. Lots of sweat and alcohol, plates running pink with the juice of fillets.

If it had been left to Robert, there might have been no invitation at all. It felt slightly wrong to celebrate something with Caroline in the hospital—on her deathbed, it later turned out—but she had encouraged me to go, to see if I could *put in a word*. An invitation like that, she reasoned, must have meant something. I had doubts. It took him a few bourbons, but Robert finally talked to me, threw an arm around my shoulders, promised to visit Caroline when he and Leslie were back from their honeymoon on the Amalfi Coast—her sister's money, he threw in, as if I would ask if he had any extra. Already booked; nothing he could do.

That was when my mother finally gave out. Lymphoma had wormed into her bones, so she was no stranger to the hospital.

Once, when she was cogent, she asked me if he was coming back soon. She wanted to see him one last time. Then one night, she popped out of the morphine and looked up at me with adolescent eyes.

"Don't ever hurt your daddy," she whispered.

"I won't."

"I know you get like that sometimes."

"I said I won't."

"That's good. Real good." Her eyes dipped to the window. "Almost here."

There was no telling whether she meant Robert or death. A few hours later, Caroline Adekins was gone. She left the world without a rattle. Just a fading heartbeat, as soft as the life she lived. The bizarre appropriateness of it all almost made me laugh: she died waiting on a promise from Robert Woodhouse. One last time, for good measure.

I threw her ashes into the Gulf. No ceremony. No one there but me. Who would have come? I drove as far west as I could get, which turned out to be Colorado—a clean place with clean water. I meant to start fresh. But Colorado never suited me. A lot of luxury multifamilies were going up, homes with prefab doors and internet-order keypads that never needed someone to install them. One apartment manager had to let me go because, in his words, "I can just YouTube it from now on."

I drove nowhere in particular. I never thought about Florida, but whether you intend it or not, home always has a magnetic pull. Locksmithing, odd jobs—they might have felt random, but over time, I was dragging southeast. About a year later, I found myself somewhere in Florida, cheap and inland, swatting mayflies on my wrists, hating the heat again, growing ornery. Life was tough but simple. My job was fixing locks and getting chewed out by stressed-out property managers who always threatened to call a locksmith whose car never broke down. Evenings were my only respite. I used to go to a bodega down by a lake and sip Mexican Cokes.

That was where it first happened.

A property manager had texted for me to come and redo the lock of an old lady who failed to understand the dynamics of a basic keyhole. I trashed the Coke bottles and threw myself into my car.

But inside, it was all wrong. Fuzzy dice on the dash, a skunky scent buried in the upholstery.

"What the hell, man?"

A young guy—beady eyes, blue snake tattoos coiling up his neck—pulled me out by the shirt, and as I threw a look back at the car, I saw my mistake. He shoved me again and I went swinging against the brick side of the bodega.

"What are you, dumb? You don't just open random doors."

"It was an honest mistake." I pointed. "Look—my car—"

We both drove the same species of early-2000s rust box. Even down to the color, Pinto blue. But he only shook his head. "I don't give a shit. Your bitch mom didn't raise you not to get into other peoples' cars?"

At which point there is a sore, yawning gap in my memory.

I remember the aftermath, though. Scrubbing the bedroom of my duplex. Latex gloves on. I panicked, cleaned the whole place over thrice, hands shaking, wondering where the body might go. When everything was clean, when I was *certain* of it, I took the long drive out to the coast—that unconscious, magnetic pull again. My lungs were still hot as I rang Robert's doorbell.

He answered it with his hair matted: sweaty from nine holes of golf. He invited me in. I sat down. And I told him. I told him everything. Caroline's ashes, how no one came, Colorado, how there was no work, then back to Florida, yelled at by landlords, how unclean everything felt now, how I only liked drinking out of glass bottles, and then the gap in my memory, everything up to that moment.

Robert took this all in with a sniff. One staticky cough to clear his throat.

"Bullshit," he snapped. It was all he said. I tried to tell him more, but he cut me off. "If you think this is funny—get therapy, Wes."

"No. Seriously. I need your help."

"You came to the wrong place. Police, therapy. I'm not equipped for this, Wes. And I'm done trying. Let them figure you out."

I stood up, wiped my fingers on my jeans. "Not Wes," I told him. "Weston."

What Caroline had named me.

I can still recall the little details of the day on Robert's doorstep. The word *Senectitude* in its proud cursive above the door. I remember stopping at the coatrack, rubbing the fabric of a silky overcoat. I could smell remnants of Leslie. Something floral, maybe rose water. His life was so fragrant now. Robert was right: he had moved on. He had a wife who would not embarrass him, he had a home *with a name*, he was free of my mother, and he was finally rid of the son who had brought him so much shame. I had even made the same mistake Caroline had made: placing even the tiniest shred of hope in Robert's sense of loyalty. *Loyalty* is a peasant word. People like Robert, they laugh at it. So I walked out to my car that night, working my wrists, rubbing them until blood budded in my sleeves, throwing one last look at the hard triangle of his neck where the muscle meets the jugular.

Caroline made me say I would never hurt him.

Fine.

But he could still hurt in other ways. After I drove away that night, I found an app for the local police scanner and heard about nothing but a grease fire in Belle Glade. I started packing. Month to month, I remembered. Really, I was all paid up.

I spent that first night in my car, wrapping my mind around these new problems, never able to sleep, my whole body tingling with anxiety. Any second, I was sure, a police officer would *thump-thump* on the glass and my life would be over. Somehow it stirred up the memory of Halloween as a child: Caroline ripping up a bedsheet so she could sew it into a costume. She only got as far as cutting out a mask. She handed me a black marker and said that once I put on the mask, I could be whatever I wanted. The thought electrified me. I cut out two small dots for eyes, drew *X*'s over them, and called myself a corpse.

It was one of the best nights of my childhood. Wearing the mask, I had no problem ringing strange doorbells, shoving my recycled Winn-Dixie bag in their faces, threatening them with tricks if they gave me no treats. Pouring a stranger's entire glass bowl of candy (TAKE ONE) into my bag. Dropping it to see if it was strong enough to smack on the concrete without shattering. Shoving a kid who ran into me into the tall grass. Showing him the glint of the broken glass I still held between my fingers. Watching the panicked, muley way he ran off.

It took a corpse's mask to do it, but I felt alive again.

The memory of that night was enough to soothe the tingling in my fingers. This was a solution of sorts. What if a face like Robert Woodhouse's could be a different sort of mask? What if my hair was white? One eye the wrong color? If I was careful enough, it would all lead back to him. I could do whatever I wanted. Anything at all.

Now, sitting in a coffee shop, sipping something with far more milk than coffee, I realize I forgot one variable.

Leslie.

I never gave much thought to her then. And what should I make of her *now*? Maybe her presence is a good thing. Maybe Leslie could help. That seems worth remembering. Worth exploring. And what would I call her, if I met with her again? *Stepmom* is a sawed-off word, a hedging word, far too fractional to describe the way I feel.

But I can think about that later. *Will* think about that later.

I pack my laptop into my bag, drain the last of the latte, and walk out into the sun with my hands packed comfortably in my pockets.

LESLIE

When I get home, June is pulling a load of laundry out of the dryer. "What happened? Did you get the alibis?"

"No." Then I add, "Still here?"

June nods wearily.

After some more work on the case and a late dinner, I put on a pot of coffee. I like to make coffee when it's dark. I don't always drink it. Sometimes I just cup the mug inside my hands, inhale the earthy steam. Night is when people most need the touch of something warm.

Normally we'd get ready to call it a day, but at ten we still find ourselves in the dining room office, shuffling through papers, hoping there are obvious things we'd missed. That doesn't seem so far-fetched. I'd missed so much about Robert already.

June pushes her chair out and pinches her forehead. "I know these are four-letter words to you, but we need to at least talk about a plea deal with Freeland."

"Plea deals are for guilty people."

"And for people who leave DNA evidence at the scene. You don't deny that, right? At least a plea deal gives you a chance to reset expectations, postpone things, look for something that exonerates him. We're already short on alternative explanations."

"You're assuming Robert would even say yes. And if he did, we'd still be giving Freeland two first-degree murders. That's life in prison. Two lifetimes. Even with a plea deal."

"Think of it as negotiating *down* to two lifetimes—"

"Why are you suddenly so afraid?"

June sighs. "The DNA witnesses are coming down the pike. If that buries us, we'll regret not talking it out with Freeland when we had the chance. We'll look back on it and say, 'Right after the Tiller testimony, that was when things looked best. When we should've gotten Robert the best deal we can.' That's all criminal defense is, right? You do your best."

"That's not our best. That's least bad. We're not fighting for least bad."

"Call me crazy, but I think Robert *living* is a pretty good deal."

My throat clicks when I swallow. "I can't bring this to Robert. The *best deal we can get* doesn't mean we start saying pretty please to Freeland just because we hit a roadblock."

"I wouldn't call it a roadblock. It's more of a gaping canyon."

I ignore that. "If you were accused of murders you know you didn't commit, what would you say when the lawyers told you that you can get a better deal if you just admit to one or two of them?"

"Of course. But it's about what we can prove."

"We don't need to prove anything. Freeland does."

"Freeland has DNA. What do we have?"

"What's more important here, June?" I snap. "My husband? Or having a clean case so you look good at Williams and Moore?"

Her head snaps back like I splashed water in her face, then pushes her chair back in. "No, it wouldn't hurt if the media thought I did well on this case. That's why I'm *trying* to help."

"But that's what this is. You trying to look good."

"Is that so terrible? Some conflict of interest? Every lawyer wants to look good. I've never been more interested in helping a client."

"Neither have I."

June is staring into the spotless white void of a cloth napkin on the table. The one she threw in the wash for me. She turns, eyes me down. "But that's the only reason I asked to lead, Leslie. You know it's true—people shouldn't represent their spouses. You stop seeing the right moves because you only consider one option. But, okay, let's play this out. We call the owner of that gas station, present the evidence of the Madre alibi, and try to hammer this idea that if he didn't commit one of them, he didn't commit any of them. Freeland counters with DNA at two scenes. Even then, does it sound like a winning case?"

"No," I demur. "But it never does at this stage."

"And it's all right, by the way. I'm stressed-out enough; I have no idea how you feel. I would have cracked by now."

I nudge her. "Is that what I just did? Crack?"

June shrugs, then slips her bifocals up her nose and turns to her laptop.

My own research takes me to my bedroom. I walk up to the bookcase and pull out the thickest tome I own: an encyclopedic directory of every saint. Lives and patronages, a Christmas gift from Steph. Of course I made a passive-aggressive joke about that: Is there a patron saint of being abandoned by one's child? She'd just gotten into Wharton—thrilling news, and all I could bring up was how far away she'd be.

Setting aside these thoughts, I thumb through the *M* section. I wonder, half jokingly, if there's a patron saint of murderers. And sure enough. St. Julian the Hospitaller.

I push the book in, next to the giant family Bible that Robert once bought me as an anniversary gift. He thought I was dropping hints every time I said I wished we had a big family Bible to study. I wasn't. He'd simply listened. Robert calls himself an agnostic, always couching it with a sugar glaze: "But I'm an aspiring believer." Now I'm not sure if he ever meant it. Maybe that's just him cushioning himself for me. Still, the gift was thoughtful. He'd done the research—which translation was best, made sure he bought it from a Catholic gift shop—then wrapped it in an expensive ribbon and promised to go to Mass with me for at least a month. He went exactly four weeks. His honest best.

Lately, it seems like I only can look at him with double vision. Which husband is he? The one who notices my tiny comments and makes gifts from them, or the one who makes me wonder if there's a black hole inside every person?

"Hey."

I nearly fall through the bookcase. June is standing with her arms crossed in the doorway.

"A little light research?" June asks.

"Just thinking it couldn't hurt." Hands shaking, I let go of the book I just pushed in. Should have started with *F*: the falsely accused. "You're right to pursue the alibis, but we have to be ready for the possibility there aren't any alibis for the last two. You okay if I shift focus to look at the alternatives? There's something not right about how fast everything came together, especially with the DNA."

"What do you expect to find that wouldn't feel like another Leslie Woodhouse special?"

"You'll have to define *Leslie Woodhouse special*."

"You know, Leslie Woodhouse. Wins on technicalities. Sets guilty people free."

That presses something sharp into me. "Don't take this the wrong way, because I'm grateful. But my husband is in the fight of his life and I'm praying for a technicality. As long as Robert's free, I can handle it if the public thinks he's guilty. Sorry if that irks Williams and Moore."

"It will. It will irk them. I told you."

"And you?"

"It would irk me . . . a little."

"Still here, though?"

June offers a stiff smile. "Still here."

ROBERT

The sound of keys jangles up the hall. A few seconds later, someone knocks. "Visitor. Fifteen minutes left."

My feet clap to the ground; my spine goes firm. Another chance to see Leslie? Earlier today she and June Daswell came to start prepping me for what they're calling "DNA day." But this time, when I shuffle in, the figure waiting for me on the other side of the glass is sharp and gaunt.

"Wes." The name slips out of me. He would probably prefer a *hello*, but I can't help it.

He holds the receiver to his ear, eyes pinched. Like he's waiting for a translation.

"Why are you here?" I ask.

No response. The same pinched look.

"Well, if you're not gonna talk, I guess I don't need to be here." I stand, wiggling the receiver in the air—*if you still want to talk.*

"I was just checking in to make sure we have an uneventful day tomorrow," he finally says. "When I testify."

"Uneventful?"

He doesn't answer. He stands, pulls a phone from a pair of stiff black chinos, holds it up to the glass.

And there is Leslie. The image is fuzzy and out of focus but it's unquestionably her rosy-white hair, and that is unquestionably our kitchen window behind her, unquestionably the roll of paper towels hanging under the cabinets, the one Leslie always insists has to unroll in proper overhand fashion. Her eyes are wet and the tendons in her neck are tight and snappy, mapping all the stress I've made for her. She's talking to someone off-screen, someone I have to assume is June.

As if he doesn't already have his claws in me. As if I don't know what he can do. I would need to see our whole world— mine and Leslie's—all gathered, guarded, behind bulletproof glass, just to tell her what I know.

Maybe he just wants to rub salt into that gaping wound.

Wes pockets his phone and leans so far away from the receiver, I can barely hear him. It sounds like *See you tomorrow.*

* * *

"At this time," Freeland announces, "the state calls Weston Owen Adekins."

Wes walks up to the stand with slow, stiff rhythm. He's wearing pleated slacks and a navy blazer over an oxford button-down. His hair is trim. His nails are neat. Though I've never seen him wear a watch, the Timex he wears now comes with a strap of red, white, and blue. Only I know that this is a costume.

I rub my thigh through my jumpsuit. Leslie rests a hand on mine.

The nod Wes gives the bailiff is casual and polite. The Bible does not burn his hand like acid when he swears in. The bailiff does not smell the sulfur under Wes's deodorant. Judge Bates does not turn, glance down the bench, and catch even a whiff of murder. The crowd in the gallery does not lean in to hear the self-conscious way Wes mutters his name for the record. People think they can smell danger—*I should've known who he really was, he was exactly the type*—but mostly, people guess wrong. We think too highly of our hindsight.

As Freeland runs through the basics—Robert the absentee father, abandoning Wes to an alcoholic mother—Leslie watches my knuckles shine. She scribbles a note.

Sorry. Should have prepped you more.

More scribbling.

Don't worry. Just a character witness. Waste of time.

I don't smile. Waste of time: it only feels like that if it's not your character being witnessed. The world is about to hear the story I had snuck through a lifetime to avoid.

"Is there anything," Freeland is saying, "that your father did when you were young that sticks out as particularly traumatic?"

Wes leans into the microphone. "Well, I am under oath, so I feel obligated to tell you he convinced me to jump ship from the Rays to the Marlins right before the Rays made the World Series."

A smattering of laughter from the gallery. He is a minor *hit*. And, not true, of course: we never talked anything as tender and intimate as baseball.

"But clearly this was a fractured relationship," Freeland pushes.

"Yes. He was not around often."

"You've had some personal experience with him recently. Why? Why still work on that relationship?"

"I would describe it differently. Not working on the relationship, exactly."

"Then what?" Freeland lifts a page from his folio. "We have records that indicate you returned to Florida within the past couple of years. Can we assume you saw him a few times over that span?"

"Well, he *is* my father. And I had no idea what else was going on. Yes. I visited. I wanted to reconnect first."

His words are light and chirpy: the birdsong of a son who forgave his father years ago. He is making himself a nonstory. Just a normal-dude son of a psychotic father. If the press barely covers his testimony on the evening news, he'll have achieved his goal. He is as serious as the situation demands of him, the poor unfortunate victim, but that's all. He gives us nothing else.

Leslie once taught me a trick to spot a liar: watch for micro-smiles, tiny flashbulbs of enjoyment on the lips. Especially when they're getting away with it. It's called *duper's delight*. People can mostly control their demeanor, at least if you're looking at them from thirty feet away. But they can't always control their morbid twitching.

Wes never twitches, never smiles inappropriately. He never even looks at me. A duper without delight.

Freeland continues, "Were you ever able to, as you say, 're-connect'?"

"No. I called him often. But he was frequently . . . *unavailable*, I guess is the word. Which was odd, I thought, for a retiree. He never had so much free time."

Leslie's chair squeaks as she turns to me. I only flit my eyes in return: *Absolute bullshit.* Called *me* often? The man is a phantasm who rarely keeps a phone number for longer than six months.

Now, I think. *Now.* The courtroom is secure. Wes can't get to anyone. What would happen if I stood up and told the world it was him?

Nothing, probably.

Maybe a piqued brow from Wes. A gavel pound from Bates. A smile from Freeland. And a hit tonight on the news: *Chaos in court today as accused Gulf Coast Killer Robert Woodhouse blamed son for crimes.*

There is a low blasting sound somewhere, a fan or something, and only when Leslie puts a hand on my fidgeting knee do I realize it's the way I breathe through my nostrils when my heart rate rises. A couple of jurors glance over.

Freeland is unaffected, still pulling threads. "What was life *like* for a young man like you?"

"Not easy." Wes swallows. "I had very little idea I was supposed to have some guidance in life. My mother stayed with me but never raised me."

"Who raised you?"

"Dan Rather."

"You're saying she wasn't around often?"

"Without her, I relied on screens, I guess. TV. The internet. You learn to google things."

"Help me out. 'Things'?"

"How to do a load of wash. How to shave."

"A load of wash. Shaving." Freeland lets the words hang dry in the air so we can hear the silence of it all. "And why do you suppose that your father wasn't around—"

"Objection," Leslie calls. "Speculation."

"Sustained." No hesitation from Bates.

"Well, I can move on," Freeland continues. "In your opinion, did your father ever give you any hint that he was capable of crimes like these? Any indication at all—"

"One of my first memories. A birthday party. Mom—Caroline—had a couple of people over at a boyfriend's house. A couple of neighbors. My—well, Robert. He was there. I remember being out in the backyard, just him and me. Someone had filled one of those dinosaur kiddie pools, you know, the ones with ripples in the plastic for scales? The kinds you fill with a hose? He kept trying to make conversation. Even young as I was, I remember thinking, 'Why does he talk like this?' Anyway, something I said, or maybe something I never said, must have set him off. Because one minute I was with my toys and the next minute he had me by a fistful of hair and was shoving my face to the bottom of the pool."

June rises. "Objection—relevance."

"Your Honor," Freeland shoots. "She's interrupting the witness."

"Overruled. Witness is here to speak, Miss Daswell. Mr. Adekins?"

Wes watches this play out with a look of gloamy patience. "Not sure I even fought him at first, like maybe it was a joke—but then I remember taking a breath and only sucking in water. Then I started flailing, screaming—as much as you can scream underwater, anyway—and I remember being so sure that I was going to die. I remember that word being in my head. *Die.* I probably blacked out, because next I woke up coughing out water with Robert over me, Caroline hugging me, crying. So, yes, I've known he was capable of violence from a young age. Crimes, maybe. I never knew which crimes. But I grew up with that always sticking in the back of my head. My father tried to kill me until he thought better of it and changed his mind. And when I saw what was happening, when I saw he was arrested as a suspect, I thought—'Well. Something about that adds up.'"

The only sounds in the gallery are cameras whirring. Sniffs and a few soft breaths. I shouldn't move, shouldn't dignify any of it with a bodily response for the cameras, but I can't help the hard bite in my jaw. Leslie's eyes trace my hand, up my arm, then to my eyes. She looks uncertain. *No*, I whisper, which is the wrong word. It makes my mouth go inappropriately kissy.

"Nothing further, Your Honor," Freeland announces.

"Your witness."

Wes's gaze makes a slow arc over to Leslie, who shares a few whispers with June before standing. "Weston Adekins. How old were you when this happened?"

"Not sure. Three? Four?"

"And you have no other memories of him being violent toward you?"

"No."

"Nothing further," Leslie says.

Wes stiffens, Bates dismisses, and the bailiff escorts the witness back to the gallery. I do my best to regard him with sympathetic eyes on his way down: maybe a juror will read that in me, a touch of empathy, the aftertaste of betrayal, *he lied*. Leslie gives my hand another squeeze and I shoot her a brighter look. Freeland announces the next witness, a grocery clerk from Estero I've never met, and finally I can't help but shoot a glance back at Wes as he takes his seat in the gallery.

He just returns my look with a smile.

LESLIE

The whiplash of Wes's story sends my ears ringing. Bob? Can't-gut-a-fish Bob, holding his own son under the water for no reason? Usually I'd say no, but there was something about Wes's complete lack of hesitation that fills me with doubts.

Sitting down, I throw my notebook on the table, along with my pen, my keys, my purse—it all crashes to the table with a shattered-glass sound that's more violent than I intended. "Is it true, Robert?"

"What?"

"The story Wes just told. Is it true? Even a sliver of it?"

"Are you getting a sense of how he is now? Of *who* he is? Can't you object, go after him for perjury, something—"

"That's not what I asked. I asked if it was true."

"The guy will say anything to get what he wants."

"Robert!" I throw my fists into the table. The *thud* they make rings hard, too, but there's no pain. Only a numb, nervy shock. "Just tell me."

Robert eyes the door. I wonder if I've been too loud, if it will force guards to come in and see what's happening. But after a beat, it's clear no one's coming in to save us from ourselves.

"No. It's not true. I was worried something like this might happen. He lies like this sometimes."

"Then tell me *that*. You don't think it would've been helpful to know? I *asked* you if there was anything else I should know about him—"

"And I said no because look how well you handle it."

"After you lied! Or didn't tell me about this story of his, which is the same as lying. You knew he might say something like this and you never told me what kind of character witness he would be. Me. Your lawyer. Your—"

The word *wife* rots under my tongue. I have never felt like less of a wife. As a lawyer, yes: clients have lied to me before. *Two drinks, Leslie, I swear—their Breathalyzer must be busted if it said one point five.* But it never hurt me because it was never personal. Clients just wanted their lawyer to believe their story. It's different as a wife. Why shouldn't I know the truth? Why don't you trust my knowing? Do you not respect my intelligence? Have you met me? Really met me? If you don't trust me, do you not love me? After too many lies, it never feels like I'm getting real answers. Words, yes. Conversations, plenty. But never answers.

And now, Robert Woodhouse's lawyer wonders what Caroline would say if she were alive and next to take the stand. Maybe she would only have complicated things. Robert Woodhouse's *wife* might not want to hear those things. Digging truths from that family history is like pulling out some rotted tooth, which, when finally gone, only reveals a great yawning abscess underneath. "You should have told me if you thought Wes would lie about you."

"I'm sorry. It's unpredictable." He rests both cuffed hands on the table. One opens at me, a blossom of bones and pallid flesh.

And his hand waits there, me with my arms crossed, steeling myself. I'm not sure I like the strange Dutch angle of his smile. Years ago, I did. Years ago, I would take his hand, accept the answer of unpredictability, and forget all of my red-flag questions. It settled me as little then as it does now, but then, finding a man my age without the spiritual baggage of divorce felt like winning some sort of prize. To be a wife again—a real wife. During my wedding I kept saying how overjoyed I was. In retrospect, that was such an apt choice of prefix. *Over* is so rarely a good thing. Overwhelmed. Overserved. Overpowered.

"Robert," I whisper. "Did you ever hurt anyone?"

And there it is. The question I never asked—of course he's innocent, he always said, I always assumed.

"Never," he says.

"They found your DNA. And I can't square that, Robert. No matter what I think I know about you, no matter how many scenarios I run through my head, I can't square it."

Robert's hand wilts on the table. He's always looking at his own hands, which is fast becoming habit. I read once that narcissists tend to look at their hands. They struggle so hard to see beyond the skin they love. "You want me to explain the unexplainable. I don't know, Les."

"Tell me *something*."

He opens his mouth. Considers his words, draws a breath. There's a slight crackle in his throat. Then he sighs with a long, deflating whimper in his chest. "There's nothing to tell. Maybe next time, I should just talk to June instead."

My fingertips rush with blood. I pick up my key chain, ready to storm out and pop the car open, maybe drive home angry, but the keys slip through my sweaty hands and go flying hard into the wall, where the key fob bursts and sprinkles to the ground. At least it was against the wall and not his face, the face that can't even look at me, the face of a man who can't even acknowledge all I've done to fight for him.

June's words ring hot in my ears: *People shouldn't represent their spouses.*

I sweep up the mess I made, then collect everything I left on the table, my folder, my purse. Robert watches me with a supplicant look in his eyes. Will we embrace? Will we even say goodbye? I don't have answers now. I don't know what comes after this. I only know I can't be his wife again.

Not until his lawyer is finished here.

Soon I find myself at the Madre Island McDonald's, alone in a crowd of parents toting children, closing my eyes as I go kiss-deep into the twisty mound of sugar and guar gum. I know this because the list of ingredients is only a finger tap away on my phone. There's never been anything dishonest about ice cream.

Diet soda is a bad choice, and the caffeine has my heart still reeling from my crashout with Robert, but people watching soothes me a little. Any distraction would be pleasant right now. I'm waiting on a family Doberman to finally make his move on the loose nuggets near the end of the table when my eyes start swelling with tears. *I should just talk to June instead.*

"Leslie."

I look up. Clay Ingram is standing with a tray, sipping softly. Given that he has me by a good hundred pounds, the tiny peep of his voice is always endearing.

"Fancy seeing you here," he says.

Yeah, fancy that. But where else would we meet? It was a trick in my glory days: if you wanted to run into someone in a small town, camp out at a McDonald's. You'd run through the entire population in about a week.

Especially if they have kids. The much-texted-about Evie Ingram is standing next to him, shifting her weight, squeezing one of her elbows so hard it bends her arm the wrong way. The clumsy rope of ponytailed brown hair she wears has to be Ingram's handiwork.

"Clay," I say, wiping the wetness out of my eyes with a napkin. "Yeah. I don't cook much these days."

"Makes sense. Are you all right?"

"Just stress. Have a seat."

"Don't want to disturb."

"Yeah." I shoot them both a paper smile. "This is fine dining and you really shouldn't *disturb*. Sit down. And, oh, this must be Evie. Hello, Evie. I've heard a lot about you."

Evie regards me with that pinched look—*Heard* what *exactly?*—that comes so naturally to twelve-year-olds. But she follows her dad's lead and sits. Her presence makes it a little hard to press Ingram for anything he might leak to me about my husband's case. Small talk, then. Evie's favorite class is algebra. She wants to be an engineer for Boston Dynamics one day. I throw a look at Ingram: *See? Boston.* Daughters are so slippery. The tighter you squeeze 'em, the harder they shoot out.

Only when Evie goes to the bathroom can I start needling Ingram. I try to keep it light. Anything he might have on, say, Teagan Cook? Illegal search and seizure? Process errors?

He picks up one of Evie's fries and folds it into his mouth. "You're bordering on witness tampering."

"I'm just asking for the truth."

"*The* truth, as in total, objective truth? That I don't have. I only have my little slice of it."

"Then I'm all ears."

Evie walks out from the bathroom with a hitch in her posture that reminds me of how people walk when they're squeezing something between their knees. She leans in and whispers something in Ingram's ear. His eyes flicker. He glances at me, swallows. "Oh—uh—really? Now? I—uh—well, let's see."

Then it hits me, too. The bathroom; her crab walk; Ingram's obvious itch to run away, fly to the beach, and jump into a deep chasm under the Gulf. Evie's flailing ponytail screams how bad he is at these things. I grab my purse and stand up. "Clay, with your permission? Evie, I think I can help you with that."

Wretched and desperate, she looks at Ingram.

Ingram looks at her. "She's not a stranger. It's okay."

I take her by the hand and lead her back to the ladies' restroom. I think back to Steph, how we were in the same place years ago. Feels like weeks ago. At my age, everything feels as if it were just weeks ago. The first thing Evie will want is privacy, so I stand guard at a stall while I pull a pad from a dispenser and hand her what she needs. A woman comes in to use the changing station. I wash my hands, rewash them and rinse them, create a little white noise, and then when we're alone again I whisper what to do and how to do it. But mostly what she needs is knowing this is normal, she is healthy, her father would want to help if he knew how. I pop in my car for some dry clothes, an old Marquette hoodie. Then I walk out to see if I can speak some blood back into Ingram's drained face, which is fixed on the ketchup overflow of a condiment cup.

"It'll just be a minute," I tell him.

"You're a lifesaver. I thought I was so ready. But when the moment came—"

"It became a reminder of who isn't here." That thought freezes him, and I regret the words when they come out, but only slightly, a pop of guilt on the tip of my tongue. If there is a crack, if there was a reason I felt compelled to buy ice cream here instead of at the Balanced Diet and wait for him, it's this moment. "It's why you're still in Madre, right?"

"Yeah. I'm from Tallahassee, that's where all my holidays are. I came to Madre for my wife. When she passed, I just kind of . . . stayed. Evie had school, my wife loved that school. It always felt like leaving *here* would be leaving *her*." His eyes are wet. He sips a little Diet Coke. "I don't know if that makes any sense."

"It makes sense," I say, my voice small. An hour earlier, Patricia sent me a video. Nurses at her clinic had recorded her ringing the bell after her first cycle of chemotherapy was over. They cheered. They roared. One gifted her a cupcake crowned with tiny champagne-bottle candies. I wasn't there. I was busy at McDonald's, thumbing my phone, watching toddlers wail, finding new ways to make six-piece McNuggets and diet sodas last me hours.

This needs to be worth it.

"I'm sorry to harp on this, Clay," I push again. "But I think you're an honest person. If there's anything dishonest I should know about—"

"I don't know. I don't know."

He says it twice. Something more there than what happened with Evie? Before I can press again, Evie walks out, posture corrected, hoodie cinched around her waist. She's ready to go home.

* * *

I'm in bed reading about St. Dominic Savio, patron of the falsely accused, when Ingram's text comes through.

Thanks again. And for the hoodie. Evie has been asking questions about the kind stranger all night.

Before I can reply—*don't tell her how you know me*—a link bumps onto the scroll. The screen lags as it loads, then blips to life in a single-page file.

There, on a green evidence table, under the glare of a smart-phone's flashbulb, is a newsboy hat. Look familiar? Ingram asks. If not, ignore. Otherwise . . . ask questions.

My heart sinks.

This is what I've been working Ingram so hard for? All that time, all that patience, for the newsboy hat? A piece of evidence in our files since day one? That they obtained the hair with Rob-ert's DNA from the hat specifically has been public knowledge since the arrest warrant.

Then I sit up.

Ask questions.

"What's going on?" June stirs from her nap, pokes her head above the couch. "Leslie, tomorrow's DNA day. We agreed. At this point, the best prep is sleep."

I throw my phone at her. "Look at this."

June pulls my phone tight—she doesn't have her contacts. "Okay, but this is old news. This is from Ingram? We knew about this since we saw the warrant."

"That's what I thought at first. But *Ingram* sent this to me. *Ingram*, good faithful police officer. *Ingram*, who I've known for several years, wants me to have this picture and thinks it's important that I ask questions about it. Why would he think that?"

"Sleep, Leslie. This is what staying up too late does to people."

"Because Ingram filed it. He knows Cook, and if there was any mishandling, he'd know. Something is clearly sitting wrong with him. All we have to do is find out how she got the hat. In specifics."

June finally straightens. "It's not exactly the magic pill you were hoping for, right? We get Cook on the stand and she'll just squash it. She can say Robert left it in the car. Abandoned property, DNA valid. Then Bates tells us to move on because you know Bates thinks police can do no wrong."

Maybe. There's a strange quirk in federal law and in most states: *abandoned* property is fair game. What defines "abandoned" property before a judge signs a warrant is more nebulous. If you smoke a cigar down to a stub and toss it in a public trash bin, that cigar is fair game for prosecutors. But if you're smoking a cigar and an FBI agent yanks it from your lips before you're done—private property, DNA inadmissible. Yes, it's the tiniest of cracks. But a defense lawyer sometimes has to live in these boundaries between *evidence* and *unconstitutional search and seizure*.

"Maybe Robert will say otherwise," I tell June. "Maybe Robert will say she took it."

"Which becomes he said, she said. Again, Bates won't like that."

"But if there's something there, I can try to trap her, see if she commits to some lie. She's not expecting questions about the hat. Let me have a crack at her tomorrow."

"Oh. What, like badgering the witness until she admits it? What about my questions? And you're still assuming there's something for her to lie about. What did Robert say?"

"Nothing yet. This is new. I'll follow up with him."

June pulls up her phone and glances at it. "When? We're well past attorney hours."

"Tomorrow, then."

June stands from the couch. "Okay. Here's my summary. Tell me where I'm wrong. So we have nothing but *old* evidence from your cop friend, no answers from Robert, and no time to consult with Robert. There's the possibility that Cook just takes these questions and laughs at us, the possibility that DNA Day is a flop for us . . . and this is the big Leslie Woodhouse curveball you've been waiting for?"

"I wouldn't word it that way, but, yes. Assuming Robert tells me the truth—which is becoming iffy, I grant—it's at least an option. There has to be something there. Ingram doesn't trust her, I know it. There has to be a reason."

"The hat is old evidence. 'Abandoned property.' There's nothing new here."

"We never *asked* Robert if he abandoned it. And Ingram telling me to ask questions has never happened before, either. I've known him for years. What did I always used to tell you? Half of the law is interpreting code, but the other half—the more important half—is interpreting people."

"I don't see it. Alibis, those I see. I've been putting that together a while now. This is—just speculative. For all we know, Ingram's messing with you."

"Maybe."

"Then what makes you so eager to roll with this tomorrow?"

That stops me. It's just a feeling. Have I proven to be the best judge of character in my sixty-two years on earth? With Cal, yes. Robert . . .

"We don't even know what Robert will say about the hat," June adds. "Maybe he really lost it."

"I'll ask him tomorrow morning. But it has to be tomorrow, because we can only catch Cook by surprise tomorrow. I'm not confident I can trap her if she sees it coming. But *if* there's something here—you know what it means."

"Sure. I'd love for it to be true. But if it isn't? Then we've only cemented the DNA evidence in the jury's mind, anyway. It's make-or-break."

"DNA Day always was."

"I'm still leading it, right? We agreed. I've been sitting here, day after day, memorizing every piece of paper down to the letter—"

"And you will. Unless—"

"No 'unless.' Promise."

Something makes me hesitate. "Promise."

My pulse still electric, I walk to the kitchen, deciding not to push the issue any further. June is already nervous enough. I pour myself a glass of milk, I break off a generous nib of a cinnamon biscotto, I head to bed. Before sinking into the pillow, I pray a Hail Mary and hope for green-thought dreams.

ROBERT

The next morning, a guard turns up early and tells me my lawyer is here. Usually he says *wife*, because *lawyer* could also refer to June Daswell. Then he drops me in the consultation room, where I'm alone with the dim blue glow of the sun.

Leslie walks in, clacking hard in short heels. I try to make my face look soft. It's not easy given how I feel. If the eyes never lie, my look is dry, prickly, all razor wire and singed nerves.

She barely looks at me as she pulls out a folder and starts talking through a list. These are the witnesses for DNA Day, the questions June will be asking Special Agent Teagan Cook. I fiddle with the metal rim of the table. Maybe Leslie's life would take an immediate turn for the better if I simply pulled it out at the screws and jammed it in my own neck.

After she's done, Leslie runs me through the usual prep: sit up straight, keep my reactions cool, but never icy. I nod through this. Then she folds the file.

"One last thing," Leslie says. "I'm not going to explain this one because I need absolute truth if it's going to have any impact on the case."

"Okay. Shoot."

Her eyes narrow. "This is not a 'shoot' question. I'm telling you I need absolute truth, Robert."

"I said yes."

"Absolute truth?"

"We're going to run out of time if we do this merry-go-round thing every time we have one question—"

"The day Special Agent Cook drove you home, you left your hat with her. Did you lose it, or did she specifically take it from you?"

Strange question. We've been through this in one of the many millions of our consultations, which are now melting together in my mind as the same memory: one everlasting, life-shortening sludge of fight-or-flight anxiety. I'm sure I told her what I remember. My hat was on the dash that day. I set it down, and when I got up to go, it was gone. Cook told me she'd check the lost and found. No, it had clearly been on the dash. But what was I going to do? Fight the FBI over a hat?

"Define *took*," I venture.

"Did you ever ask for it back?"

"That I can answer. I remember asking. I thought it was weird."

"You're sure?"

"Yeah."

I meant the word to come out friendly, but Leslie balks. "Don't *yeah* me, Robert. Don't say it just to placate me. You're *absolutely* sure?"

"Yes. *Yes.* Will you take my word for something one goddamned time?"

Maybe it's my tone, maybe it's taking the name of Leslie's Lord in vain, maybe it's just the way the case is going, but Leslie huffs with such desperate strength I'm certain I gave her the wrong answer. She gathers her papers and her purse in one hard swipe and rises to leave. "See you in there, then."

LESLIE

June and I swim through the crowd that's formed in the courthouse lobby. The air is electric, a thousand conversations at once. I'm surprised Bates has allowed it to come to this. There are lawyers and court officials and TV producers stressing about the autofocus mechanism on their cameras, men wearing CNN polos, women pulling the long wires of their CourtTV mics. Walking from around the corner—I don't like parking anywhere reporters know to find me—I passed a makeshift podcast streaming live from a gastropub.

As June and I take our seats at the defendant's table, the conversations sink to whispers. The benches are full every day, but today there's overflow. A security guard has to escort out a couple of photographers just to avoid a fire hazard. Then the bailiff enters and some guards walk Robert in. As I asked, he's fresh for the day, cleaned and groomed, his white hair brushed into a neat cap over his scalp.

"DNA Day," he whispers to me when he settles in. "We feeling good?"

"Just remember," I tell him. "Cool, never cold."

Then the bailiff strides in, which means Judge Bates isn't far behind.

Showtime.

Wearing a tan blazer and skinny jeans that wrap her a smidge too tight, FBI Special Agent Teagan Mae Cook swears to tell the truth, the whole truth, and nothing but the truth. Ever since her good-cop, bad-cop routine at the Madre Island police headquarters, there's a strangeness I pick up from her—a cross-eyed stare like she'd rather look at my nose than grant me the intimacy of fixing her black-olive eyes onto mine. Her chest is up, her chin is high. She's clearly feeling good today, a woman who believes both God and the facts are on her side.

Freeland has her first. He stands in the hot lights, slowly, painfully chewing the scenery. June tells me that this thespian act of his is starting to grate on the crime sleuths of the internet. They hate him. At least there's one point in our favor.

"Special Agent Cook," he finally says. "I'd like to start with the DNA found at the crime scene in North Naples. Can you confirm that you were the first one to sample the defendant's DNA?"

"That's correct."

"And what was the source of DNA at the scene of the murder in North Naples?"

"Objection," June throws in. "Speculation."

Bates barely stirs. "It was a murder scene. Overruled. You can answer, Agent Cook."

June shrugs at me: *Worth a shot.*

"There was hair found during a scrub of the crime scene," Cook says. "It matched similar hair found at the scene at the Estero killing."

"But until more recently," Freeland says, "it didn't match anyone else."

"Correct."

Freeland asks for the bailiff so he can hand over a copy of the DNA application Cook filed on the twenty-ninth, after Robert's official buccal swab. "Special Agent Cook, can you confirm to me the findings of these DNA results? Whom do they match? Can you read that for me?"

"Robert Alan Woodhouse."

And off Freeland goes with the DNA questions, as expected. June scribbles in her pad. I'm watching Juror Number Three whenever Freeland talks, looking to see if there's a sharp appetite for the Fourth Amendment on the jury. If there is, it'll come from him. Right now, his arms are crossed, but his face is slack. Neutral position.

After about a dozen questions, Freeland rests. At least that's smart. He spelled out the evidence, plain as day. He wants to leave no extra surface area for us to grip.

Now it's June's turn. I slide a bottle of water her way and she takes a hard, loud click of a swallow. "Special Agent Cook, why did the FBI first send you to Madre Island?"

"I was assigned to the Gulf Coast Killer case after Estero."

"Meaning your specialty is in—"

"Violent crime."

"Does that include serial crimes—serial arsonists, serial rapists, murderers—"

Cook whistles out a breath like she's holding in laughter. "Yeah. Those all count."

A few chuckles. Bates glances at his gavel.

"And in your experience," June continues, "do serial killings typically follow consistent patterns between crimes?"

"Not necessarily."

"But in this case, the six murders charged by the state *do* follow a consistent pattern . . ."

"Again, not always. It can be case by case."

I jot down a quick note. *Too subjective. Nail her down.* June glances at it, nods. I watch her finger trace her sheet, skipping a question. "In your assessment—and according to what the FBI told the public—each crime was most likely carried out by one person alone. Is that right?"

"That's right."

"So if my client were, say, seen at a gas station during the abduction of Barbara Tiller—"

"Objection," Freeland shoots. "Speculation."

"Sustained. Rephrase, Ms. Daswell."

"Agent Cook, my client, Robert Woodhouse, was in police custody at roughly the time Barbara Tiller reports being set free by her abductor. How would you explain that?"

"I wouldn't. Barbara Tiller was delirious and in a state of extreme dehydration. She had no way of knowing when she was set free."

I watch the jury. A crowd of calm, stoic faces. Their attention is flagging. One woman's gaze runs near the ceiling on the opposite wall, where a clock is counting down the seconds until lunch. The *thud* June was worried about has landed in full. It just doesn't belong to me.

Now or never.

I put a hand on the small of June's back. "Let me."

Hail, Mary, full of grace . . .

June doesn't budge at first. She swats my hand away. I tug her blouse. She clears her throat and shoots me a side-eye dipped in a searing, desperate rage. All the weeks of prep work. She thinks she's going somewhere with it. Maybe, but not if we lull people to sleep. This could go on all day if we let it, and there's only one chance to ruin the first impression Cook makes on the jury, and some long-forgotten nerve in my legs is screaming for me to step in—

So I stand.

June hardens, clicks her sheets together, then admits defeat. She sits as I take the podium.

"Special Agent Cook," I start. "Paint me a picture, just so I'm clear. The day before the arrest, Mr. Woodhouse attended a witness lineup, and you gave him a ride home. Can you share what happened exactly?"

Cook's head bounces back a little. She straightens her hair. "Yes. I drove Mr. Woodhouse home sometime that afternoon. I don't remember what we discussed, but it was pretty surface level. He seemed nervous to go home. Then I dropped him off in the driveway and drove the SUV back to Madre Island PD. I spoke to Sergeant Clay Ingram about the lineup, then later, we ordered dinner in."

"Ordered dinner in? Was it a late night?"

"We had a lot to talk through. And, despite my name, I'm not much of a cook."

A chuckle shoots out of the gallery somewhere, but my face is numb. Sometimes the witness stand is a dance like this. Especially when crime enforcement gets defensive, wants to joke their way out of any hint that they did something improper. But I file a mental note for later: she's nervous. "According to the warrant, at some point you noticed Mr. Woodhouse had left a cap behind."

"I did."

"How exactly did you notice it?"

She hesitates, drops her eyes, her mouth whispering through the response before she verbalizes it. "It's a habit of mine to do a sweep of any car I drove that day in case something's been left behind. If there is, it becomes abandoned property. His hat was under the dash, so I took it in."

And she breathes. A low shiver works across her cheeks. She's suppressing a smile. This is the shrug-off: *Yes, Ms. Woodhouse, I know the law as you do, and I pulled your husband's DNA fair and square.* But there's something here. Something brittle in the timeline. A kind of defensiveness under the hard slate of her eyes. That she had to practice that response, right on the fly. And I've gotten her to commit to a story.

"All right," I say, buying time, which is fast slipping away. Is there anything to work with there? Anything at all? I glance at the lights above one of the cameras, that bright pip of red. The iris of the world fixed on me. "Then there was a match between Mr. Woodhouse's DNA and the DNA found at the crime scene, and you had your warrant. Just so I understand?"

"Objection," Freeland puts in. "Repeating."

Bates's eyes are hard with attention and the answer comes quick. "Sustained."

I shuffle through my papers, an obvious nervous tic, but I'm running out of ideas. I hear June shuffling through hers. Would it look like a disaster if I gave the stand back to her?

But I've already committed.

"Special Agent Cook," I say, "how long does it take to run a DNA test?"

"That depends. It can be two days, sometimes fewer. Obviously, in this case, we found a clear match before making the arrest."

"Is that usual?"

"No. But they put a lot of resources at this case's disposal and they have great labs at Quantico. That's why they sent me down."

"So this was not usual—"

"No." Cook's chest stiffens. She can feel herself winning. "Quantico is very fast."

This time, even more chuckles.

"Objection, Your Honor," Freeland says. "We're repeating."

"Sustained. Ms. Woodhouse, I don't want to sustain all day. If you could move on to the next topic you have prepared, or maybe narrow your focus."

I search around again, unable to speak, eyes darting, the lights going hot. I feel silent the way someone choking can only point to their neck. There's nothing to do but to give control back to June. I imagine the court reporters tonight: *There was the famous Leslie Woodhouse curveball, an unexpected line of questioning—but instead of a clean strike, it took a fast and disastrous turn into the—*

Then there's a sharp tug on my skirt.

June. She slides a copy of the warrant over to me, points at the corner. I shrug at her, helpless, still choking—*Can't speak, help me*. She pulls out a pen and circles the time of the DNA application.

It's 3:47 p.m.

The time, in plain ink. Electrified, I raise my head toward Bates. "Your Honor, if I could just follow up on one detail?"

He raises a palm: *Go ahead.*

"Agent Cook," I say, trying to thread the story in her mind as she's presented it, "you said you like to do routine sweeps of cars you drove, in case there's anything abandoned by a suspect. Typically an end-of-day routine?"

"Yes."

"And that's what you did this time, too?"

"That's right."

"Good." Feeling my pulse quickening, I suppress the urge to smile. "When would you estimate you found Mr. Woodhouse's hat? What time did you sweep through the SUV that night?"

"I'd guess about ten."

"And what time did you give Mr. Woodhouse a ride home?"

"About three o'clock."

"I'd like to pull the court's attention to the arrest warrant filed June twenty-eighth." I motion at the bailiff, a short, squat man who looks like he's melting in the heat, and hand him June's copy to bring to the stand. "This DNA application was filed at three forty-seven p.m. Which means the only way you could have run Mr. Woodhouse's DNA would be if you had discovered his hat in your SUV the moment you drove back to the police department. Did you forget when you filed the application?"

Cook picks up June's copy from the bailiff and blinks at it. "I didn't file this."

"Who did, Special Agent Cook?"

"It says Clay Ingram."

"To whom you handed over the DNA, knowing questions like these might come up. Agent Cook, you've already lied to this court. Either you took my client's hat without his consent, or you found it in the late evening, several hours after this application went through. We know the latter isn't true, so please answer on the former. Did you *take* the hat for yourself, Ms. Cook? Without him knowing? Because if you did, this was his personal property, had never been abandoned, and therefore is completely inadmissible as evidence, which means everything gathered *after* that is also—"

Freeland stands. "Objection—speculation—"

"Overruled," Bates snaps. "Witness will answer."

Cook swallows. Out of the corner of my eye, I pick up Juror Three leaning in over his knees. I can hear the electricity buzzing in the camera lights. No one coughs. No one even clears their throats.

"I didn't *take* it."

I press forward on the podium. "Did Mr. Woodhouse ever ask for it back?"

"Those days run together. We had the chance to save Barbara Tiller's life—"

"Which is why everything was expedited. DNA lab research, the posting of results, even how quickly you took Mr. Woodhouse's DNA without his knowledge so you could have a warrant by the next day."

"That's not so fast—"

"But, Special Agent Cook, you told me just now. Quantico is *very fast*."

Now the small current of chuckles from the gallery is moving with me. Bates smacks his gavel. "Order. Ms. Woodhouse, please watch your tone. Ms. Cook, back to the original question."

Cook is not a woman who shrinks. But now, cringing, she wraps up tight. She glares out at me. Then her eyes dart around. All those bright, burning red lights.

And she whispers, "He did ask for it back."

"You're referring to Robert Woodhouse," I say.

"Yes."

"Your Honor," I announce, "the DNA evidence presented in the application submitted June twenty-eighth was taken from private property, not *abandoned* property, and is therefore inadmissible because it violated my client's Fourth Amendment rights. My client should have never been arrested, and any evidence produced under any pretense of obligation is therefore—"

"Objection, Your Honor," Freeland says, "further DNA evidence would have come to light through the course of the—"

"Bailiff, if you please." Bates's voice is a low rumble of frustration. He makes a come-hither motion. As the bailiff moves, noise rushes up from the gallery behind me: jeers, whispers, a dozen mottled conversations. Robert looks up at me with a bright look of appeal in his eyes: *Is this what I think it is?* Bates pounds the gavel, then pulls up the DNA application for another look. The pissed-off way he yanks it up to the bench makes me worry for a moment.

His eyes cool as he reads. "Given the witness admitted how this evidence was obtained, I think we need a recess."

He pounds the gavel.

Amen.

Then there's a hot-breathed rush of activity: cameras panning, conversations spiking. Instinctively, I spin around to find June and throw my arms out for a hug she doesn't accept.

"You promised," she says. "Today was my day."

"I know. I did. I did and I threw you aside. Do you hate me?"

June's eyes fall. "I can't say I'm not bummed. But at least now I don't regret weeks of prep work. It's good I knew the numbers by heart."

"Three forty-seven." My new lucky number. I even like the sound of it on my tongue. Even I didn't expect Cook's breakdown would be so complete. "A number we must have looked at a hundred times."

"Until Ingram gave you a reason to look closer."

"Yeah. I'll send him a box of cookies or something. I can't believe it. The number was sitting there for us the entire time—"

"That's how it always is. I told you a lawyer shouldn't represent her spouse—"

"Oh, shut it." I smile. "What do you think? Will that go down okay at Williams and Moore? Everyone's going to blame it all on Cook."

"Let everyone think whatever they like. I mean, no DNA, no positive ID from Tiller—we're in great shape. We can put Ingram on the stand and ask him every question this opens up. It's just dominoes from here."

Then Robert breaks in with a few questions, a giddy smile tacked on his face. He opens his arms. I just stare at him. But I can read the soft, cringing lines of his face: *Was that it? Did we just crack it?* I have a superstitious lack of answers. Best not to get ahead of myself.

But when I spin around in the commotion and see Randy Freeland slinked in his chair, staring vacantly across the court, I can't resist shooting him a shrug and a look of sympathy. It's only later, during the evening news with all the BREAK IN THE CASE crawls typed along the bottom, that I see this moment play on repeat: my look of sympathy came out as a faint and impish smile.

WESTON

About five rinses through a hand wash, I hear my neighbor flipping through channels on her makeshift patio. Game shows and local weather and *a stunning turn of events in court today* and you can have this amazing necklace for only five easy payments of $19.99—

Wait.

Stunning turn of events.

I step outside. My neighbor is grilling a can of beans, which makes me nervous, but I say nothing. Her wifebeater is tight, too; so tight I can see the purple of her areolas. She tosses me a limp wave.

"Switch the channel back," I tell her.

"What, weather?"

"The court news. Did you hear what happened?"

She pops a button and her laggy HD stick takes a while to snap on the right channel. Gone to commercial. "I did read a little on the bottom," she said. "DNA thrown out. And I'll bet they throw out a lot more because of it, too. You know how that shit goes."

"But what are they saying on TV?"

"Vibe I got is that things could end real quick. You know these legal things—you pull one thread and it all goes to shit, suddenly they can't do a thing." She spits. "A shame, too. I know that Woodhouse guy is the killer. Somethin' in the eyes."

Yes, the eyes. Windows to the soul. Which is why Robert's are different colors, one for each version of his life—Caroline and Leslie. The day I took Barbara Tiller, she should have seen Robert in me—the hair, the contact lens, all that pointless preparation—but no. Whatever is wrong with him is no costume. The rot lies somewhere in the marrow.

I pull on my collar, finding the air suddenly smothering. That may be the hot molasses from my neighbor's smoke. For a moment I think I might pass out, that the world is crushing into a cube with me inside it, but I put a hand on the trailer, breathe, squeeze my shirt at the collar. *Things could end real quick.* I try to be thorough, but the thought that I would lose simply never occurred to me. There was DNA. I fairy-dusted his stubble all over western Florida for every cop to see, and they *still* bungled it.

A thundering squall of a migraine wraps around my temples. I bite down, hard enough to see red, hard enough to taste blood. Every worry squeezes out of me except for thoughts of what comes next. What *does* come next, if any of this is going to end well for me? I think of Robert. In the eyes of the public, he is the Gulf Coast Killer. I have accomplished that much. Let him rot in that name for the rest of his life. But what if police ask more questions? What if the case isn't closed? Then I think of Leslie, and the squall around my temples dissolves into utter relief. Leslie Woodhouse, the lawyer who sets guilty people free.

Leslie.

She was always the key. I just never saw it.

"You all right, Wes?" my neighbor asks with her lips open. "You're all pale."

I look at her. The dumb, froggy mouth. The careless way her breasts hang. The bovine dimness behind her eyes. I bet if I scooped them out and went digging for her brain, all I would find is plaster and nicotine pouches. What is the point of pretending for people like this? All my pretending is over.

I slap the can off her grill. It pops in the grass, spraying its beans in fleshy red streaks. "Weston. My mother named me Weston."

PART THREE

LESLIE

Not guilty.

The words follow us everywhere. They're pinned to the air like the moon chasing you down the highway:

Not guilty.

At the grocery store in bold font, over a tabloid snap of Robert being dragged into the courthouse with unshaven cheeks and his mismatched eyes staring aloft. Staring someplace, the reader must imagine, dark and evil.

Not guilty.

At the 56th Annual Madre Island Policemen's Fundraiser ball, where No-Gates Bates sees me coming for a scoop of watermelon punch and suddenly receives a phone call he has to answer outside:

Not guilty.

At the mailbox, where I receive notice of Freeland's appeal. He believes Judge Bates abused his discretion and should never have allowed cameras in. Flimsy as it gets. But his career is shot, and the county's outraged. Freeland is willing to do anything that avoids looking like he's sitting on his hands.

If *not guilty* left an echo, if you only heard the last word repeating as it bounced through the streets, you would hear the real whispers:

Guilty.

At Jefferson Lane, where after June moves back to Miami, *not guilty* manifests in lonely ways. Our neighbor Charlotte hasn't returned from Jekyll Island and now a real estate agent's dropped a FOR SALE sign on her half of the yard. There are tough questions in store for that agent. Who are the neighbors? *Gee, funny story about that. Have you heard of the Gulf Coast Killer? Well, your neighbor's DNA was damning but inadmissible. But on the positive side, there's a very modern kitchenette.*

At our garage door, where on the first night after the verdict, someone spray-paints GCKILLER in freckly red streaks. Robert spends the better part of the morning sponging it up, but the color has already set in. The leftover smears make the condo look like a crime scene. We'll have to paint it over.

At Patricia's, where I sleep the night after the spray paint rattled me. And the next. And a few thereafter. We devour more desert-island shows, but the pretense of binge-watching television evolves as I notice Patricia struggling to stand up on her own. I become a live-in nurse. I keep her stocked in lotion and the good rosemary-oil shampoos for her short, white hair, which is flowering brilliantly on her scalp like some tenacious orchid. (Of course it is; she's Patricia Colton.) I rationalize that she needs me there.

At home with Robert, my husband and I have a half dozen zombified conversations, mostly logistics: Who buys which groceries when? How are we on butter, bagels, Beefeater? Robert is a strange shell. He texts me grocery lists instead of going out because of the way people stare at him in the aisles: all those gluey, paranoid side-eyes. One cashier outright refused to serve him. When I'm home, we only talk in fits and starts. Every time

I remind him of this, I notice my throat rising or have the urge to break another key fob, and I stop myself, making excuses about Patricia needing me, heading out. Barricading myself from the hurricane of a conversation Robert and I still owe each other.

At the Madre Island Police Department, where I occasionally drop in to see if Clay Ingram is willing to speak to me yet. Not long after the trial ended, a rogue journalist took to his Substack and dug into Clay Ingram with a five-thousand-word series about how the police sergeant could never have tipped me off if he wasn't—to chop five thousand words into three—in on it. Clay only replied once. He wanted me to know that Evie's best friend's parents won't let her sleep over anymore.

One day, after several nights at Patricia's, I stop by our condo for toiletries. Robert is sitting at his laptop in the living room, unshaved, uncombed, losing his roasted-garlic tan. The TV news is blasting without his attention, and there's an overbaked look in his eyes like he's been staring at the laptop screen for hours. When I walk in, he slaps it shut.

"What were you doing?" I ask flatly, aiming for blasé.

"Nothing."

"You can tell me. Naked women?"

A joke that would have sent him cackling and riffing if I had made it months ago. Now he only laughs enough to dislodge a little phlegm. "Ha."

"Seriously. You okay?"

"Just . . . thinking."

"About what?"

"What I'm gonna do."

I stare at him. Do—"with what? His afternoon? His relationship with me? His remaining retirement years?

None of it would surprise me. *Not guilty* didn't hit Robert like I expected: he shot down Patricia's offer of a family champagne party because he said he wanted to keep a low profile, and anytime I catch him alone, he seems to be puzzling out something in his head.

The deodorant I came for is waiting for me in the medicine cabinet. I pop it in my purse. I inhale deep. I had told Robert that Patricia needed me. A second round of chemotherapy is an awful thing to lie about, I know. But time with Patricia really does decompress all the coiled springs of dread left over from Robert's trial. Seeing Patricia's hair grow, her appetite return— it's better than vitamins. If she's her old self, I'm my old self. It steadies me.

Still. Not quite there.

Back in the living room, I've prepped a dart of small talk about how wet it's going to be tomorrow, windy, too—maybe leave on a pleasant note. But Robert's staring at the squawking TV, his temples seized up, his veins gone garden hose.

Citing the ongoing threat to the public, FBI sources tell NBC News they are reopening the Gulf Coast Killer case . . .

WESTON

. . . based on, quote, a "reassessment of the underlying facts of the murders." We have no way to know what that means in the specific,

but it appears some Justice officials are not fully in alignment with the widespread public opinion that Robert Alan Woodhouse is, in fact, the true Gulf Coast Killer . . .

The car radio's button is stuck. I throw a fist at it, meaning to crash on the *down* button, but instead the volume explodes with a shriek of the reporter's husky Transatlantic:

IN FACT, THE TRUE GULF COAST KILLER—

Slam.

Pound.

The plastic knob bursts off; the volume swings to a whisper. The reporter keeps droning on, muffle-mouthed under the idling engine of my '07 Chevy Aveo. It was never my choice, exactly, what with its burgundy, bloody-vomit paint and a smell in the back seat like an egg has been rotting there since the dark ages. But it keeps me mobile.

The true Gulf Coast Killer . . .

My fingers wrap around the gear stick. Either the car is shaking or I am. Now that I live in my car, yes, in theory I will be harder to find. But not here. Not driving a beat-up Aveo in a neighborhood like Pheasant Crossing. Every home looks the same, all dotted with the same white Mediterranean tiles, the token gator-gates. And everyone drives one of three makes, Lincoln or Mercedes or BMW.

Today I just need to see if the code I wrote down is current: 1957, the code to Patricia's house, which is another code, really. The code to Leslie. Leslie adores her older sister.

Justice officials are not fully in alignment . . .

Leslie overshot the mark. She should have taken the plea

deal. Robert serving six life sentences would have had a certain anticlimactic feel, but at least an acceptable one. They might have thrown one in for Caroline, make it seven. Too much to hope for.

But the DNA failed to land in court and *everything* proved too much to hope for. I remember staring at the bottle of Clorox in my former trailer, wondering if there were flavors of Clorox like there were flavors of lollipops. Would it be the sweet, mild perfume of soap? Or, once it burns, more like drinking molten lead? I almost found out. But an image flashed in my eyes: a useless man conked out in a useless corner of the world, face down in his trailer, wrists rubbed raw, toes twitching, an empty bottle of bleach tipped over in the sink. And once the news came out, there would have been people gorging themselves on the satisfaction of my death. Most of all, Robert.

So. Alternatives.

Leslie has always been the key to Robert's happy Senectitude. I wonder how much she knows. Lawyer-client privilege—she could know as much as Robert does. Still, this is Robert Woodhouse. She could know absolutely nothing. Would she defend me if she knew it all? Would she *respect* me? Would she leave Robert with a giant, wife-size hole in his life? Delicious possibilities, all of them. Everything hinges on her.

The garage door of Patricia's house suddenly bangs to life and knocks me out of my daydreaming. A tick later, Patricia herself bounds up in her silver Mercedes, a chirpy Pomeranian leaning against the passenger window. I hold up my binoculars. And, yes, confirmed—1957. Cancer has made her a little lazy. A woman of her age should change her codes more often. Especially with the True Gulf Coast Killer skulking around.

Tap-tap-tap-tap. "Excuse me. What do you think you're doing?"

Outside my window, a white-haired woman with cat-eye sunglasses is holding some muttering toy breed under her arm. I pump the window down. "Oh. Hello."

"Yes, *hello*. I asked, what are you doing? You don't live here."

I shake the binoculars. There is no other answer. "Bird-watching."

"Bird-watching. Yeah. Just stay right there, okay?"

She pulls out her phone and takes a half step toward the hood of my car and I know exactly where this is going, so I palm the skull of her dog and shove it through her arm until it falls to the ground and yelps. The woman squeals and turns, dropping the phone, running to protect her precious mutt, and then the way is clear. I slam into first gear and take the long way out of Pheasant Crossing.

Southwest toward Madre.

ROBERT

Leslie leaves to pick up groceries. Patricia wants to bring dinner to our condo as a thank-you for all of Leslie's support over the summer. She's ordering takeout, but of course Leslie wants to stock up on all the things Patricia likes, dill pickle spears and

Beach Plum Lacroix and, I'm guessing, an obscenely expensive bottle of chardonnay.

The dinner idea annoyed me at first. Then I thought, *Me, Leslie, Patricia, all in one place?* I haven't heard from Wes since the not-guilty verdict. Maybe he's been forced to go into hiding. Imagine he wasn't even in Florida anymore. If I knew everyone was safe, tonight could be the night. I could finally be free of it all. My laptop was all tabs—surprise-trip bookings for Philadelphia, googling whether it's possible to purchase plane tickets under pseudonyms, all to bring us together. And then fate dropped this on me, easy as pie.

Tonight, then.

Tonight I can tell her. Leslie will know what to do from there. God—it's been so miserable for her. For both of us. To think it might be over soon.

It's late afternoon, the dregs of autumn still hanging damply in the air. The neighborhood is quiet. Shades are drawn, cars are parked inside garages: a standard afternoon on Jefferson Lane since my trial. I wait on the porch because Leslie's favorite store is only a few minutes away. I want to be a good sport when she gets back. Maybe I'll say something nice about the chardonnay, I think, as her sedan trundles up . . .

. . . only it's not her sedan. It's an old Chevy hatchback with a ruddy paint job.

Weston Adekins throws open the door, slips out, stands tall. He's wearing a long-sleeve button-down that should be soaked in this heat, only it's not. "Is Leslie here?"

I stand. "You can't be here."

"I heard a news report this afternoon. It said they plan on reopening your case."

I eye the empty finger of Jefferson Lane, bending under the oak trees toward Fontaneda Boulevard. *Keep shopping, Leslie.* "Really, you have to go—"

"Can I come in?"

"No."

"Ask Leslie. Is she here?"

A thousand different sentences firework through my head. The truth: *She's out for groceries.* The lie: *She's on vacation by herself.* What I really wish I could say: *She's gone to stay somewhere else, somewhere untraceable, so don't ask about Leslie, don't even say her name, you monster, you absolute mistake, you stillborn psychopath.*

"No," I only whisper. "She's out."

A black cloud of disappointment folds across his face. "Out? Out where?"

"I won't tell you that. But she could be gone for weeks."

"Weeks?"

"Weeks. And, yeah, I saw they're reopening the case. But it's not my case, is it? I'm done."

The cuff of his sleeve seems to itch him. He fiddles with it, then pulls something oblong from his pocket. "Just tell me where Leslie is. I can wait."

"What do you want with Leslie?"

"Let Leslie worry about that."

"You're never going to reach her. And I should tell you that police are constantly driving through here now." Something of a bluff, but close enough to true. Madre Island squad cars never used to drive up and down Jefferson Lane before the case; now I see them at least once a day. Fortunately, Wes seems to buy it; he checks over his shoulder, shields his eyes as he glances up toward Fontaneda. "I'm not going to say anything to anyone," I tell him. "If that's what you're worried about. If they call me to testify, I won't. Like I promised."

After you threatened to kill her.

"No one cares about your testimony. I want Leslie to hear what I have to say."

"Well, like I said, she's not here."

The itch has spread to both cuffs. He tosses the object from his pocket from hand to hand, working either wrist with no effect. What it is—silver, matte, oblong—now becomes clear. It's a box cutter. *The* box cutter, maybe. Miraculously, it's still sheathed. "I need her. She can help."

"Help with what?"

"Help. *H-e-l-p.*" He snicks his tongue like he's run out of words. "Just help."

"I don't even know what you mean. But if you want to stay a few minutes, I'm sure a patrol will come through—"

"I said *help*!" He pushes through.

Unthinking, I reel back, dig my back foot into the porch stoop, and shove two fists into his ribs.

I don't know what I was thinking. Startle him. Shake the box cutter loose. Turn and slam the door. Something. Even the obvious hardness of his body—skin and rib cage and nothing else—should have hurt. But the shove barely moves him. It only makes him pause. He reexamines me. Wes never looks at you, really. His eyes only trace the bones in your face. And even when he does make eye contact, you get the feeling your eyes don't register as real, that you're a separate person. I've seen butchers trim the fat off their meat with more appreciation for what the meat once was.

The box cutter clicks open.

Then whatever he sees in me must spark some old memory. He flexes his fingers around the cutter, relaxes.

He steps back. "Apologize for that."

"What?"

"Apologize. Watching my mother believe your lies for entire decades—I could handle that. Watching you find Leslie and move on with your life when all we ever wanted was your acknowledgment—I could handle that, too. But never telling me sorry? No. That might be my fault. Maybe I should have expected nothing more. An apology would require that you put a hand over your heart and use that beat-up throat for something other than a lecture or a lie. It would require that you speak to someone who embarrasses you. I bet you apologize to Leslie, though. You do, right? You would do anything for Leslie. Say anything for Leslie. As long as it keeps you in dollar-store polos and your little beach house. Well, I can tell her the truth. You are an absolute poison who infests every life he touches. And rather than reason with me, rather than talk to me, your instinct is to sweep me away before *the missus* comes home. So go ahead. Prove me wrong. Apologize for shoving me."

My throat clicks. If it's some sort of verbal trap, all I know is I'm not sorry for defending my wife. "I'm calling the police—"

"Oh. The *police*. No apology, then." He picks a torn slip of paper from his pocket. "Thirty-three Pheasant Crossing, passcode 1957; 2938 Seventy-First, unit 7G. Do I have to remind you?

"No."

"Yet now you feel fine threatening me with police. What changed?"

I say nothing.

"And you should have so many other questions. How do I know the passcode? Have I been there before? And if I did, what did I leave there?" His eyes run down the white pillars of our porch. "Even here, how can someone be home every hour of every day? How can you know what I see or hear? What I have planned for you?"

"What are you talking—"

"Just promise. No police. Let me be the one to speak to Leslie."

He pockets the box cutter. A pissed-off gale of wind swings in from the ocean, upsetting the palms and oaks. It settles just as quickly as it came. I want to ask how he knows these things, does he know where she is, did he talk to her or what—but there's no chance.

"See you soon," he says.

A twist of his feet, a door slam, a wailing grind in the gearbox, and his Chevy pulls away.

I turn inside and lock as many windows as I can, draw the shades in the bedroom and guest room, and, on a whim, throw a Swiss Army knife from our miscellany drawer into my pocket.

It's only when I stop in the living room that I catch the hummingbird tempo of my heart. I tear up the sofa cushions, feel through curtains. Is he *listening* somehow? Does he know? And if he does, how can I tell everyone? What happens if I do? What happens if I don't? What if he decides a police patrol is nothing to worry about and comes back? What if he comes back *tonight*? In five hours? Five minutes?

When Leslie comes home a few moments later, I hear her muffled sounds: the paper bags crinkling; the keys clinking; the heavy, inevitable *tink* of the chardonnay.

"Robert?" she calls.

I think that's what she calls. I'm not sure. Because I'm in the bathroom when she shouts it, dry heaving into the toilet.

LESLIE

"Oh *no*."

The words spill out of me when Robert walks into the living room. He wipes his lips on his sleeve. All color has drained out of him except the pink rings of his eyelids.

"Let's not have dinner here." He staggers past me, his breath carrying the scent of mint. It sounds like he gargled with thumbtacks. "Let's go out. A nice restaurant on the mainland. Somewhere big. Crowded."

"What happened? Are you all right?"

"Just hear me out. What was that place Patricia took us years ago? With the coconut shrimp?"

"You haven't been out in so long—you said you can't take all the stares—"

He dips a finger into the window blinds, peeking out at Jefferson Lane. "Well, maybe I can handle stares tonight, you know? Maybe it's time to try."

I move toward the kitchen to unpack: dark-chocolate bars and a tub of the Greek yogurt he likes. "Patricia will be here soon, and she probably already has the food. I'm sorry. I know the idea is that it's for you. Robert, seriously, are you all right?"

He follows me in and leans against the bay window, crossing his arms. A whisper inside me wants to warn him about the danger there. If it cracks and he falls through . . .

"It's fine," he says. "I'm all right. But you saw what they spray-painted on the garage door. *GC Killer.*"

"I saw."

"There could be someone out there—after us—"

"On second thought, we can cancel if you want." I set the plastic bag on the counter, careful not to knock it with the glass. "Is it better if we cancel? Maybe it should just be you and me tonight. It's been so long since it's just been us two. We need it, don't you think?"

He sighs: I'm reading too much into him again. I thought it's what he wanted me to ask. Ever since the trial, we've been in different time zones.

So I start unpacking. Paper plates, Solo cups. Tonight could have been our victory meal. But what victory is there, really? That I pounced on a quick-trigger verdict that left questions unanswered? That I freed my husband and, for my reward, have become roommates with this Robert-shaped stranger? Since the case, I don't know who he is, this creature skittering around the house. He's like a hermit crab, rushing from shell to shell, this one too small, that one too broken.

Robert crosses the room and cups my shoulders, rubs my arms. A warming gesture, but my skin goes prickly. "I can do dinner. Yes. Let's do dinner. I'm sorry—it's the idea that someone out there painted our house and we were inside the whole time, sleeping."

"That's all that's bothering you?"

"Christ, Leslie. Yes. *Yes*." He grunts and nudges up from the window and throws his hands in the air as if strangling something in it, and it's in my direction, this thing he wants to strangle.

I flinch, backing up to the counter, knocking the tub of yogurt to the floor and nearly slipping in a gluey wad of mixed berry.

Robert looks at it. Looks at me. There's a broken-spell feeling in the air. "Don't stop anything on account of me. I'm gonna go change."

And then he leaves me here. I grab a paper towel and start mopping up yogurt, already thinking of excuses for Patricia so I can cancel and have the sit-down Robert and I have been putting off so long. *Robert is under a lot of stress—he has an excuse to be freaked-out about the spray painters—and, no, Patricia, we have yet to address how the Gulf Coast Killer might have his DNA apart from Robert's litany of I-don't-knows.* His theory is that the killer randomly saw him one day, realized that he looked just like him, and stalked him until he had DNA he could pull. Pure dumb luck.

I'm still toweling up yogurt—Greek yogurt on hardwood has a sort of baby-wiping eternity to it—when a car pulls up outside. Its squeaky brakes suggest it's not Patricia. Its height says it's just a sedan, and not one I recognize. The beveled glass inside our front door prisms it into a Picasso of reds and blacks.

I throw open the door and shout, "This is private property. We said no more media, or we're calling the police."

"Leslie Woodhouse!" comes a voice. And when I see her almond eyes and honey cheeks, I feel like an idiot. "Stephanie Tressler, *The Daily Pennsylvanian*. Did you or did you not jaywalk last night? Confess!"

Steph.

The car drives off as Steph promises a five-star review, and then it's a blur, a rush of apologies, hellos, hugs, multiple hugs. My Steph. She's stopped growing, but she's still surprising. Her height, Patricia's height, half a head taller than me, and her hair, which dips well below the shoulder-length cut she wore when she left. I squeeze her and drown myself in Steph scent, her sweet-and-salty sweat mixed with mango sunscreen. And something new, something earthy. Philly, maybe.

"Sorry," she says. "Aunt Pat said I could come straight from the airport and she'll meet me here."

"Oh, *did* she?" I'll have to make up the guest room, then. And the talk with Robert officially has to wait, unless I want Steph overhearing what's bound to be an argument. But it warms me to hold my daughter again, picking a tuft of lint off her shirt, thinking about little things like whether we have clean bedsheets.

"She said you could use a surprise. You're not mad?"

"I'm never mad to see you. But don't you have class?"

After her stubborn roller luggage finally hops up over the curb, Steph huffs and smiles. "It's a weekend thing. I'll be back Monday morning. My ticket is round-trip. You're sure this isn't crazy, right? I know things have been heavy. Aunt Pat said I can stay at hers if you and Bob decide you hate surprises."

"Nonsense," I squeak—but stop short of telling her what a perfect antidote she might be. "Come in."

"Seriously. Bob won't mind?"

"Never mind what he minds."

Then I motion her in first so I can lock the door properly behind her, once and twice and thrice.

Turns out I owe Patricia five dollars after all.

Steph has a boyfriend.

As she loads her laptop, she drones on about him: Drew, not Andrew but Drewson, how they met in Corporate Finance when they formed a study group, Finance Fursdays, and isn't that cute, Mom, everyone in the group got at least an A-minus, and I reply with a thousand-yard stare as I think back to the night Patricia got her diagnosis and I incorrectly listed off the myriad reasons Stephanie was too busy for boyfriends. All wrong. I grab a wineglass from the kitchen and get the char-donnay flowing early. I tip the glass to my lips and think briefly about starting a wine company that pumps it straight into you via IV.

"You want to meet him?" Steph asks from the coffee table. "We can Zoom. You can put him in the Chair of Inquisition."

Ah, yes. The joke-not-joke I used to make with all her boy-friends: I'd sit them in a chair and pretend to *cross-examine* them about politics and religion until catching them on some incon-sistency. Thinking of it now makes me want to cringe into hot oblivion.

Before I can protest that I'm not feeling particularly intimi-dating today, the boyfriend maximizes on-screen and Steph slinks back into the sofa with me. A big loaf of broccoli-haired forehead greets us. Patricia was right again: she even knew which guy it was from the photo. The big guy, the goofy guy, the wrinkle-free pleated-khaki WASP I was so sure wasn't Stephanie's type. He has thin, eel-fin lips that stretch his smile into something vaguely resembling stress. His little finger-wave so tepid that I immedi-ately think, *He lacks a hunter's instinct. He can't provide for her.* Something in my chest warms, thinking these tiny worries again.

"Is this the Chair?" he asks after the introductions, settling back, making a show of it.

"The actual Chair has spikes." I feel myself slip into an old rhythm. It's supposed to be all in good fun, this Inquisition. And even if there's currently another man I'd prefer to have on spikes, I enjoy the feeling of asking questions that receive answers. How did they meet? While Drew talks, I find myself sinking into Robert-centered daydreams: having him on the rack, the spike pit, the iron maiden, shouting, *Is it really just the spray paint,* tak-ing Patricia's big boat and sailing out to sea so there would be no one to interrupt us. I come to as Drew is describing an incident in which Steph spilled noodles all over his lap. "It was," Drew says, milking the moment, "pre-pasta-rous."

Steph leans in, a tiny squeal whistling out of her throat. "Pho-nomenal."

"*Nice*, babe."

God, help me: they are pun people. One year in the Ivy League and I don't recognize my own daughter.

There's a lull in the conversation when Drew asks if Robert's here, too, whether we can all make an appearance on the laptop, but Steph shoots him a cutting-neck motion to put the kibosh on that. We say our goodbyes. And as I try to end on a polite note—I'm not really an Inquisitor, it was all a joke—I can't help but observe Robert sneak into the room, slick haired and trousered. Steph leaps up and wraps him in a hug.

"I hope it's okay I'm here," Steph says. "Aunt Pat wanted it to be a surprise."

"Of course," Robert says. "I think we could use the company."

He sloughs to the good rattan chair as we catch each other's glances. I shoot a good-natured shrug: *Steph! Isn't it nice?* But his look is pure meerkat: high neck, bugged-out eyes that drag to the window.

The doorbell chimes. I go to unlock it. Patricia doesn't wait for an invitation inside; she struts in with a paper grocery bag in one hand and cat-eye sunglasses in another.

"Aunt Patricia!"

"My favorite niece. Fancy seeing you here. Mua, mua." Patricia makes kissy noises when she pecks you on the cheek, as though you needed a reminder of what she's doing. She's at home working a room. "Bob, you'll be glad to know I brought pharmaceutical amounts of wine."

"So did I," I announce, throwing a thumb toward the kitchen.

"Good," Patricia says when she eyes my bottle, "you got yourself one, too. See, you're learning."

As Steph heads to the kitchen, I stand to greet my sister. "Steph told me you paid for her tickets, Pat. You know how I hate secrets."

"Yes. You. Secrets. Never."

"So what was the idea, then?

"Dinner's the idea. Just dinner." She pats me on the top of the chest. "Why? You had other plans?"

I look at Robert for moral support. He's got his fingers through the blinds and seems far more interested in the front yard.

WESTON

Patricia's home is even bigger on the inside. Open concepts everywhere, vaulted ceilings. This is the kind of home you might think any aroma would get lost in, but sliding open the door, the air is immediately choked in something sharp and spicy floral. Cloves? Cinnamon sticks?

I step in from the deck, pop off my shoes. The gate out front would register my entry on her app. Fortunately, Patricia is no security expert: she only has a camera at the front door. Easy enough to slip by. A woman of means has so much driveway to cover.

I walk into the living room. The sunset filters through her bay window, a pale strawberry color. All the lights are off. That was obvious as soon as I pulled up, but I had hoped to spot the blue crackles of a TV going, maybe find Leslie dozing inside.

Instead the place is empty. Out for dinner again? They were the other night.

A puzzle is splayed on the coffee table, though. A sunny-blue city, maybe charming *Paree*, with most of the pieces still scattered and no sign of the box.

Leslie has been sleeping here lately. Before Robert's case was reopened, that had been a good sign. *Not guilty* was a slap in the eyes, yes, but if I somehow pulled them apart, that could have been something. Not enough, but something. Someone had spray-painted their house with GCKILLER—not me, just a happy coincidence, there are some real crazies out there—and that probably spooked her.

After doing a quick roundup of the hallway, I walk back to Patricia's back door and pull on my shoes. Where to next?

The other night they had dinner at a seaside gastropub. It would have taken too much nerve to approach her there, but desperate times and all that, so maybe I can try that place again. Leslie is a woman of consistent habits. Failing that, I will try Senectitude once more.

Before I step out, I notice a laptop on the kitchen counter. Asleep, but—

One press of the space bar brings it to life.

Patricia had been using her browser, still logged in to a website so she could check the sales listing on her yacht. Currently moored in the Madre Island marina. Seventy feet. Flybridge style, white as a shark's belly, with tinted windows and a hydraulic stage that dips down to water level. *Great for water activities!* Except fishing, apparently: listed for six months, no bites yet.

Evidently, Patricia's listing agent hopes for three million dollars. She should drop that. She never uses it. After several visits to 33 Pheasant Crossing—just watching, learning—I never once saw her go out to the water. This is the first sign I ever saw of it. She might have forgotten it entirely. I imagine Patricia casually checking up on it, once a month. Something quick before heading out: *Be right with you, Les. Just wanted to see if I have an extra three million in my account. No? Oh, well. Always next month.*

Never once worrying about your next meal. Your next meal *ticket*.

The peace it must bring.

I stop. Look around. Pinch the stem of the spiny plant on her kitchen counter, testing it for life. It crackles in my fingers. Not fake. I should never linger, but the thought of living in a home like this is dizzying. How many miles is this from Seaside Paradise? From where Caroline was born? I could measure it in minutes. And yet Patricia has known so little else. She lets entire millions sit collecting barnacles in a marina. And with so many better uses for it.

So I have no guilt about this next part.

LESLIE

My normal routine is to set the places for dinner. I like the control of it: aligning the place mats to north and south, wiping water spots out of the silverware, seating everyone symmetrically even if there's an odd number of plates. And, yes, I insist we use plates. Usually. Patricia is not a cook, so she brought Chinese takeout. Between the Styrofoam boxes and mismatched wineglasses Patricia pulled from the cupboards, the entire feng shui of my kitchen is in tatters.

Robert heads out to the deck for a "quick walk." I think briefly of what kind of excuse I can offer for his strange behavior, but nothing makes sense, so I say nothing. Steph is telling Patricia about Drew, and Patricia is asking about all the inappropriate things I wish I had the courage to: religion, money, politics, do you use protection—*Goodness gracious, Patricia*—Steph parrying each thrust with lighthearted jokes about how it's still too early for all that. Maybe it's because I'm here. Patricia makes grand, theatrical exits every time she gets up to grab more drinks ("More wine, Les? Want a glass, Steph?"), with her eyebrows raised at me as if I should read the subtext as plainly as captions under her head. Instead, I'm thinking about Robert and the conversation still stuck in our gums.

At one point, Patricia's phone dings. She picks it up for a glance.

"What's that?" Steph asks.

"Movement at the doorbell." Patricia sets the phone face down. "Getting a lot of that lately. Deer, I think. But I never catch them on camera."

Robert pulls the door open and walks through, slapping sand off his thighs as he shuffles to his place in our little nook. We'd be in the dining room if it weren't still stacked with papers from the trial. I haven't been around to file them away, and Robert hasn't wanted to look at any of it.

"You've been quiet, Bob," Patricia says as Robert settles.

"Sorry," he spurts. "It's been a strange summer."

Patricia snicks her tongue. "Yeah? What'd I miss?"

This receives the raucous laughter only Patricia can get.

Later, with bellies swelling with wine and ice water and too many chicken dumplings, I walk Patricia out to her car. The sun is invisible, setting behind our condo somewhere over the Gulf. It's that time of the evening when the cul-de-sac glows in citrus colors. I like the sweet pungency that comes out in the evenings: mowed grass, dewy palm.

"I was kind of angling to stay at your place tonight," I tell Patricia.

"I brought dinner over. Thought you'd take the hint."

"It's just—with the trial—"

"Don't tell me you think . . ."

"No. Nothing like that."

"And Bob's all right?"

"I think he's still shaken from the trial."

"Can't blame him." Patricia squinches her lips. "Well, you're always welcome. I just hope things aren't as bad as all that."

"Forget I said it."

"I think I had half that wine. I'll remember none of this."

"You good to drive?"

"Yes. Just point me in the general direction of the mainland, would you?"

"Har, har. Take an Uber. You can pick up your car tomorrow. Another excuse to see Steph, anyway."

"Smart. You were always the smart one." Patricia smiles and starts tapping at her phone. "Book smarts, anyway, because I don't think you know. Steph's pregnant."

"What?"

"She didn't say anything. But water and no wine, for a girl her age? Please. Did you know Drew wanted to fly out here, too? They had something planned. They were so desperate to see you in person, I suspected something was up. I'm telling you now because I don't want you to blow your lid when it's time." Uber booked, she looks up and flashes her ordered and symmetrical teeth. "If you don't believe me, we can go double or nothing."

ROBERT

The guest sheets have been collecting dust in our closet since June left. By way of apology, I pull them out of the guest closet before Leslie has the chance and start slapping them clean in the hallway. Steph sets up camp in the (momentarily sheetless) guest bedroom; I can hear the walled muffles of her on the phone with her boyfriend. *I told you my aunt is crazy . . . No, crazy in a good way . . . No, maybe tomorrow.*

Leslie walks up coughing and waving dust out of her face. "You should really do that outside."

"They'll get damp outside." *Slap, slap.*

"Can we talk now?"

"Of course."

"In our bedroom?"

No more excuses to postpone that, I suppose. We go. Leslie closes the door behind her, one hand still crunched around the knob. "Patricia was asking about you. About how you don't seem well."

"It's just my stomach."

"Your stomach is what's eating at you?"

"Yes. Well. You try being the Gulf Coast Killer for a day. See how your stomach feels."

"Of course—I'll never blame you for that. But I think this is something else."

My temples ache. That's life with a cross-examiner: to Leslie, I look like a pile of clues. My jangled sleep, my pallid skin, the erosion around my fingernails where I've been chewing. My stomach. The white tufts that get stuck behind in my hairbrush lately. "I know."

"Just tell me what, Robert."

"I'm freaked-out, is all. The spray paint. The way people look at me."

"You know, you startled me tonight, Robert. When I spilled the yogurt."

Robert again. We're in the same room, breathing the same air, but we speak in the formalities of the long divorced. "I'm sorry."

I scan the room. Is it paranoid to imagine that Wes might have something in here recording us? The thought is stifling. I had practiced for this with late-night searches: *Ten tips for coming clean with hard truths. Step one: Take a breath.*

"Because," I go on, "I didn't mean to scare you like that. I wasn't going to touch you, I wasn't going to hit you. And then I didn't help you clean up because I was embarrassed. The trial had me crazy. Still has me crazy. But that isn't an excuse for any of it. I'm sorry."

A knock at the door, three quick taps. My heart goes jazzy for a second.

"Sorry if I'm interrupting," Steph's voice comes. "Can I get those sheets? I'm wiped."

"Coming," Leslie says. She reaches. I provide. It's a smooth handoff between us, all cotton sheet, no skin to skin. And then she shakes her face into a motherly smile, opens the door, shuts it carefully behind her.

After a minute, when I'm sure Leslie is locked into conversation with Steph, I walk out to the deck and let my gaze linger on the Gulf. Glassy black, faintly sizzling. I patrol a little, making a circle around the property. All quiet. Wes has made idle threats before, I reason, moving past the garage where GCKILLER is still foggy through a fresh coat of paint, and only some of them have come true. Then I'm at the deck again. The Gulf sends whispers up and down the sand, breathing like a sleeping spouse.

Strange to think there's an invisible ocean underneath all those waves. Maybe that's how it should be for me, too. Maybe it never had to be all of us in one room. Just Leslie. She'll have better ideas about what to do next. With her, I can start small—*Step one: Take a breath*—and work my way up to the full ocean of the truth.

First, an anonymous warning to Patricia. Maybe using the spray-paint incident to remind her to change her gate codes. Maybe the police will send an extra patrol her way. Steph will be with us all weekend, so there's safety in that. She doesn't have to know anything.

Leslie, though. How do I tell *her* the truth? Before Wes came, I felt ready. Now what? *When* do I tell her at a moment I can be sure everyone is safe? When Steph is back in Philly. Then I can call Patricia and ask if she's out somewhere nice and public. Then I can tell Leslie.

Something small. A text. A private dinner. Then a long and florid confession note. It would be hard at first, hard for me, hard for Leslie, hard to answer police questions about how I almost let myself die in his place, but it was never *his* place, it was always Leslie's, and it's not really an obstruction of justice when there's a knife on your throat, is it? Leslie will know. She knows every law. She might even forgive me. She'll fret and she'll rage and she'll ask all the *How could you?* questions I've been dreading, that Stage IV fear that started as a tiny black lesion in my stomach and swam to my liver and lungs and is currently spreading its dread through my lymph nodes, and there will be tears and hard treatments and therapies, but eventually, as all storms do, it will pass.

One safe, perfect moment is all I need.

One moment.

I head back to the bedroom. Leslie follows in soon, closing the door with a soft *swick*.

"I can sleep on the floor if you want," I tell her. "If you're worried about Steph asking why I'm sleeping in the living room."

"No. No, it's fine." She eyes the bed reluctantly. "You're my husband. I can sleep next to you."

She settles with a groan and peels off her socks. She fluffs a pillow. It's the closest we've been to our routine in months. We lean against the headboard, her with a paperback and me with my phone, discussing the day's events. Leslie wonders if Steph is pregnant; Patricia's idea. I explain that's how Patricia is, every human being a spark of gossip and she is the tinder. Maybe, Leslie admits. Then she puts down her book and stares into the ether for a while, and I think she's going to ask me a question, but instead she turns away, burritos herself in the duvet, and clicks off the light.

That leaves me with my phone glowing in my lap. I can't sleep. A little piece of me aches for the cocooned sleep of jail. The comfort of leaving today's questions for tomorrow. The strangest thing about being back on the outside is finding how much freedom I found in those bars.

Step two: Give yourself grace. Even the act of thinking of an apology as big as this one can be a start. Plant the thought and let it bloom.

A slice of Jefferson Lane glows through the doorbell app in ghosty-gray night vision, all hibiscus and pavement. For now, it's empty.

WESTON

The marina twinkles on the Florida-facing side of Madre Island. My wrist throbs as I pull into the gate. A crusty, unclean feeling has crawled up my arms. That will need sanitizing soon.

Getting in the marina only requires a card scan, which is easy enough; that was in a drawer near Patricia's garage. I drive down to where the pavement meets the dock, park, and pull a visibility vest from my trunk. No one questions a man in a visibility vest.

It may be a little overcautious. This is a moonless, overcast, sixty-degree letdown of a night and not one soul is out in Madre Island Sound, even for a pleasure cruise. Not exactly PortMiami.

The *Gutted* is easy to find. Largest boat in the docks, the only double-decker. It barely even sways in the waves. From there, I leap aboard. I hop the stairs to the bridge and look in all the familiar places for a backup key. I find one in the first compartment I check, attached to a bright red MADRE MARINE floatie that might as well be a bull's-eye. I twist the key in the ignition and let out an ill-disciplined little yelp of joy when the fuel needle spikes up to *F*. That must be for the listing agent, in case they need to take it out for a spin.

I kill the engine. All right. Good to know. The internet tells me a boat this size can get a thousand nautical miles on a tank, maybe more with slow cruising.

The primary plan is a chat with Leslie. Alone. I had imagined a reckoning with Robert, but he can duck that all he likes, and besides, maybe Leslie needs a more chemically pure version of the full story of Robert Woodhouse. Leslie is the key. If *she* knows who he is, I can face anything.

If not? The backup plan is firmly in place.

I hop to the dock, back to my car. I shut the door. Hear myself breathe. Senectitude is only five minutes away, and probably where she is now, but the hour is late and the itch in my wrists is now a septic, all-encompassing exhaustion in my veins. I turn the key and take the familiar road back to the parking lot of a twenty-four-hour supermarket, slapping myself awake along the way. Then I can sleep. What happens tomorrow is too important for me to be anything but my sharpest.

LESLIE

"I made Aunt Pat leave her car here," I tell Steph the following day as we eat a late lunch of turkey sandwiches and fried plantains in the nook. "Wanna help me drive it back? We'll need to drive over two cars. But we can be on speakerphone the whole time. It'll be fun. A convoy."

"Sure. Dibs on Aunt Pat's."

The Mercedes SUV. After Steph takes Patricia's key and gets her AC revving, I call a goodbye to Robert, who's taking advantage of the low tide by walking circles into the sand and spearing up trash with a litter picker. He barely waves back.

Steph and I drive off, me out in front. I insist that we carry each other on speakerphone like truckers using CB. Now I can put her on the stand. Tell me about Drew. Religion. Are his parents still together? Yes, and he wants to follow them into pharmaceuticals. At a red light, Steph pulls up behind me, and I ask more intimate questions. Good stomach? Digestion? She tells me these are boomer questions and, no, she does not keep a daily BM chart. And her workload for the next semester? She's all good to go? No major changes on the horizon?

Steph's voice crackles through the speakers, making her sound miles away. *Yep. All good, Mom.*

Patricia greets us at the door wearing white jean shorts and a floppy sun hat, and though I can tell there are new hollows under her eyes, she brightens. She wants to show us the new doggy purse she got for Mr. Fluffernutter, who barks incessantly at Steph, but not at me. Will we stay for drinks? she wonders. It's five o'clock in Bermuda. Steph wants to. She'll take a virgin daiquiri. Patricia flutters her eyes at me, shakes a quick cocktail, then runs out of steam. We end up collapsed on the couches, watching slow Saturday news.

"Another virgin daiquiri?" Patricia asks.

"Sure," Steph says.

"Wanna know the secret ingredient?"

"Is it rum? Nice try."

Patricia throws a shrug at me: *Worth a shot.*

Evening hits us. Right as the shadows outside start to get long and lean, I go to the counter to find out whose phone was doing all the buzzing. Steph has a missed call from Drew, who's still listed in her phone with the full DREWSON BENTLEY. Bentley. I shouldn't judge people for their last names, but there are bad last names. Stephanie Bentley. Even worse somehow, like some on-the-nose porn star character they added to an updated version of Clue. Stephanie Bentley, with the Candlestick, in the Library.

As it turns out, the buzzing phone was mine. There's a stack of texts from a number not listed in my contacts.

> Hello, Leslie. This is Weston Adekins at a new number. ☺.

> There are some things I need to tell you that are maybe best not shared over the phone.

> Proper punctuation. A man after my own heart.

> When is convenient to meet? I should be just a few minutes away.

ROBERT

Wes won't answer my calls.

He never answers my texts, either. There are still a few green bubbles in our conversation in iMessage, verbal pips of all the times I got nervous and tried to reach out. Hey. Hello? They're so small against the black backdrop, I can almost hear their sad little echoes.

And there's a draft saved in the text box that would've looked out of place if anyone had found it. *Hey maybe I can* is as far as I got.

I had to give up my phone when the trial started. If police ever saw the conversation, they thought nothing of it. The draft simply sat there for months. A gym sock at the bottom of the bag, soggy and forgotten.

Select all.

Delete.

Since it's a steamy, staticky evening, I mix up a pitcher of sugar-free lemonade and bring a foldout chair to the front porch. My neighbors tend to go inside when I do this. The other day, a woman was halfway to her mailbox before she saw me, and when we made eye contact, she stuck a foot out and swirled, with soldierly precision, 180 degrees back to her door. Surprisingly nimble for her age. Adrenaline does strange things to people.

Like going outside to stare at the cul-de-sac with a glass of lemonade, just in case I can see his ugly red Chevy before he sees me. Wondering what would've happened if I hadn't listened to my fears and instead sent that text to him. Wondering if I'm a fool to believe someone like him is capable of feeling regret. Wondering what it means if I have nothing *but* regret. Does that make me a good person who's in a bad spot, or a bad person who should know better? What *would* happen if I walked into Madre Island PD right now, put my hands out on the big desk in the lobby, said, *Cuff me, lock me up, do what you will, but here's the truth about Weston Adekins and it's time somebody stopped him?* Will those words finally come to me when Leslie gets home? Will they feel like the right words? Even if they feel wrong, I have to say them. It only takes a few seconds. All this torture, and it'll only take fifteen seconds of saying what feels like wrong words to have finally done the right thing. And that sounds right. The trick is simple, and it's the same one everyone's dealt with at some point or another: the first step out of hell is the hottest.

A few minutes later, a boxy silver Mercedes turns into Jefferson Lane and pulls up our driveway.

"What's going on?" I call.

Steph lets the window down. "Cool, right? Aunt Pat said I can have it for the weekend."

"Where's your mom?"

"That," Stephanie says, opening and shutting the door, then pointing a finger gun at me as she snicks her tongue and tries to think of the words, "is a good question. Um, she said your son wanted to see her, actually. They were just going to have a little chat and then she'd catch up with me at home."

My chest clamps. "With Wes?"

"Yeah." Steph's wide-lipped smile. "Unless you have more kids we don't know about."

"When did she leave? Where? You can tell me. Where are they meeting?"

"Holy shit, Bob. I don't know. About ten minutes ago? Same time as I left."

"Give me your keys."

"This is Aunt Pat's—"

"You parked me in. Just give me the keys, I'll take this back, we'll figure it out later, but give me the keys. In fact, come with me. But I'm driving."

She holds the keys up, dangling above her shoulder, leaning away. I pluck them before she can pocket them. She flinches; that's fine.

"Just—relax. Go on your phone and—" What do I say? *Warn your mother? Call the police? Wes is the killer and I'll explain later?* Maybe none of it's necessary. Hopefully. *Please, God, let it be unnecessary. If not, well—today is the day, then.* "Let's go."

LESLIE

I expected the Mercedes in the driveway, but when I pull in, only Robert's car is there. No sign of Wes, which is good. Mentioning the name out loud in Robert's presence would risk giving the poor man a coronary. Springing Wes in the flesh would risk the full widow-maker.

But no one's home at all. Robert must have taken Steph for something to eat. When I check my phone, there are a few texts from him, but as I clink my purse to the dining room table and pause to read them, a new text from Wes bubbles to the top.

Out on the beach. Nearby. Join me if you like.

High tide. Waves hugging the dunes, foam rolling up the fresh sand. The sun setting with a rusty-red color behind a wall of clouds. Only a few people are out—a man walking a Yorkie and a young couple helicoptering their toddler, picking at seashells, working their way south.

And then there's Wes.

He's wearing a black field jacket, endless pockets. He has a fresh pair of tennis shoes, and that's what he's watching: the tips of his feet near the foam, as if measuring the tide.

"Hello," I call, oh so gently. He seems lost, like he'd startle easily.

"Leslie?"

"Didn't expect you here so soon," I say. "I didn't see your car."

"Parked a few blocks up. Presidio."

"Well, glad we have a minute to talk."

"Me, too." A stiff nod, a stiff smile. Weston looks more like Robert than I remember: the same lean cheeks, the narrow shoulders. He's wearing a black button-up underneath the jacket. "Glad you could join me. Care to take a walk down my private beach?"

"Your priva—" I whirl around. There aren't too many people here, but no one would confuse this with a private beach.

"That was a joke," he says.

"Oh. Ha. Sure. Let's walk."

As we do, the wind stirs up. I have to strain to walk as slowly as he does; he watches his feet, tracking the edge of the waves.

"Tell me one thing," I say, "that day in court. Your testimony. Was that true?"

"Which part?"

"The whole thing. About you and Robert and—the kiddie pool."

"For sure," he says, no hesitation. "One of my earlier memories."

"But memories are tricky. You're that sure it was Robert? Not some friend of Caroline's boyfriend? Someone else?"

He crouches, presses his palm into the foam, washing. "This is exactly why I asked you here. Do you want to know what kind of man you married?"

"I do."

"There was more to it than what I said in court. I was hoping they would ask it. I remember being on the grass while he beat the water out of me. Did you hear? *Beat* it out of me. Then pressing on my chest, as though he was saving me. Caroline thought he rescued me. Technically, he saved my life that day—but only saved me from himself. And this is what really strikes me, this is the tag on everything: I remember Caroline *thanking him.* Do you know why? For saving me. He was Caroline's hero. I was the only one in the world who knew he had shoved me into the water and nearly held me underneath it until I was dead. That was when I knew who he was. Who he really was. And that I could know something about a person that no one else does. And I think ever since that day, I feel—forgive me—a little numb when it comes to all things Bob."

I stare. "I don't believe you."

"Caroline never did, either. Why would you? All you see is the Robert who was doing CPR. You never stop to think: Just how shallow was that water, anyway?"

I had expected Weston's story to crumble under questioning. But he says it so plainly—just a pinch of sadness—that there must be something there tattooed in his memory. Even so, heaven knows I've built a career on the fallibility of memories. "He can't even stand to gut fish—or cook lobster—"

"Maybe because he scares himself."

The words fill me with a sudden chill. "How old were you?"

"Old enough that I can still taste how hard that city water was."

His voice cracks on *hard.* He looks out seaward to hide his eyes. I've interviewed enough people—enough people being tested to their limits, in the fights of their lives—to know when to stay quiet.

I follow his stare. The sun is a dull glow, nearly set. The sea is dappled in whitecaps. The breeze is pulling in the cool air. Rain can't be far behind. "Let's walk back up," I tell him. "It's a little hard to hear out here, and we could have a drink. What do you say? Just you and me."

That cheers him up. "Yeah. Just you and me."

The fridge is all leftovers. There's some water cooling inside, Zephyr-hills. I take one and hand a bottle to Wes. He stands at the kitchen nook looking out the window. The way he fiddles with the cap, not quite knowing what to do with his fingers, reminds me of the way a fish will beat its fins to shake itself out of a tide pool.

My phone buzzes, but before I can go grab it, Wes breaks the silence. "I always got the sense he wanted to do more than that to people if they upset him. Do you want my honest opinion?"

"If that's why you're here, yes."

"I think Robert killed all those people." The flatness of his voice makes the accusation easy to ignore. I'm not sure even he believes it.

"There's the possibility he was framed, but I'd need to get more specific than that. I just have a hard time believing someone picked up your dad's DNA by coincidence—"

"Dad? He was never a dad, really. That word *dad*—it makes me think of changing diapers. Is there any word more intimate than *dad*?"

I shrug. *"Mom."*

His head jerks back, harpooned. "The simplest explanation, to me, is that my father is behind it all."

I'm a nervous sipper, already halfway through the bottle of Zephyrhills. A corner of the label is peeling off as the adhesive sweats away. I pick at it, but when the rest of the label won't un-glue, I rub it flat again. Then I set it on the counter and twist the label until it faces wherever I guess is north.

Wes points at it. "Turning it north?"

"What? Oh, I suppose."

He nods, eyes foggy and distant. "Do you think you could teach me?"

"I'm sorry—teach you what?"

He leans in. "I have this thing. A bit like a parasite. With my father—with Robert, Bob. If any thought of him enters my head when I scrub down a dish or blow my nose, I have to do it again, thinking nothing but *clean*. I even imagine the word in big cloud-letters. Against a blue sky. *Clean.* But my father will be there somewhere. And nothing about that should bother me, but it does, like even a whisker of a thought. So sometimes, if it catches me when I wash my hands—" Then he turns his palms over. They're raw, pink, massacred. "The irony is, I bleed. Which exposes my immune system to the air. But I see no other way to get clean. Truly clean. So how do you do it?"

I look at his hands. They're beyond me. His compulsions have bombed him into scabs, creases, premature wrinkles, and my own compulsions feel so tiny in comparison. I like it when labels face the right way, I pay attention to which foot goes first when I walk under a door: *Ha ha, look, I am so OCD.* "Well. I don't know, Wes . . . ton, but like I said, exposure therapy is the only one that ever worked for me."

"I tried. I can never get it out of my head."

"So don't. The first time, try to count up to one second of waiting, not washing. You'll see that you didn't die in that second, nothing happened. You're not sick. Next time, you aim for two seconds. And then you keep doubling it. Breathing, counting, four, then eight. And you keep going. You resolve never to wash until you hit your number, and you tell yourself you still can wash if you want, only later. You just have to hit your number."

"A number. A number! That I can do."

A rainbow of relief washes across his face. And before I can say, *But I'm no psychologist, you should talk to a psychologist*, he comes around the counter and wraps me in a hug.

The power of it surprises me. The bite of his fingers in my back. I pat him on a shoulder blade, tap-tap, friendly-friendly, hoping he'll let me go, but he's buried in me now, so close I see the dandruff on his scalp, smell the hardness of the water he washes with.

"Thank you," he keeps repeating. "Thank you. Thank you."

"Oh, honey." The only thing to say. "You're welcome." I'm not quite sure what I did, but that's the diplomacy he seems to enjoy. Another tap-tap at his shoulder blade. *Please let go.* I have the discomfort of hugging some antique. I'm wary of tipping him over, sending him to the ground, because maybe if I do, he'll shatter on the floor. If I told him to get a therapist, right here and now, I think he would listen. I think he'd do whatever I say. "Is it crazy if I don't know what I did?"

"You answered."

Something tells me to walk away, put some distance between us. I move to the living room and draw the curtains. Some dim light leaks in, but not much. I look up the cul-de-sac, then down our driveway. "I don't see your car out there."

Wes is under the archway now. "I parked somewhere else. Wanted to walk down the beach."

"Oh? Where'd you park, again?"

"Presidio Heights."

I am suddenly nauseous. I excuse myself to the bathroom— Wes extends his arms, *Please, please.* I close the door and lock it as softly as I can.

The face in the mirror is a ghost.

A feeling, a screech, a caterwaul like the tornado sirens of my Wisconsin youth goes gusting through me. Presidio Heights, the strangeness of him, the quivering fingers of Barbara Tiller, the uncertainty in her eyes, the alibis, Robert was not the one, was not the killer, he never was, and then everything else, the long missing chapters of Wes's life, the holes in Robert's experience of him, the vinegar and Lysol presence of him, the cleaning, the control, Robert's DNA, Robert's. As if the killer had been able to walk up to him and pluck the hairs from his father's head.

Steph. Robert. Where are they? I pat absently at a pocket and get nothing but cotton. My phone is in the dining room.

Out there. With him.

My heart is pounding against my ribs. I press against them, suck in a hopeless breath. Coming up to the house had been my idea. Maybe it's a good sign he wanted to meet me in public.

Everything that comes next is just about survival. Of not letting him see the worry in my face. I grab a tissue, wipe a glob of rheum out of my eyes, force up a smile. My lips are a flat edge.

What I would do for Patricia's easy smile right now.

Wes is still hunched in the dining room when I open the bathroom door. He's breathing into a hand. My presence doesn't seem to register. I think of how hard and needly his fingers felt when they had me in the back. I walk through, pointing to the kitchen. "I didn't ask. You hungry?"

He shakes his head. "After sunset."

Whatever that means. I open the fridge and dig out a carton of lo mein. It would rot in my belly if I ate it right now, but I want to hear the casual, all-is-well hum of the microwave. I plate it, bring it out to the living room, feeling lost without my phone, and not at all hungry. Longing for the days when there were landlines tacked to every other wall.

Wes is standing over my purse. Over my phone.

The plate is steaming uselessly in my hand. I set it on an end table, piling up thoughts. He wanted to meet, but he wanted to do it outside—whatever "it" is, he was fine if it was public—which means I'm not the target. I hope. I throw a hand up to my temple. "Stuffy in here. Do you wanna take a walk?"

"We were just walking."

"Not up the beach. Just around the cul-de-sac."

"Cul-de-sac." He throws it back at me like he's never heard the phrase. "No. I like it here."

"Come on. Some fresh air."

Wes lets my phone slip into his hands. "You know, then?"

"Know what?"

But the question dies in the air. We both know what he meant. And suddenly it's not my house anymore; it's his now, a killer's territory, and anything in the room harder than flesh is a potential weapon. And me with my safety knives. What else? The plate on the end table? Melamine, shatter resistant. The glass of the dining room table? He's there now. The TV remote, the loose pen on the coffee table, the lampstand—laughable. Even a delicate creature like Barbara Tiller was younger than me, stronger than me. I wonder what would happen if I run straight out the door and out to Jefferson Lane, how my body would take it, whether I'd shuck a hip bone like an old beater car losing a rim, whether he'd catch me before I got to the other houses, before I got out of my own yard, even. When was the last time this body went above four miles an hour on its own power? Years.

Wes has been watching my eyes, reading all the obvious thoughts in them. "No, just sit. Listen." Then he pulls my phone tight to his body with a brightening look in his eyes. "I think you should know your husband. Really know."

ROBERT

I drop Steph at Patricia's, promising I'll explain later. Explain what? I don't know. I don't even make it to the Madre Island bridge before I have to pull over near a utility pole to catch my breath. Rain-spittle wind. Cars whipping by me. Madre's dimply lights winking on for the night. I pull open my phone, tap *9*. It suggests *1-1*.

As my thumb quivers in the air, the phone pulses. A push notification drops down: text from LESLIE. Some tiny flash-lit photo waits for me in the margins. All right. I tap that instead.

And there is a photo of Leslie.

She's sitting in a chair, flush against the empty beige of drywall. Obviously she's tied to it somewhere; it's holding her posture stiff, choking her breasts under her linen shirt, folding cringe lines into her neck. Her eyes are the worst part. Big full moons in the flashing camera, flooded with tears, pupils enormous and obvious against the green. The sharpness in them—I fell in love with that sharpness—has blunted to a raw animal fear. And it's my fault. The entire summer, the last few years, are nothing to me now.

Pulse, pulse. No police, it reads. Or you know what happens.

Pulse, pulse.

Come home.

LESLIE

"On his way," Wes says as he fingers the blinds. "Imagine. Robert actually coming when his son invites him."

The way he looks at me—lips cupped open, tartarly smile—demands a response. A laugh? A *harumph*? Was that even a joke?

He paces into the living room as I work my wrists. The lamp cord is hard and tight. It was startling how easily he pulled the cord straight out of the lampstand, this scrawny man in his over-size clothes, but it pulled out slick. He even apologized for how tight he tied them.

My plate on the end table is no longer steaming. Wes clacks a fingernail against it and turns to me. "Did you want this?"

I only look at him.

"I could feed you. But only if you really want it."

I shake my head, swallowing the look I really want to shoot him: alarm, annoyance, utter disgust. Have I lost *every* old in-stinct? The alarms were all blaring so loud for Robert, the ones for Wes went through me in silence.

Wes shoots a *Suit yourself* look and sets the plate back on the end table. Swirls his finger around it. Picks at a chunk of noodle, rolls it in his fingers until it seems to come alive, a mag-goty little pellet, then slips it in his teeth.

He walks over to the dining room, conscious not to let his toes land square in the crack between hardwood and carpet, and sits across from me. "We have some time before Robert gets here. Do you want to know who he really is?"

"You told me."

Wes shrugs: *One story among many.* "Yeah. Not believable?"

"Not exactly." I catch the curtness in my voice and a memory flashes through me. The lunch. The drugged look of pleasure rolling through his eyes when I offered the simple courtesy of a *thank you.* "Sorry, Wes, but no."

"Will you ever believe me?"

"Why is it so important that I do?"

"Because then he has nothing."

"No one kills as many people as you did because they had a terrible father." I can't help it. The words come spitting out of me. "You did this on your own. And you want to blame him because he's an easy out. But he didn't make you do *any* of it."

Wes chews on this, cheeks swallowed in his hands. He tilts the chair back. "Would you have defended him if you knew what he was hiding?"

"I can't answer that."

"Why?"

"Because I don't know."

"You defended guilty men before."

"Robert was never guilty of this."

"Never guilty?" Weston pulls the jacket, folds up his shirt cuffs. Chemical burns cuff his wrists, meaty red. Unhealed black scabs dot across them. "Your husband ruined a woman's life because it was more important to him to preserve his good name. She was nothing to him. Nothing. In all those years. Just an accident, a big, everlasting hit-and-run. She never had a chance. You see that, right? She dropped out of school because of him, went back to minimum wage because of him, had to find whatever way she could to survive because he never married her. She would have had his insurance. And what then? Caroline might still be alive. What about him? He only seems to get healthier, wealthier. He has a life. He has a *condo* on the *beach*. He meets people like you. You and your sister. You ask nothing about his past. You are happy to have *him* because he is happy to have *you*—a perfect match. If you would just *acknowledge* who he is—"

"Even if that's true, that's not who he is anymore."

"But it *is*. How do you not *see* it even when you stare right at him?"

There's a *hub-bump* outside. Tires catching the steep border of the driveway. Then an engine settles, shuts off. A shadow falls over the door, and Wes rises to meet it with his hand folded neatly under the jacket cuff.

"He came when asked," he whispers. "First time for everything."

ROBERT

SENECTITUDE. Black, signature-style letters hanging on our front porch: the faux luxury of it, a home that has a name. The irony makes me want to spit.

The door opens. Pissy-yellow light spills from inside. Wes moves through it, antsy, almost skipping. A box cutter in his hand, glinty and obvious.

"Robert." He holds the door open. "Slowly."

I move through and he frisks me. And as he shoves me in the chest and pats under my arms and hacks at my crotch, I wish I'd been clever enough to think of that: sneaking something past him. A safety razor tucked behind my credit cards. A fountain pen. It wouldn't have taken much. Isn't he proof of that?

When he's done, he nudges me forward with a knuckle in my back. "All right. Sit down, please."

I do as he says. Leslie is still in the corner. Tied up, still straining flush against the wall. Her shoulders have ballooned in her sleeves. Her legs are closed. She's making herself small. She looks at me. I look at her.

Even the act of thinking of an apology as big as this one can be a start. Plant the thought and let it bloom.

Wes stands at the doorway, then pulls a cord from under the table and moves behind me to lash my hands. Not into the chair, but immobile enough, enough that it can't be two against one. Our dining room juts out to the side, bay-nook-style, ostensibly a luxury feature, but small, like most luxuries. It has a claustrophobic effect at night. The ceiling is so low, I can hear the air in my lungs come whispering back to me.

"Well," Wes says. "All of us are here."

"Untie her," I say. "It doesn't have to be like this."

But he's looking at Leslie. "You know how police work. What would a confession from Robert do? How would police treat it if his case is already dropped?"

She shoots him a gastric look of disgust.

"Indulge me," he says.

"I can't speak for the police."

"Imagine I made you answer."

I look at his hands. Raw, pink.

"If there's some new evidence I don't know about," Leslie says, "a confession out of Robert might only make your case worse. If they have something that suggests . . . another killer . . . was responsible, they may want Robert as a key witness. Find out what he knows." She turns to me, but her eyes don't meet mine. "What do you know, Robert?"

I hadn't planned on having the spotlight. The attention stings a little, in the esophagus. Tough to speak.

Let it bloom.

The only thing that comes out of me is a shrug.

"You see," Leslie snorts. "That's the trouble. They reopened the investigation because of new evidence. We don't know what that is. After the trial, they'll be more careful. But it's probably something damning. Something like new DNA at a scene. So even if Robert writes up a perfectly worded confession, even if the country thinks he is a killer who got away with it, they're not going to buy it."

Wes receives this information with surprising calm. Standing with his hands pinched under the beam between rooms, too short to reach it. He catches me looking and smiles his underbitten smile. But he isn't a threat, not the way he hopes he is. I hadn't noticed how thin he's become. He's wearing jet-black denim and his waist is so tight I imagine putting my hands around it and strangling him into two pieces. He's pretending to be big, in the way daddy longlegs are big until you pinch them in a napkin.

"Obstruction of justice," Wes throws out. "They could have him on that."

"Under duress," Leslie replies. "That case could go either way."

And the wind comes out of Wes's sails. He sits at the dining table, tapping his fingernails on the glass.

But it's Leslie who speaks next. "Robert. Bob. The story he told in court. Was it true?"

Wes's head swerves over. *Good question.*

"No."

Wes shakes. "Tell her the truth. Bob."

"That's the truth."

It only makes Wes laugh, exposing molars stuffed with black amalgam. Extensive repairs. But in him, it still looks like a disease.

Leslie sniffs. "Just be honest with me."

"I'm not on the *stand*, Les—"

"That's exactly where you are!"

Wes has been playing with the box cutter: two notches up, two notches down, clickety-clack. "Yes, Bob. The whole truth. Nothing but."

"Why?"

"She has to see who you are. She has to *see*."

Thirty years ago now. The memory has no more tread on it, no more texture. It's not quite real. If it was, I would think of something like sticking wet grass, the gluggy, bubble-gum sounds his throat made. I think of none of it. What I have is only a generalized, pounding-head annoyance, then a sniff, my consciousness in some swirl between blackout and waking life, then coming to with Caroline shouting for her child and Wes hacking up water and me staring at the pink, rashy flesh of my hands.

But it's there.

LESLIE

"I never felt any anger," Robert says. "And then something happened, like a switch clicked, and I had him underwater and all I could think to do when Caroline came running outside was pull him out like I had saved him."

"You see." Wes drums a fist on the table, but it makes nothing flare in me. If the glass breaks, good. "You *see*?"

"I never wanted to be alone with him again," Robert says. "I told you I was a terrible father. I know. But I hated myself for that more than anything else."

I avoid Robert's gaze. My gentle, squeamish husband. The man who can barely unhook a bluegill without wincing. Hates my true-crime shows, wants to know what else is on.

Not squeamish. Self-avoidant. I should have known. Or, if not, I should at least have wondered why.

"Leslie," Robert is saying. "Leslie—look at me."

But when I do, something in my eyes flips, the feeling of looking in the wrong end of the binoculars. He is so far away. He is so small. I'm not sure if it matters if I believe it. There is something jagged and broken between us.

Wes senses none of this. "So. Bob can write his confession to the murders. Whatever comes next, Leslie, you can defend me. Like you did Robert, or that other man—"

I look at him. One of his eyes catches a shimmer from the streetlights, those upsetting LEDs with their alarmy blue hues. The effect is familiar, slicing him into two different people. Maybe I can't blame Barbara Tiller for having a tough time distinguishing this face from Robert's.

"I can't represent you, Wes."

His mouth darkens. "Weston."

"Weston." My breath catches in my throat. "I'm so sorry, Weston."

"Why not?"

"I have to believe in what I'm defending."

"You *have* to believe it now. You *have* to know who he is. And you can defend me because you will understand why I did what I did."

"I can never understand that."

He shrugs. It's a fast and empty gesture. The shrug of someone who knows the answer but doesn't want to say it.

"And Bob won't write a false confession, either."

Robert clenches. "Leslie—"

"Robert won't believe a word he's telling the police," I interrupt. "He won't be able to answer questions about how he did it. The evidence won't line up. Nothing about it will line up, Weston. If you really want out, the best thing you can do is—" I stop. "You want me to act as your lawyer?"

"Yes."

"You really want my advice?"

"Yes."

"Then, as your lawyer: Turn yourself in. Confess, the way you want Bob to confess. Then take the best deal you can get. I'll even negotiate it for you. But if you have this idea that I can make miracles happen in your trial when everything is stacked against you . . . that's not how it works."

"It worked for *him*." Weston chews the word *him* like a wad of rotten meat. "Everything worked for him."

Weston starts rubbing his wrists together.

"What if there was something else?" he asks.

"What else?"

"Another option."

"Weston—"

"Imagine if I fled. If I never told you where I went."

"It's the federal government."

"If I left the country, then. If we did."

I ignore that word *we*. "If they know who you are, and they want you, there isn't anything I can do that will change that. Barbara Tiller is still out there."

"Safe and sound," Weston acknowledges.

"Imagine someone showed her a white-haired composite of you. How easy do you think it would be for her to spot you?"

For a moment, Weston considers this. His eyes have a habit of moving down and scanning, almost like he's hoping for the invisible captions that translate our words. "Quite easy. I spoke to her."

"And she'll know your voice."

"Yes." He's working his wrists again. "But will you help me?"

"If you turn yourself—"

"No. *Help. H-E-L-P*." A saucy, wet pool forms on his lips. "It was you, Leslie. Always you. Finding something, making magic. Please. I read all about it. You always found something for someone who needed it."

What to *say* to that? The man is a serial murderer. The case is reopened—which never happens without new evidence—and now this. His father and his father's wife, tied up in the living room.

All I can say is what he needs to hear. "Okay. Okay, Weston. Okay."

"Okay what?"

"I'll defend you. But I'm telling you, the only way for us to have any leverage whatsoever is for you to turn yourself—"

"I said *no*!"

Robert squirms. "If she's telling you to do something—as your lawyer—then you need to listen to her."

That Robert had the gall to speak to him, give him advice, sends blood straight to Weston's head. His neck gets tight and his temples bubble. He slinks back to the couch over in the living room, leans against its back. The box cutter is still in his fingers.

Then he pulls his hand in a high arc and brings it down, smashing it through the glass of the table.

WESTON

"Leslie. Bandages?"

Leslie's stare is fixed at the table, trancelike. I track her gaze. A piece of my hand is still bitten off there, small and wet, a ribbon of skin where it caught the glass. Or the glass caught it. The pain itself is only faint dullness, someplace separate. The glass took a piece of me, but only a pointless piece.

But Leslie. Her face looks like *she* had bled out.

"Leslie. Bandages."

"The—kitchen—"

I go, suddenly aware of the hot leak trickling down my wrist. What was I thinking? I need this hand. Right-handed all my life; the left might as well be vestigial. I pull open their drawers. Safety knives in one. Miscellany in another, pens and pads and rubber bands. Finally a first-aid kit. I have to do it myself, so I sift through until I find a big, gauzy rectangle labeled ISLAND DRESSING. Seems appropriate.

The first slides off. Right. I run their faucet, watch the steam batter softly against the sink. I can smell chlorine in the water. Awful to drink, but clean smelling, so I rinse my hand under it. Thinking suddenly of Robert. Robert's water. Robert's faucet. He has come in from long walks on the beach and poured himself a glass, right here, slurped it down, all loud, soupy, never caring who heard all his ugly body noises. The same water is in me now. If septicemia is a feeling, I have it already.

Despite all this, I find no need to clean it off. Bigger fish to fry.

I cotton off the wound, padding up all the blood I can. The dressing finally sticks. I feel my senses returning. I pocket the box cutter and walk back to the dining room, tennis shoes crunching on glass. The glass made too much noise, and if there is someone in earshot—a neighbor, maybe, these condos are so close together—it is entirely possible someone will call the police. I need to be one step ahead of that. Not turning myself in, as Leslie suggests, but still: the rest of my life, if it can ever be a free life, will require her by my side.

And she, for a reason that escapes me, requires Robert.

Which means we all have to go together.

ROBERT

Weston unknots Leslie from her chair and forces us into the garage. *The keys?* he asks. In my pocket. Weston reaches inside, pulls them out, and taps the Aviator to life. He won't have us in the back seat, that's too dangerous, so he makes us crumple in the cargo department, and I fold my legs into Leslie's. The hugging presence of her fills me with hope.

That and the shard of table glass I snuck between my fingers.

"Heads down," Weston says as he pulls out of the cul-de-sac. Jefferson Lane's streetlights roll across our faces.

He turns south instead of north. North is the fastest way to the mainland. I lip a word at Leslie: *Where?* She shrugs. Avoids my gaze. Her knees are crunched into mine, so close I can smell her, mostly sweat, but other things, too, soft notes of patchouli soap. I know her questions. How much of it is true? And if she's wrestling with that thought, all the other ones I've been working so hard to avoid are bubbling under her skin right now. How much did I know? Was I ever part of it? Why couldn't I tell her? Just how much of that is me being a coward? How much is she willing to forgive?

I know she's thinking these. So many of them are my questions, too.

The lights of Fontaneda Boulevard pulse through the windows. It's only so far until we'll find the lighthouse near the southern tip of Madre, at which point the boulevard becomes a two-lane sprint up the coast: marina, wharves, a couple of restaurants, then the bridge.

We stop at an intersection, no more bumping. I push out the shard of glass and work it until it rubs against the cords, but there's almost no friction. Easier said than done.

"Cuba," Weston announces. "Leslie, what do you know about nonextradition countries?"

She cranes her neck, throws her voice into a crease next to the back seat. "Almost nothing."

"You must know something."

"Sure. Cuba. You'd be safe there." But the look she gives me is uncertain.

The light goes green.

I'm not making much progress with the glass. But I can show it to Leslie. I hold up my wrists, flick the glass in my fingers, then hold a finger to my mouth. She leans forward as far as her knees will let her.

"Don't let him see," she whispers.

"I won't."

Her voice cracks. "He wants to kill us. Maybe all three of us. Just keep quiet until you find your chance."

"When?"

She shrugs: *Like I know?*

I nod and keep working the cords. It's possible they won't cut at all. The glass is sharp in certain places and square in others. It shattered smooth, so there's no bite to it. At one point, it pinches the fleshy part under my pinkie, and the hot wetness that follows means it's eaten into skin before it ever caught any of the cords. Still. What else is there?

I can't change the past. I can't take back the trial and I can't unspool all the lies I told Leslie. But if I end it—if I find my chance with Weston and take it—I could potentially dig us out. There would be some redeeming value in that. And as for the rest, what was it Leslie said? *Under duress.* In the eyes of the law, I'd be blameless. Not in the eyes of Leslie, maybe, but it's the best I can hope for.

I keep cutting, but it's slow and slippery work, especially if I can never let go of the glass. It's my one key out of this.

The Aviator slows and turns, throwing my knees into Leslie's. I hear the *whish* of a window being lowered, the *bee-deep* of a card being scanned, and then the ground flattens smooth under us. The smell that carries on the cool air is crabby and briny. Then the car shutters to a stop.

Leslie whispers, "Wait. Until the right time."

But that's my problem. I've already waited too long.

LESLIE

Pelicans watch us from the gateposts as we pull in. Somehow, Weston knew Patricia's code. The barrier beeps, then raises, squeaking with a multijoint come-hither motion that makes me want to wretch.

He steers us down a dip in the pavement, as close to the water as the parking allows, then kills the engine, gets out, takes in the scene. A cabin cruiser, for the island's nightly dolphin tour, is just pulling in on the other side of the marina. A bevy of out-of-towners pop out and scurry to their cars—you can always spot them shivering at night in their skinny polos and crop tops, never expecting the weather to go cold.

Once they've cleared, Weston clicks the button to open the Aviator's back liftgate. It peels up, revealing the box cutter still in his hands. He's glaring at Robert. "Your hand is bleeding."

Robert regards him grimly. "Dining room glass."

Weston's eyes are dead for a moment. He lets the Aviator keys slide from his fingers and crash their sleigh-bell sound into the pavement. We're on a one-way trip.

He pulls me up to my feet, presses the box cutter until I feel it pinch the small of my back. "Robert first."

Robert leads. It isn't hard to spot Patricia's boat out on one of the long docks. The *Gutted* is swaying on the water, one full story above the rest. The belle of the ball. Most of the boats are for dolphin watching or deep-sea fishing, but Patricia wanted it near me and Robert, saying, *Think of all the evenings of champagne and sunsets*, which never materialized as often as they should have. Few champagne dreams ever do.

Robert hops on board at the gangway and offers his hand. "No," Weston shouts. "Both of you in the cabin."

As I watch my feet hover over a black sliver of water and unmoor from the dock, I regret what I whispered to Robert. Waiting for the perfect opportunity is still waiting. And what if the opportunity had passed you? Then it's *only* waiting. For something that never comes. A feeling Robert must be familiar with by now.

"Cabin," Weston blurts, pointing the cutter at the main room behind Patricia's tinted windows. We walk in wobbly and Weston follows: *Sit down, shut up.* Our legs make popping sounds against Patricia's waterproof couch cushions as Weston digs through a utility closet. His bandage is already soaked through, and when he drops his hand, it sends threads of blood across the carpet.

Robert's face is straining. When he catches my glance, he stresses into a smile and winks. Progress on the cords? Giving me false hope with body language? I can't trust his winks anymore.

Wordless, Weston yanks my wrists and drags me to the grab rails by the stairs, ties me. It's a loose knot: the rhythm of tying a shoelace. But strong enough to hold.

He does the same for Robert on the other side, Weston's eyes thick and glazed, then he walks outside to work on the moorings.

"The glass," I whisper.

Robert is working his hands. The blood is an awful black streak running down his forearm now. "It's hard. I'm doing my best."

Weston's footsteps pound outside, *tha-dump, tha-dump*. Stepping up to the bow. The boat sways a little. Then the clattering sound of his feet as he climbs the ladder to the bridge.

The engine starts. The boat kicks, the floor shuffles, a gentle glide.

"He wasn't serious about Cuba," Robert whispers, sawing at his wrists now. "How much gas is in the tank? How long's it been in there? Doesn't it lose octane?"

"I don't know." My throat clicks when I swallow. My heart is thundering.

"Please. You have to see what's happening here," Robert blurts. "He's going to kill us both. We have to get out now."

"So *cut*."

Robert doesn't say anything. Still sawing, still grinding, still biting his teeth so hard I can't tell if he's catching more flesh than cord, and it seems pointless, we have so little time before we're stuck with Weston, before we're stuck beyond anyone's help—

"*Robert*," I spit.

The gravity in the room shifts. Outside, the marina slides into view—we're turning—and gratitude washes through me as I realize the *Gutted* is so big and clumsy, Weston has to steer us carefully through the docks before we hit the water of Madre Island Sound. Minutes. Seconds. I don't know. But time.

Robert keeps grinding away as I look at the water outside. How deep is that black water? Deep enough, marina-dredged, safe passage for boats. And what about me? My heart feels like it'll give out just waiting on Robert. When was the last time I swam in anything remotely wild? Suddenly I hate how I ignored my doctor's advice, skipping the gym so I could lie at home with Robert in my illusionary, oh-so-peaceful life: I am a grandmother's age, I am not a natural swimmer, and my genes are my father's, the thick Wisconsiny stock of a Holstein farmer. I'll probably have to swim like one, all torso and twiggy legs. How far can that get me in open ocean before I exhaust myself, slip into the water? If I jumped out now, maybe, if Robert gets the stupid things *loose* ever, maybe, but soon Weston completes his turn and we're making for open water.

Pop. Something hard and tendony snaps in Robert's hands.

"Yes," he whispers. "Yesyesyes—"

My heart leaps with him. *Yes!*

The cords fall away. Weston's shoelace knot to the rail is easy to untie after that. Free and smiling, *Yes, yes, yes*, Robert turns to my cords next. The engines are kicking up now, catching more water, more thrust.

"I love you," I tell him. "We'll get through this."

A stupid thing to say. Stupid and distracting. Robert only nods through it, working my cords now, sliding, slipping, his hands frictionless with all their blood, and the engines gear up another notch now, near open water, the hull *slap-slapping* against the waves, throwing Robert off, making the glass shard miss the cords and pinch me, and something sinks out of my stomach when Robert starts cursing. He sleeves off the sweat from his forehead, wasting precious seconds. Hyperventilating. I whisper to calm down—slow is smooth, smooth is fast—but my words don't catch. His eyes go buggy and wide, scanning the windows. How far will we have to swim? How distant are the docks? One dock is still in sight. Swimmable. Reachable. For both of us. And the hull jerks again as Weston pushes on the throttle.

But no progress on my cords yet. Robert stops. Looks me in the eyes. One green. One blue. I don't know whom I'm looking at. I have never known.

And he whispers, "Don't think badly of me."

"No—*don't leave me—*"

"I'm sorry, Les."

He tosses the glass shard to a couch cushion. Turns to the door, throws it open. And when he points his fingers flat and steps to the rail, out to the water, ready to dive, when I finally accept what he's doing, the realization blading through me, I have to turn away.

It's worthless. No matter how far I turn, I can still hear the splash before he starts swimming to the docks.

WESTON

The *Gutted* cuts into black infinity as we emerge from Madre Island Sound. The Gulf does strange things around the southern tip of Madre, but here, the water is not so pissy choppy. A chilled peace takes hold. Crisp, cool air, maybe a fleck of rain. The lights of Madre and the mainland cradle me now. Cradle us. I finally have time to ease on the throttle and let the tide do some of the work.

I heard noises before. I have to check on *that scene* below.

There is rain on my soles, so I take my time down the steep, uncertain stairway to the cabin. The lower I go, the more blood there is. The plastic is smattered with it. The rails help only a little—some of the blood will be mine—but when I emerge, I notice only one person is tied to them.

No.

No. His cords were *tight*. I yanked the knot. Even *tested* it.

I swirl around. Someone kicked the door open. Leslie calls something—"He's not here"—but the words are meaningless, of course she would say that, so I check the bow, I run to the stern. *Great for water activities,* the ad said, not *great for diving into the ocean to save yourself while your wife is still on board.*

Somehow he got out. He was trapped. I finally had him trapped. And somehow, even I, the person who *knows him best*, had never considered that he would run.

I feel woozy. Famished. I should have eaten something. Lately I only eat dinners. When finally sure the rest of the *Gutted* is empty, I return to the cabin and sit on one of those marine-grade, plastic settees that line the windows.

"He really left you," I tell Leslie. I want her to hear it. "Left us."

Leslie's mouth is a wide line. "Yes."

"*Now* do you see who he is?"

She says nothing. Which is as good as a yes.

ROBERT

I'm safe.

The swim isn't much—fifty yards or so from dive to dock—but I hyperventilate my way up each step of the water ladder. I turn to the water and wretch. Swallowed too much seawater. It leaves a salty, scraped-out, exorcised feeling in my throat. Everywhere on my body. Exhaustion and guilt and the salty pain in my hand have vacuumed the life out of me. I check my pulse. Still beating. Still going. I really am safe.

Call the police.

But where is a phone? The Aviator is up there. Hadn't he tossed the keys to the pavement? I can go *get* help. That's what I'm doing. I'm going to *get* help. Soaking, hotly breathing, I find the keys where Weston left them and crawl into the Aviator. My clothes sponge to the seat, everything heavy.

And I drive.

To the Madre Island Police Department. Fast as I can. To tell them what? That I knew about the killer, always knew, and left my wife to have it out with him? No. I skip the turn. The Aviator drags me across the bridge, toward the highway. Road studs wink at me at seventy miles an hour, golden pips curving and dancing, turning it into a wormy runway. Or maybe I'm seeing stars. I should pull over. I don't like the way my breathing has become a frantic pulse of inhales. Long ago I had a chain-smoking uncle who had to get a stoma—he'd make the same noise. I can hear my larynx click. And that fills me with panic: I can hear my organs, I can hear them failing, I am full of holes, I am dying, Leslie may be dying, I killed Leslie, I killed everything. I need to pull over right now.

The Aviator's neutral female voice picks up: "Call from: Patricia. Would you like to answer?"

YES/NO bubbles up on the screen.

I do some quick math. Seventy-five plus seventy-five, the combined speed of my Aviator and a random driver on the other side of the highway. Like hitting a wall at a hundred and fifty. At that speed, would either of us ever really feel it?

I try to tell the car no, but again: my invisible stoma. It comes out stuttering. "Nonononono." I fumble with the dash, accidentally flip on my hazards.

My car doesn't understand. "Call from: Patricia. Would you like to answer?"

YES/NO.

"Yes." I say it because I don't have the guts for anything else. Halfway over the median, the whole thing could flip over. The only man wearing a halo brace in prison.

"Bob!" The speakers send a blast of Patricia's wide, throaty mezzo-soprano. "What the *hell*, Bob? What on earth is going on? Steph and I are *sick*."

"Madre Island Sound," I tell her. "I don't know."

"What is happening? Did you see I called you ten times?" Pause. "Eleven. Leslie's not answering my texts."

"Call the police. Madre Island Sound. She's out there in the *Gutted*."

"You make no sense. What am I calling them for? Why haven't you called them? *What is happening?*"

I kick the gas above seventy-five, change lanes. Why does it feel like a rush? No one's chasing me. I don't know where I'm going. Away, that's all. Quickly away. As fast as I can go without getting pulled over.

"She's with Wes. I don't know what he plans to do."

"You went to see her?"

"Just—send help."

"Were you with her? What happened?"

A semi pounds by on the other side of the median. A big sucker, cab over engine, probably hauling twenty tons. What a spectacular wreck that would be. Spectacular and painless. The driver? Maybe a little whiplash, a little PTSD, nothing therapy couldn't fix.

"I'm on the road," I say. "I can't talk."

I tap the icon to kill the call. If I'm lucky, it will say *Call dropped* instead of *Call ended*. But if not, at least I told her where. Madre Island Sound. The *Gutted*. I said the words. Filed the report. She can't say I didn't try. I took her call, I told her where, I was rushed and twitchy and frightened and cranked on adrenaline and I was doing my best.

I drive into the night, square and steady in the lanes.

LESLIE

Weston is tearing apart the cabin. Where does Patricia keep the first-aid kit? I don't know; we've never had to use it. His cut has already soaked through the bandage, and when he swings his arm, ropes of blood swing with him.

But at least he's distracted. I shuffle down the couch, hoping my hands catch the shard of glass Robert threw away.

Robert.

The sound he made in the water when he jumped out of my life. The soft, pathetic smallness of his body. He has always been that small. I'd just refused to see it.

Weston digs out a first-aid kit from a storage bin and starts peeling off his old bandage.

"We're not very far if you want to make it out of the country," I tell him.

Weston shrugs. He's slapping cotton clumsily to the wound, like if he beats it enough, it will lose the will to live. Each slap sends a pulse of fresh blood.

The carpet is already soaked with it. It's changing him. A minute ago he asked which was closer, Cuba or the Bahamas, then when he didn't trust my answer, he went sifting through nautical charts. Of course, the maps wouldn't show much beyond Madre. Now he's sitting on a waterproof couch, just running his thumbs across it. Staring at it, caressing it, as though his blood could be the catalyst revealing some invisible-ink path to salvation.

"Yes," he says finally. "Cuba?"

"We'd have to *go* there first."

"Then you can . . ." His voice dies.

"Solve all your problems," I promise. I have to. Yes, me and my hidden ways out, the magic lawyer powder I keep in my purse for such occasions, Cokie Dean and Robert Woodhouse and, now, Weston Adekins. Whatever he needs to hear.

Finally Weston tightens the bandage, ties it up in white tape. It blooms up red. "You see who he is now."

That *splash*. Robert's slight body, an enormous ocean. "Yes."

"So I succeeded."

No comment. I don't know how Weston defines success or failure. Failure: Will he get anger, frustration, murderous rage? Success: A boredom and emptiness so profound, he would feel there was nothing left to *do* but kill me? He wipes his wrists, all fingers and frantic energy. His heart is working too hard. It's squeezing the blood out of him.

Better that I play the mother. Say reassuring things. Rescuing things. Yes. Cuba.

Another tiny scootch. This time, my hand catches on something sharp between my thighs. I take a wide, self-soothing swallow of air. Weston shouldn't know I have it. I turn outside, scope Madre Island dim through the window, hundreds of yards away now. I can make out the elbowy shape of its tip, the light-house, everything hairy with live oak. And what is my plan exactly? Getting loose? Diving in, swimming home? Robert would tell me how silly I'm being. Ignoring the facts in front of me.

Or hoping that he's serious about Cuba?

Weston has been circling the ship. He dips under the door-way. "Is there an anchor?"

"On the bow. It's automatic, I think."

"Something heavy, then."

Heavy.

He stands, switching scratching hands against his wrists, looks around. Patricia left a pile of life preservers strewn about, the foam orange ones she never makes anyone wear but keeps on hand in case a police boat does an inspection. Weston gathers them into a pile, then heads out to the deck. This time there are several splashes.

"What are you doing?"

No reply again. If this conversation were a text thread, all my bubbles would only read SENT. He walks past me, piles up another load of orange foam, dumps it into the water. They float away with surprising speed. I can picture my head like that, see myself thwacking uselessly at the water, swallowing salt, losing my breath, dragged away in the undertow. No, I can't swim home. There is only this boat.

"What if we need those?" I ask.

SENT.

He jumps up the steps to the cockpit. Even lashed, my hands almost rise: *Be careful.* The muscle memory of motherhood. A few seconds later, the motors give a big kick-drum *thwump-thwump* almost in unison. The boat rattles and makes a steady beat against the water, but not south, not along the coast to Cuba. Straight west into the Gulf. Weston probably up there, thinking up uses for *something heavy.* Working those wrists again.

I start working the glass against my cords, no longer ignoring the facts in front of me.

ROBERT

Three miles on. Less than three minutes of road time: that's how far I made it before I had to pull over and vomit. And it's a gusty night, which means I'm half blowing on myself, the warm oatmeal of this afternoon's water crackers.

The occasional car swishes up the highway. I have my hazards on. I get back in my seat so people don't think they need to stop and help. My lungs still won't work; every breath is like the first after breaking the surface of a deep pool. One car slowed down and looked ready to offer help, but I held my breath steady, waved them on, there is nothing to see here, I'm not weeping, there is no man here who committed the greatest sin of omission a husband is capable of, there is not a broken and absent father who helped raise a serial killer, a man who is rethinking his entire life from the entry of Caroline Adekins on, and even before her, what kind of man was I all along if I could sleep with a woman and never want to be around her again, never want to be around the walking reminder of it. No. Nothing to see.

Patricia calls my phone twice more. For some reason, that gives me energy again. The wet air fills my lungs. I can pull back into traffic. I can drive away from that.

LESLIE

The first time the glass catches my skin, I start praying Hail Marys.

The cords are impossible. The glass is dull. There's too much intermingling blood. I squeeze the glass between my pointer and middle finger, sawing uselessly. All the while, a chorus is ringing in my head like I'm holding a seashell to my ear. Something singsong, from miles or years away. Soon I realize it's my own voice. The voice of a hundred thousand prayers finally catching up with me.

Pray for us sinners, now and at the hour of our death . . .

Amen. Hail, Mary . . .

On my third *Mary*, the engines cut out.

The sudden deceleration nearly slams me into the windows. Sea legs: not a myth. My hand flashes red, and I blink, seeing sparks in my vision, but then my hands turn blue. And red, and blue—

A megaphone crackles. I can barely make it out. "—the engines—off. Slowly—in the—air."

I throw my hands up, just in case.

The flashing lights start to syncopate. A second police boat is curving in the water behind us. It sparkles across Patricia's tinted glass like a strobe.

Nothing from upstairs. I wonder if Weston is complying, whether he has his hands behind his head and is waiting for them to toss a rope. It was smart to slow down. That's what I'd tell him: *As your lawyer, always comply, everything is negotiable until you resist, and then there goes all of your innocence.* You don't have to talk, you don't have to like it, but you have to—

A fresh *thwump*. The boat slides on its haunches, shoving me down into the couch.

The police lights dim behind us. The shadows get long. The *Gutted* gets a loose, swerving feeling, like Weston is losing control of the ocean.

"All right," Weston says.

He's propped himself in the door between two of Patricia's tinted windows. The *Gutted* is plowing through the water, driverless, and it crashes on a wave like all it wants to do is curve to port and moon its way back to the police boats. They're following at a cautious distance, bouncing through our violent wake. I don't blame them for holding off. If Weston wasn't holding on with two hands, he would have gone over on one of the ocean's swells.

"All right?" I scream back at him. "All right what?"

He only waves at me and kneels to a foldaway cushion near the door. Inside are some supplies: flashlights, zip ties, spare fuses, electrical tape. He tosses the bag of zip ties at me.

"What do you want me to do?"

"Tie your ankles."

Another slap of ocean water under the hull. I watch him sifting through the next carton of goods, still searching for something. I pull my ankles together. Still working my tongue under my palate. *Hail, Mary . . .*

"It's too hard," I tell him.

"What?"

A wild thought staggers up from some ancient fight-or-flight lobe in my brain, then blinks to life as if jingling around in my eyes: *Get him close. Let him get really close.*

"My fingers," I shout. "The salt water—it's tingly—"

We're still raging through the water, fully tilted port now. The police lights flash distantly. But they're there. Weston shoots up with a huff of exasperated air and staggers over to me. He cinches the zip ties around my ankles, then gets another pair, cinches that around my wrists with a stiff yank. It sends a real tingle through my fingers.

"When I find the rope," he says, "you can do mine."

"What are you doing? There's no one up top."

No response. He jumps back over to the couch, intent on finding rope—I'm sure it's rope.

A sharp wave hitches under the hull. The engines kick over to the other side and we sway before hitting some *rat-a-tat* pattern in the sea that knocks Weston over. For a second I think he's out—finally, the blood loss got him—before he pulls himself straight up. Coffin-style.

Full of grace . . . the Lord is with thee . . .

"Ha ha!" Weston stands and turns. A tangle of thin rope

is dangling from his wrists. He ties a quick knot to a storage bin, then starts tossing in anything with any weight to it, the induction cookware, unopened wine bottles, binoculars, piles of hardback books. He scooches next to the bin and ropes his own ankles before tossing the loose end to me. Then he stands, wobbly.

"You and me," he says. "Just you and me now."

Holy Mary, Mother of God . . .

I do my best to make a show of it. The rope is black and veiny and barely bends, hard as licorice. Something Patricia bought but never got any use out of. I can't wad it up around his ankles.

I hold my hands up. "Whatever your plan is, at least help me."

Pray for us sinners . . .

Weston considers it, barely nodding on his feet. Then he leans down. I smell the human rust of the iron in his blood, the spiced anger in his breath. My hands are bunched together for his to cinch to the rope, wrist to wrist. As though in prayer.

Now and at the hour . . .

Weston pulls my hands up close so he can see, almost up to his chin. And when he's looking past my fingers, busy with the rope—

I think of Steph and Patricia and Robert and Cal, my first husband, and my mother and father and of twenty-five years putting off confession and the gym and the statin I'm supposed to be on and the five-year-old girl I once was and for some reason I think of the minty-weed dandelion smell of a freshly mowed lawn in a Wisconsin summer . . .

. . . of our death.

I balance the heel of the glass against the trunk of my pinkie. It will hold. Then I extend the needly end of it, unseen, unheard, just two or three little inches of metal shank underneath his jaw—

And then I shove it into his neck with all my strength.

His eyes bulge white. I pinch away, close my eyes, but that doesn't hide it at all, the wormy lung sounds, the hot squirt of blood on my cheek, so I open them and watch in case he's going to thrash, in case he's got any strength left in him to throw something back at me, but all he manages is a tight claw with his fingers, grasping the air, for nothing, for absolutely nothing, and soon he totters to his knees and collapses onto the floor. A hot pond of blood growing in pulses under his throat. It makes me want to wretch, but I watch, a tick of blood, and I wait, a tock of blood, because I want to be looking when the blood stops beating out in ribbons and his heart stops pumping and there's nothing left of Weston Adekins but the shattered remains.

Amen.

"Gulf Coast Killer" Identity Revealed as Weston Owen Adekins After Coastal Confrontation with Police Leaves Murderer Dead Killer Had Abducted Lawyer Leslie Woodhouse, Who Remains Safe

Madre Island, FL—The FBI and local Madre Island police authorities announced early Sunday morning that they have identified thirty-four-year-old Weston Owen Adekins, the son of acquitted suspect Robert Woodhouse, as the man behind a recent streak of murders along the Gulf Coast of Florida.

According to police sources, Adekins was killed during a confrontation with police boats south of Madre Island. The incident reportedly involved Woodhouse's wife and legal representative, Leslie Woodhouse. FBI authorities are expected to share more details about this confrontation during a press conference this afternoon.

The revelations come after the FBI reopened the "Gulf Coast Killer" case several weeks after the acquittal of Robert Woodhouse, though there was not yet any public indication that Adekins was a suspect. Authorities now believe Adekins had been attempting to frame his father for the murders, which took the lives of six innocent people over the last year and a half, and abducted Leslie Woodhouse in the apparent hopes she might represent him. Though the sixty-two-year-old lawyer was unavailable for comment, police sources report that she is safe and resting comfortably.

Police were alerted when Ms. Woodhouse's elder sister, Patricia Colton, grew worried and phoned Robert Woodhouse. Describing him as "shell-shocked" and "erratic," Colton went on to say that Adekins and Mrs. Woodhouse had been spotted aboard a boat moving through Madre Island Sound, and that Mr. Woodhouse had asked her to call the police.

Robert Woodhouse did not immediately respond to phone calls seeking comment.

PART
FOUR

LESLIE

Months later

The floral light of an early-May morning pours through the windows of St. Lucy's Memorial Hospital. It's misting outside, the lawns plump and weedy. It reminds me of my first place in Florida, an upstairs/downstairs apartment where my neighbor used to cackle every time summer had a rain delay: *Lived here seventy years, and you ask me, the weather people are full of it. April showers bring May showers.*

The room belongs to Patricia, who's sitting up in her hospital bed and scooping at a tub of coconut yogurt. Maybe her appetite is back. Her blond hair—once her carefully pruned pride—is coming back in, a few weeks after she put the kibosh on her final round of chemotherapy. It gives her a bleach-white cap that makes her look like an angel about to high-dive off the top platform.

"Thanks," Patricia says when she's done. "You know what's funny about hospital food? They're supposed to be healing you, but they hook you up to IVs of Oreo creme."

"It's not that bad."

"I'm not joking. Lunch came with a pack of Oreos yesterday. I wanted to puke just looking at them."

"But how do you feel?"

"I don't know. Mega-stuffed."

I glance at the tub of yogurt. Half full. She ate forty whole calories. Something about that tugs on a primordial nerve. "Well. I'm gonna step out for a bit, check on Steph. Want anything?"

"Some new skin, maybe. See if there's any lying around."

I flash a morbid smile. "I'll see what they have."

When I walk out—making sure it's my right foot that clears the doorway, never the left, always thinking green thoughts about Patricia's next scan—I notice some nurses at the desk turning away and dipping their noses into paperwork.

I have this effect on people now. There's no in-between: the presence of Leslie Woodhouse inspires only rapt absorption or abject fear. The morning shift is the abject-fear nurses.

Certain names stick in the country's teeth like popcorn hulls. Even if you don't know the particulars of why they're infamous, you hear the names somewhere. Infamous murderers and victims and bystanders. And even if you try to avoid these names, they'll get into your bloodstream in other ways, a kind of informational osmosis, popping in while you flip channels or scroll through the ads of true-crime podcasts. I've come to accept Leslie Woodhouse will always be one of those names. Rooms go quiet when I enter them. Or, even worse, they go loud. I've signed a few autographs, snapped a few selfies. One person even asked me to record their voicemail message. I declined.

Robert Woodhouse is one of those names, too, except he isn't out in the world to experience it. I mostly followed his new trial online. Except this one wasn't broadcast, so that meant intermittent news reports, sketches, TV journalists logging updates from busy Florida sidewalks during little asides between the stock market and the international news.

And of course, on one long afternoon, I was a witness.

There wasn't much more to tell them about Robert and Wes's relationship, but I knew what Robert did (or didn't do, as I made sure to remind the jury). Weston was the monster, but Robert's sins of omission made it all possible, all of it, up until the last moment when I was forced to be the one to end it.

I still get nightmares about that. I've learned a lot about PTSD in the last several months. I've read about war veterans and how they build new lives. Or how they don't.

At least I don't relive shoving glass into Wes's neck every night. My nightmares aren't always about the boat. Or so I tell my therapist, but she always looks up at me with a hiked brow and says, "Oh yes, they are." The one where I'm being chased? Standard post-trauma. The one I have about driving on ice (never mind that I've lived in Florida for decades), then losing control around a curve before I slam into a pedestrian? My helplessness that night on the *Gutted*—being forced to kill. The one where I'm knocking at the coffin in my own funeral and my mouth opens but I can't speak and say, *Help, I'm buried alive*? Maybe it's Robert who left me in there.

I get that one almost every night.

I sleep at Patricia's now. Steph stays with me, taking a year off college—yes, she was pregnant; yes, it looks like I will have a grandchild. Tonight, a Patricia-size glass of chardonnay wallops me like a sleeping pill. I walk the long, whitewashed hallway to my usual spot in one of her guest bedrooms. Patricia's bedroom door is closed.

But with her scan coming up, I can't help myself. I need to feel her presence here again.

I slip inside.

The potpourri scent hits me first, bright as cinnamon. Finally I learn its source: a fat Cire Trudon candle on the nightstand, still freshly wicked. Then the bay window and its broad-armed view of the coast north of Madre. If Robert was here months ago, I'd report *low tide*. The sand is scrubbed smooth. An orange layer of dried sargassum marks where the tide started going out, and that's what sets me over. Not the candle, not the potpourri, but seeing that high-water mark, the tide gone out, the drained hourglass of my life. I sit on Patricia's bed, her fluffy white bed that bounces like very young flesh against my slightly squishy flesh, and won-der how I skipped from one to the other so quickly. Thirty years? I just moved to Florida to follow *her*. I blinked, I had a couple of lunches, I got married, I had Steph, my husband passed, I met a new husband—that whole story—then I had another lunch, then I blinked again, and now I'm here.

I cross myself, pray for a clean scan for Patricia, and fall into broken sleep.

A few days later, as I wait for Robert Woodhouse at an empty table in the Florida State Prison visitors' cafeteria, I can't shake the feeling of being watched. I turn. Sure enough, the prison guard is looking at me with his guppy lips open.

"Something I can help you with?" I ask.

He shakes, almost startled. "I'm sorry, ma'am. Just that I know who you are. Was just wondering if you'd heard? About Cokie Dean?"

"What about him?"

"He died last night. Heart attack in prison."

My hands plop to my lap. Funny how I don't feel anything, not even relief. I try to puzzle out how old Cokie was. I try to remember what color his eyes were. Neither answer strikes me. All I get is a random memory of how when Cokie Dean was free, he used to pick his teeth with shish-kebab skewers, never toothpicks.

Then the door opens.

Robert shuffles in with his blaze-orange suit, another guard holding him loosely by the cuffs. It's not as if Robert ever gave Weston any of the blades he used, but the jury found there was too much *obstruction* and not enough *under duress*. Besides, the public pressure was too great. The killer was dead, and someone had to answer for the Gulf Coast killings. It might as well be the coward who left his wife to die. If it had been a regular case, and maybe if I'd been defending him, Robert would have gotten six months, not four years.

Robert sits across from me. The chair squeaks. He eyes my shoulders. Is he waiting for a hug? No one knows better than I do that the man is impossible to read. "Who died?"

"Cokie Dean, since you ask."

He shrugs. "World's a little better for it, don't you think?"

"Has to be." Again, no emotion—just an image of Cokie Dean, the knitting way he would pick his teeth.

Robert looks flushed. So far, prison hasn't been unkind to him—three square meals and more daily exercise than he'd had on the outside—but now? He's aged years beyond the man I would have recognized.

"So, to what do I owe the—" He stops. "Why are you here?"

"Couple of things, actually. The condo, for one. I need you to sign some papers."

"And we're not going to fight, like last time?"

"I won't if you won't."

"Last time, you called me a coward."

I try to ignore his bait and pull up a manila folder marked ROBERT, remembering all the promises I'd made myself as I stuffed it with his papers. All I have to do is walk out with his signature and initials on a few lines, and I'm free of him. Legally.

"Coward, Leslie. And I've had weeks to think about it."

I throw the envelope to the table. So much for the peaceful exit. "Well, I was on a boat with a killer, and I have you to thank for that. Is there a better word?"

"It's a subjective word, though, isn't it?" Robert crosses his arms. "A lot of men who stayed home from wars were called cowards. Then a generation later, no one even remembers what the war was about. They throw up a memorial and say, 'Good job, buddy, thanks for being the fresh meat.' Well, memorials are nice and all that, but some of us would rather grow old."

"That's the difference between us."

"Oh?"

"Growing old is only important to you because you think this is all there is."

"Christ, here it comes."

"Just listen. For you, there can only be one goal: living another day. Because once you're dead, that's it. Dirt nap forever. But that's what makes a martyr so special—"

"Now you're going to compare me to a martyr?"

"Well, no. There's no comparison. We agree on that much. For a martyr, all that matters was what they did while they were alive. For someone like you, all that matters is the physical act of living. That's the difference."

A window starts *tinking* with rain.

"I think you owe me more than that," Robert says. "If I had done things differently, can you say for certain you'd be alive today? Wes was constantly poking around. He crawled around the Senectitude more than I ever told you. He even knew where Steph lived. And he made sure I knew it, too. I saw one way out. Keep my mouth shut. And the world hated me for it, yeah, but at least it kept us all alive. I was the one suffering for the sake of other people. So sure, maybe I am a little bit of a martyr. Maybe I deserve a little credit and not a hundred percent of the blame."

"Yes. That counts for something. And all the people you let die because you didn't come forward sooner?"

He's been smiling, but on that, his mouth goes limp. "I was talking about you. On the boat."

"I had to *kill* a man. I had to stick something in his neck and watch him die. Because of you."

"You ended a life that needed to end. It's good that you weren't the only one on that boat trapped with a killer."

Something in his voice—the casualness of it all—spears me between the ribs. *Killer.* He means me. All the months of therapy, the nightmares, nightmares he and his son gave me, and it's just a joke to him. Killer? I don't even like throwing wilted flowers away. Ending this marriage is different. It wouldn't even give me the slight eco-guilt of tossing out a pot of perfectly good soil. At least the dirt was real.

"Not a killer, Bob," I manage. "Just cleaning up after you." Thank my lifetime of experience for the calloused, lawyerly mask of my face: I shake, but I never cry. I pull the folder close to me. "And on that note, this is probably as good a time as any to tell you I'm seeking an annulment."

Robert's face hardens. "I thought you didn't believe in annulment."

"Since when?"

"Les, you called it divorce for Catholics. On many occasions."

"I wonder what could've changed my mind."

"Well, what do I need to do? Papers to sign, or something?"

"It's up to the diocese. There might be questions, I don't know. I'm just telling you. These, on the other hand, are for the condo."

Robert knocks back, slaps his face into his hands. That may have been my mistake. I'm not a great bearer of bad news; I tend to lid it up until the pressure shoves it all out at once. I don't know how easy an annulment will be and I don't know if I can even get one. Bishops are nothing like courts. And Robert didn't have to hear about the condo again, remember what he won't be coming home to when he's out in a few years. Then I think of the happy little splash his body made when it slapped into the water, and guilt washes out of me in a hot flood.

Robert glances back, shrugs himself in, turtling himself small. "So when I get out, I'll have no wife, no job, and no place to live."

"They're listing around a million," I tell him. "Both our names are on it, so you'll get half." I don't tell him that Charlotte's half finally sold for a fraction of that. Our agent still wanted to list it for seven figures, said there would be someone glad for the Gulf Coast Killer bargain if they love the beach enough. I have my doubts. Madre isn't priced like Sanibel Island. That's partly why we bought there. All those seaside dreams, morning coffee in the sea breeze, falling asleep to the gentle laps of the Gulf, gone. "What you do after that is up to you."

"I've had an offer for a tell-all. Several, actually. And TV interviews. But I've been told I should save that for when the book's coming out. I've been jotting down notes."

"Oh." It's all I can say. "Well. Congratulations."

"But if you hold off—with the annulment and the condo I mean—just let things cool down, maybe those notes stay notes."

"No. Write and say whatever you like. I'm comfortable with the truth."

He settles back in his chair. "For what it's worth, it wasn't easy living like I did. Never knowing what I could tell you and couldn't tell you, never knowing if he bugged our house or hacked our doorbell or what. I made a thousand mistakes I'd take back if I could, but I don't think I have to apologize for being his hostage."

"So you won't apologize?"

He shrugs. "What good would it do me?"

If there was ever a question that summarized a man.

"Well," I say, "if I do forgive you, at least I'll have the satisfaction of doing it without your consent."

I pick up my purse, spinning for the door, then stop and look back. In the blue light of the windows I can see new patchiness in his hairline. Liver spots under his neck. The subtle, broken green of one of his eyes. They rise to meet my own, just for a second, before falling back to reading the backs of his empty hands.

Then the guard leads me out and I make the prison's long, labyrinthine walk out into the rain.

The next week, I'm carrying an unwieldy box of chocolates under my arm to Patricia's hospital room. It makes awkward work of the door handle, but even when I get a good grip, it won't turn. I peer inside the window. It's dim. The shades are drawn; the bed is pressed. The machines loom in stony silence.

I try to steady my breathing as I walk to the nurses' station. There's no reason to panic. The explanation will be simple. They've moved Patricia to another room, something like that. Hospice? I would have heard. Her doctors were optimistic. The chocolates were supposed to be *congratulatory*—or, if the results were bad, emotional support. She is fine. She has to be fine.

But the face I wear as I approach the nurses must not be so confident because one of them asks me if I need to sit down.

"It's okay," I tell her. "Just—did my sister change rooms? I'm confused."

Then they shoot me giddy smiles. Their eyes point behind me.

I whirl around.

Patricia is waiting for me there in the hallway, gleaming, *standing*, a piece of paper rolled in her hand, her bright green eyes wide with expectation. "Surprise! Let out this morning." When I wrap her in a hug, she whispers, "I'm sorry. I recruited the nurses, insisted they be in on it. Funny, right?"

"So funny," I say wearily.

"Good. I've got something for you."

Then she unrolls the paper and shows off the results of her first clean scan in months.

Even at a reduced price, Senectitude stays on the market far longer than I'd hoped. The agent did all she could: a deep cleaning, then minimalist décor in beiges and grays so anyone considering a seaside condo could imagine themselves sitting in it instead of the infamous Woodhouse family. The sale price inevitably left me shellacked, and half goes to Robert, but it's enough to take me and my modest list of possessions to the only other place besides Florida that might feel like home.

To Steph.

And to Drew, I suppose. At least that's going well. Steph had waited a few months to break it to me officially, until I was at Patricia's for a big family Thanksgiving, and there was no talking her way around the baby bump by then. A pro-crastinator, like her mother. She took me into Patricia's parlor, speaking in little whispers, said the two words, then winced as if she had said, *Please slap me as hard as you can on the count of three,* instead of *I'm pregnant.* And it was a shock to my Catholic sensibilities, my utter inability to know the people around me, but Drew was spectacular through it all: they agreed to get married while Steph took a year off. And me? Could I help them in Philadelphia? Of course. I could think of no higher calling than *grandmother.*

After Steph had my first grandchild, she handed him to me. His eyes were pinched shut, his fingers were little curling beans. And I fell in love.

"Leslie," Steph told me. "Leslie Drewson." My heart popped in my chest, fireworks, candy rocks. But I must have made a face because Steph said, "Oh no. You hate the name."

"No." I smiled. "He's absolutely perfect."

Which means leaving Florida to help Steph in Philadelphia.

One clear winter day, when the thought of flying from the seventy-degree subtropics into slush and snow especially pains me, when the last of my things are potted and packed, Patricia waits by the driveway.

"This is all a joke, right?" Patricia asks. "It's like that prank I pulled on you at the hospital. I'm going to drive home and you'll be waiting there at my door saying, 'Gotcha, I'm staying in Florida.'"

"Because my life on Madre Island brought me such good fortune?"

"Point taken. Philly. And don't forget to drink more often.

You have too many brain cells, Les. It's not healthy." And she takes me in for a hug. When she squeezes me, it's with a firm strength that reminds me of better years, of our invincibility when we were young in Wisconsin. "Love you, babe. Love you even more than I hate you for leaving."

"Love you, too. And you could always come with me."

"What's the temperature there right now?"

I look it up on my phone. "Thirty-five."

"I don't love you *that* much."

And she laughs her spicy, five-alarm laugh.

By evening, I'm in the Philadelphia suburbs, where I found a five-over-one condo in a cozy neighborhood. It's too small for my liking, too modern and brutalist, and too far from any available ocean, but at least it's near Steph. I will be a neighbor-slash-babysitter. I'm actually watching little Leslie tonight—a rare date night for Drew and Steph, who promise to do all my heavy moving for me tomorrow. And, after all, it's why I'm here.

Sometime around seven, there's a *thunk* at my front door. When little Leslie is in the bassinet for a nap, I push it open. A box turns over.

LESLIE KIRCHENHAUSER

FROM: PATRICIA COLTON

Patricia will never let go of "Colton," but I can almost taste how much she relishes a chance to use our maiden name. After locking the door, I grab a box cutter and saw through the packing tape. It's an entire album of keepsakes. On top, a photo of my original family: Mom, Dad, Patricia, and yours truly. It's like looking through a thick rheumy layer of Kodachrome, but there we are, heads through the cutout animals and elephant boards at the Milwaukee County Zoo, 1970. I would have been seven years old. I was the camel. I dig a little more, but there's so much, too much, entire piles of Cedar Street knickknacks I never even knew Patricia saved.

My stomach twists. It kills me that I can't drive across Madre Island Sound to see her anymore.

Deeper in the box, I pass through a three-volume copy of *Jane Eyre*. A glance inside the cover tells me it was published in 1847. I remember this. It used to sit on a corner bookshelf at Patricia's, and sometimes I'd pick this exact volume off the wall just to smell it. Books from the 1800s have a smell that ages like wine. That leather-and-almond scent, both musty and sweet. She must have seen.

Lastly, there's an envelope. A letter and a gift card. I open the gift card—GENERAL WINE GOODS, $500—and already know what her note is going to say.

LESLIE

Bloody Mary was a good Catholic queen, wasn't she? Have a few on me, and save some for my first visit. Just don't save too much. We're not getting any younger, and there's plenty of time for sobriety in Heaven.

And by the way, if you're right, and life really is just a dream, you'll forgive me if I don't want to wake up quite yet. The people we love will still be waiting for us in the morning. And I'll be waiting for you, baby, anytime you miss me.

Your elder, wiser, eternally striking sister,

Patricia

(Not Pat.)

Feeling my heart go soft, I fold the paper and slip it into the box. The faint smell of potpourri hangs in the air.

After Steph and Drew pick up sweet little Leslie, something stops me. I don't draw my 9:00 p.m. footbath in front of the TV, don't order a Friday-night hoagie.

Instead, I get in my car.

Half a mile up the road, St. Lawrence Catholic Church materializes over a hill like a jewel in the clouds. It reminds me of small-town churches in Wisconsin, sitting atop the crest of hills, beacons above rolling waves of farm. The Wisconsin lighthouses, my dad called them.

When I pull in the parking lot and get out to look at the teary smudges of stars, I start wiping and sniffing. Patricia's letter is still stuck in my throat. No amount of FaceTime will ever brighten a room the way she does in person.

Inside, the church is a pleasant respite from the cold, the air spiced with incense, the heat biting and iron-y from a twentieth-century furnace. I dip my fingers in the holy water, cross myself, and sit down. It's only then I see that someone's placed an A-frame sign underneath the hymn numbers:

CONFESSIONS FRIDAYS.

A young priest is waiting in the pews, praying. Must be a slow night. We start a conversation: he's glad I'm here because he's seen me skipping the Eucharist. I thought I'd been sly in the back pews. And then it all comes spluttering out of me: the last twenty-five years, how many times I'd skipped Mass in those years, my guilt over Cokie Dean, the story about Weston Adekins and Robert Woodhouse, the glass shard, the boat, the zip ties, the rope, the rubber hardness of an artery when you're pressing glass through it, then watching the life drain out of him, how it gave me a macabre sort of pleasure, how it gives me night terrors.

The priest digests it all with a look of stony experience. "That's quite the nightmare. The thing about nightmares, though—eventually, you wake up. And there's nothing out there so horrible that you can't come back from it. Kind of like waking up from a dream." He rubs his hands together. "I'm glad you're here. The long holdouts are my favorites. You'll be glad to know self-defense is no sin. Nor is criminal defense. We'll have a little chat about you skipping Mass, though."

In the confession booth, he makes good on his promise of a light penance: I owe him one rosary, and I have to come back for another confession in three months. I feel so silly. Twenty-five years I'd been avoiding it, and for what? Twenty minutes of prayer?

I have time for two rosaries. One for me, one for Patricia's next scan. Normally, I'd do a third, just for safety, just to salve the itch behind my ears.

But I think two's enough.

ACKNOWLEDGMENTS

Thank you, readers, for giving me a chance. I'm going to keep trying my best to be worthy of your time and attention, and I hope we can do it again soon. Special shout-out to all the Bookstagrammers, online reviewers, influencers, and booksellers who shared *The Perfect Home*, as well as this one.

Thank you, Ronald Gerber, for all the guidance and the work you do to make it easy to focus on writing. You once told me it only takes one "yes" to change everything, which is true: I can trace it back to the "yes" that came from you.

Thank you to Sabrina Pyun for helping me untangle this knot, and for the many improvements that came from your sharp instincts. I'm constantly grateful for the journey that landed my books on your desk. I also owe a major thanks to Sophie Guimaraes, not only for your energizing faith and support, but for taking this on and sharing it with the world. Thank you to Scribner and Simon & Schuster for offering your talent and enthusiasm, especially Nicole Miller and Colleen Nuccio.

Thank you to booksellers, fellow authors, beta readers, and people who shared nice words, especially Lisa Baudoin, Elizabeth Walsh, Christina McDonald, Alex Finlay, Marcie Rendon, Jeff Hagkull, Kyle Iverson, Rachel Levy Sarfin, and Jill Newberg.

Thank you to Ben Johnson and Caleb Williams, who dramatically increased the quality of my life.

And finally, thank you to all the lawyers in my extended family who prove what a noble profession it can be. No lawyer jokes here, tempting though it may be. With that said, I'd also like to thank my parents for never saying, "Writing? Not law school?" I also need to shout-out Tom and Gwen for the big *Perfect Home* poster they keep in their house. A special thank you to my older brother, Mike, and my sister-in-law Rachel, for celebrating *The Perfect Home* with me, and especially for Mike's helpful glimpses into the legal world.